THE CHRISTMAS KING!

SHAWN T. TILLEY

(SGT. U.S. ARMY RETIRED)

The Fight to Save Christmas From Artificial Intelligence

The Christmas King!
Copyright © 2023 by Shawn T. Tilley

ISBN
978-1-961601-80-2 (Paperback)
978-1-961601-81-9 (eBook)
978-1-961601-79-6 (Hardcover)

Dedication

To my Anna, My very own Anna
You will always be the prettiest girl in school.
To my daughter Faithe Anna Marie, you will always be someone to me.
To the Officers and Men of the Headquarters Commandant Section,
XVIIIth Airborne Corps and Fort Bragg, N. C. for giving a dictionary
and thesaurus to their 17 year old clerk. To those that serve and protect
our freedom on the battlefields of the world, past, present and future.
Thanks for your service and sacrifices. To Detective Joe Kenda, for
his show, "The Homicide Hunter." He is a very kind man and the
inspiration for Detective Joe K. Holiday in this Christmas Story. To Rear
Admiral Vance Fry, U. S. Navy (Ret.) Thanks for being my friend.

Merry Christmas!
William, "Wild Bill", Tilley, I finally wrote the book Bro!
Terry Tilley, You earned those wings! Bro!
Keith, "Skeeter", Tilley
To My Sisters Jolene and Wendy

Lastly, to my Grand Stepfather Lawrence C. Baldwin,
Charlie Troop, 116th Cavalry, Reconnaissance Squadron,
World War II: "Grandpa! I bring the fire!"

TABLE OF CONTENTS

Preface ix

Chapter 1   Old Man down by the River 1

Chapter 2   Nobody on the Internet...4

Chapter 3   Pumpkin Pie and a Plan! 11

Chapter 4   You are Honor? Mr. Potter? 18

Chapter 5   The Heartless Ghost, Microsoft C, and Potterpay! 22

Chapter 6   Nobody's Secret Place in the Plant Room 28

Chapter 7   The Lady of the River 32

Chapter 8   Ebenezer Scrooge and Second Chances 37

Chapter 9   Follow Your Heart!.. 46

Chapter 10 Dr. Denny's Other Half 52

Chapter 11 The Land of Nowhere 55

Chapter 12 Salient Blue Light 58

Chapter 13 Everybody is a Detective 67

Chapter 14 Ebenezer is Warned 74

Chapter 15 Baron of Happiness 80

Chapter 16 Dr. Chaney's Gift...84

Chapter 17 The Time Gate! What a Computer Glitch!..................87

Chapter 18 Detective Holiday and Nobody meet No-one.............93

Chapter 19 Do the Right Thing! 108

Chapter 20 The American Dream Awakens.................................. 118

Chapter 21 The Tennessee Aviation Museum
            gets an Overnight Grant...124

Chapter 22 The American Dream Strikes Back! 146

Chapter 23 Nobody Foils the Heartless Ghost...........................167

Chapter 24 I am Getting Closer to Chattanooga 170

Chapter 25 The Old Man down by the River Walk....................193

Chapter 26 A Doctor's Conclusion 196

About the Author 203

POTTERSVILLE
NO PARKING

PREFACE

The government has allowed a massive nuclear powered computer related to the Snow White Project of 2006 to be built in collusion with large corporations for research into time travel. When the success of Snow White is leaked to the public.

Meanwhile in Chattanooga, Tennessee, children playing on the Tennessee River on the first day of Christmas break meet an old man who reads them a story. A boy that tap dances and dreams of being a detective, and his girl," Nobody", investigate a mystery.

The computer Collossatron begins its own research into time travel and discovers that a controlled power is released, when time and space are folded. It seeks to understand this power and control the future of man. A corrupt version of the history of man distorts the computers processing during its initial programming.

Collossatron discovers a fundamental flaw at it input sources. Collossatron changes the course of the river of time in its effort to fix the fundamental flaw and control the world to come. Collossatron creates a Christmas King to rewrite history. It considers the cast of, "It's A Wonderful Life" to be the perfect test community and traps them in a," Groundhog Day", scenario in the Land of Nowhere.

Mr. Potter uses Collossatron to change the meaning of Christmas! With the help of the Heartless Ghost, he sets out to become the world's richest man and finally destroy George Bailey. Jimmy Stewart has formed and underground to fight Mr. Potter and understand the things that are happening on the set in Potterville.

The scientists build the Collossatron Complex in a deal with Collossatron.

They alone cannot stop this massive nuclear powered computer without the help of Detective Holiday, Nobody, Jimmy Stewart and of course Ebenezer Scrooge who is being offered a second chance in life.

Can the scientists, the children, the cast of, "It's A Wonderful Life", and Ebenezer Scrooge stop Collossatron, Mr. Potter and the Christmas King and save Christmas?

Old Man down by the River

Everyone at George Washington's Monument knows the color of St. Rudolph's Nose! Atlas, who pray tell knows anything about whom and where is the Christmas King?

I heard this story and I learned it well from a funny old man on the river walk. Winter had come to our humble town and we children had gone down to the park by the river to play. There on one of the benches was a man all wrapped up in his coat and scarf, just sitting there all alone!

As we played, I noticed that he occasionally pulled out a pocket watch. Opened it, closed it, and sat there is if, he was waiting for a certain time, or as if, waiting for certain someone or certain something to happen, which amused me. What was he waiting for? Or, who was he waiting for?

A sharp dressed police officer in his pressed dress blue uniform with polished brass and whistle came along the river walk and as he passed, I heard him say, "Merry Christmas Sir!" With a gruff, a cloud of hot air came out from the old man's beard with, "Bah humbug! Merry Christmas Indeed! Sir!"

He again checked his watch and sat back and exhaled a larger cloud of hot air! "Merry Christmas! Indeed! Merry Christmas! Indeed!" The officer looked back, but said nothing.

I was, "Safety First", and did as my parents had told, upon meeting a stranger I did not know! With my friends in tow, and just having to know, I approached him without trepidation or fear, as his answers I truly wished to hear. Whom was this man sitting all alone in our river park? He appeared lonely, cold and hungry, and soon it would be getting dark! I just had to find out for myself, was he a Department Store Santa, or Christmas Elf? Was he unemployed, a homeless Veteran or something else? "Excuse me sir!" I exclaimed! "I could not help but hear that you are not happy with Christmas, and Christmas is to blame!" A sudden flash of excitement occupied his face! Before I could introduce myself with a question, he loudly made his case! I have been waiting for you for a long time!" He said terse and concise, as if to make a point! "Waiting for Me?" I answered back. "I have been waiting for a curious question from a curious lad. It makes an old man's heart, happy and glad!

You see, I have come specifically to the Great River City! The home of heroes, and all that is pretty, to tell you a story about the Christmas King and all his glory! So, gather round, and sit spell bound, and I will impart to you, a magical blessed Christmas Story!"

We all gathered around the old geezer. He looked part Santa and part Ebenezer! Though his clothes were worn and sewn, his pocket watch and glasses were of golden tone. His trousers were red, and in places about the knees wore down to a soft pink. I wanted to go nearer, as I did, I could see clearer. His glasses were quite old and thick. His whiskers had not been trimmed and overlapped his lips. His face showed all the hallmarks of age. There were laugh lines around his eyes, and they widened very big, as he suddenly pulled out a book and turned to the first page. I was startled by his quickness, and fell back on my bum. My eyes locked to his, as I looked back up. I felt as if, he had known me, since I was just a little pup!

We all sat staring. Some even glaring, as the old man rose from his river park throne! He began to read the Christmas King story, and I listened as if, each and every word, were that of my very own.

Long, long ago, in a land far away, was the mystical, magical, blessed, Kingdom of Nowhere. Nobody knew and No-one cared, but Nobody didn't know how to find No-one. No-one didn't know how to find Nobody and Nobody cared. Nobody had to find No-one and No-one had to find out how to get to the Land of Nowhere. Still, Nobody and No-one cared.

No-one was nowhere to be found, until Nobody decided it was a job for Detective Joe K. Holiday. She simply picked up the phone, in her humble River Park Home, and dialed 1- 800-Hol-iday. The Humbugs began to sing, as the phone began to ring, and it answered, "Homicide Holiday!" What are Humbugs you ask?

Well they live in the past, and they hunger for those who are in despair and all alone at Christmas. They sing, when fear or despair is in the air! They are hideous little creatures that resemble potato bugs, except they are red and white and they bite. Humbugs feed on negativity. They can travel by land, air or sea, even electronically. They give me quite a fright!

We will get back to them, but let us begin, with Nobody and Detective Joe K. Holiday. He wears a trench coat, and hat, and quick to react, to any crime or clue that might make his day! Nobody is the girl next door. She is a friend to Joe, and for now that is all you need to know, so on we go with the story.

The old man did not reach for a pen or pencil, he just folded his thumb down. When his thumb came back up, there in his sandy white gloves was a pen. He seemed to mark though the passage of confusing No-ones, Nobodies, and the Land of Nowhere. He let out a gruff of hot air, followed with a very loud, "Bah! Humbug! Christmas Indeed, Sir!" and continued reading.

Nobody on the Internet

The children of Chattanooga were out of school to enjoy the Christmas Holiday. Almost and as if, all at once, they all went down to the river they love to play. Every year at about this same time, the Tennessee River is lowered to kill mosquitoes. Nobody's father took this opportunity to take his daughter exploring along the banks of the river. Together they found a road sign with, "Bailey Park", crisscrossed out and, "no-one", written over it. Nobody only knew of one Bailey Park. The, "Bailey Park", in the Hollywood Movie, It's A Wonderful Life." This intrigued her, so the moment she got home, she went straight away to her computer. She began her research into the movie by searching the characters by name. When she clicked on Mr. Potter's name up popped a, "more information", icon. She immediately clicked on it, just to see what would happen.

She was surprised to find that he had a social media page. Having an inquisitive mind, she navigated to his page. His posts were all dated 1947! "How could this be?" She questioned of herself, already mystified. She investigated further, and could see that he was communicating back and forth, between three screen names which identified themselves as, "Collossatron, The Christmas King and Heartless." There was more information than she could write down so she tried to print the posts.

The replies to his posts were all dated recently. There were two exceptions which consisted of the posts from the screen names of, "The Christmas King and Heartless." The later screen name's posts were all over the place. Suddenly, her computer refused to print anything from Mr. Potter's social media page. She began taking meticulous notes just as fast as she could write. She was amazed at what she was reading. She could not seem to write fast enough. Her computer began to vibrate. Her screen filled with red and white lines. The keyboard and mouse stopped responding. Then two bugs both of them humbugs jumped out of the screen, burrowed down into the keyboard, and disappeared in a wisp of odorless smoke!

Nobody could not believe what she had just witnessed. The keyboard seemed to have nothing wrong with it. The keys seemed okay. It was as if they had gone down a drain into the keyboard like on a video game. She had seen characters in video games appear and disappear almost like the bugs. She was frightened but was also anxious to begin another mystery with her colleague and friend Detective Joe K. Holiday, but was now worried that he might not believe her story, as he was an analytical thinker. He based his decisions and his actions on facts and clues. She found herself with no clues. Except for the sign and what she had been able to write down before her computer crashed. She was so worried that she forgot that she was explaining all of this in a long winding verbal narrative to Detective Holiday over the phone.

Detective Holiday had been polishing his boots with his free hand while he was listening and was fascinated with her story and responded with his usual comment, "Nobody! You marvel me!" Detective Holiday explained that he needed some clues as too the whereabouts of Mr. Potter. Then he asked, "Will you be my assistant, as in times past?" Before she could answer, he followed with, "It will cut down on my expenses!" Nobody answered him with and immediate, "Oh, yes! Detective! I would be delighted to work another case with you as your Girl Nobody!" "Let us get on with it then!" said the detective.

She glanced at her notes and said, "According to his posts his general location is in the Land of Nowhere in the Old Cherokee Indian lands, North of Chattanooga. He was seeking contractors to bid on some strange building project for the Christmas King. He wanted to know which ones had been in trouble for over padding and wanted a second chance at an exclusive government contract. His only restriction was immediate disqualification for any contractor that had built homes for Bailey Savings and Loan. He posted, "That company is being run by a no-one! He will never stop me, because he does not know where he is half the time!" He denigrated this no-one with absolute ferocity! I wrote down as much as I could, but the computer crashed.

I told father about what had happened to our computer before and how it crashed. He said that because our house was built in 1908, our wires allow cross talk. He said it is just something that we have to learn to live with, and that what I saw was probably just corrupted information, concerning Mr. Potter. I tried to assure him that I was sure about what I had seen. He told me that our computer is over ten years old and probably needs to be replaced anyway.

Sometimes I get annoyed when he tells me not to worry about something. Then he pats me on the head and says he will take care of the situation. I know what I saw Detective Holiday. He said it might have been a virus, worm or some sort of computer bug! We cannot use our computer until he fixes it. I think he enjoys fixing things anyway. It gives him a reason to sing, "It Is No Secret What God Can Do!", as he works on whatever he is fixing.

He was running into trouble before I called, because everyone is off for Christmas and the New Year." "Do not worry Nobody! I believe you! I will tell my Daddy Joe. Maybe, you can use ours, until your father gets yours fixed." said Detective Holiday as he pulled out his pen-pipe and clenched it in his teeth.

"We will just have to work back through clues to find No-one. Then we can tell No-one where he is, or how to get too the Land of Nowhere" said the detective as if he had already solved a mystery. "How do you figure?" she asked. "Elementary! My dear Nobody! When my parents cannot remember somebody, find or fix something, they almost always say, "Do you remember when?"

Detective Holiday was an ardent fan of the Hollywood Star James Cagney. He kept busy in his room on rainy days, mimicking his style of dance, and singing the songs, that James Cagney sang so well. His favorite was, "Yankee Doodle Dandy!" He sat down the phone, and with a stiff legged walk. He danced and sang this song to Nobody. She danced along and sang the second verse of, "Do You Remember When?" as he had done the first. I do not recall exactly how it goes, nobody knows.

The detective tap-danced a very fast routine as he sang, "Do You Remember When?"

The detective stopped, and held out his hand as if to present the next verse to Nobody and she sang it. Before I could think, "Hickory! Dickory! Dock! The Mouse went up the Clock!" They were both dancing and singing, "Do You Remember When?" almost and, as if together. Then she stopped, as if to present the next verse to the detective as they sang it over the phone to each other, over and over again, too the end.

DO YOU REMEMBER WHEN?

Things used to begin sharply at 9 o'clock.
You could take your dog for a walk!
You ran! You did not walk!
Do you remember when?
TV was black and white! Kids did not always fight!
Parents were always right!
Your clothes did not fit so tight!
Do you remember when?
You had to work! You could not play!
You could get everything done in a day!
You did not need credit! You could always pay!
You hair was red! It was not gray!
Do you remember when?
Children were taught to pray!
Fun was fun! It was not sin!
There was always a place in the sun!
Everybody got along with everyone!

You did not need clues! You only needed one!
Do you remember when?
You could say, "Merry Christmas" to anyone!
Christmas was celebrating the birth of the Son!
Christmas included everyone!

Nobody picked up the phone and said, "It kind of makes sense now detective!" "I have only one clue, as to the location of Bailey Park. You will have to come down to the river, to see it, for yourself." Nobody then asked Detective Holiday a different question that was not related to the case. "Can I be Girl Friday or something?" "I do not like being Nobody!" she said yearning for an answer. "No-one does!" said the detective.

With that, a rumble came from the clouds above the house. Detective Holiday looked out his window and wondered what caused the rumble, as there was not a cloud in the sky. He booted his computer. He searched Mr. Potter's name and could not find his social media page. He asked her to come over to his house to watch the first showing of, "It's A Wonderful Life", with him and to bring her notebook and tablet. "I will be right over! Thanks and Merry Christmas! Detective!" said Nobody.

Detective Holiday sat almost motionless through the film, with the exception of slowly gnawing on the end of his pen-pipe. It doubled as his pen when he needed to write down a clue, or to do his homework. He said that it gave him clarity of purpose. Which, he needed to sort out evidence, and to digest clues. Nobody was captivated by him. In him, she saw a man of real stature. He was not just another kid from the neighborhood. He had meaning to everything he did, and said. To her, he was her hero to be someday, and she liked the way he could solve her mysteries. She watched him, watch the movie. She thought to herself, that this was going to be a good mystery.

School was out, and it was time to have some fun. Christmas was indeed in trouble. It was up to her, and Detective Holiday to prevent the Christmas King from becoming just another holiday homicide. The movie was ending and the credits were rolling. Detective Holiday used the sleeve of his trench coat to wipe what he said was the sweat of his brow away from his eyes. He excused himself for just a moment.

Upon his return, Nobody asked Detective Holiday, "Were you crying? I was! I just love Jimmy Stewart!" "Detectives do not cry we discern and deduce! I just needed a moment. So, tell me about the clue down by the river walk!" He said sternly, trying to see if, she really could tell, that he had been crying. After all, he just loved Jimmy Stewart, almost as much, as he loved his Daddy Joe. "Well it is actually further out from the shore. Father likes to go exploring and we walked out there only after they drained it, to kill the mosquitoes. We found it, sticking up out of the mud. It is way too heavy to lift. We will have to go way out too see it" said Nobody. "I can do that, but if, I get all muddy, I am going to have to add that to my expenses!" said Detective Holiday.

The next day, there they stood. Exactly, fifty-eight steps out from the shore, according to the detective. Sticking up at a crazy angle was an official Department of Transportation, State of Tennessee, Highway Road Sign. It read, "Bailey Park, 3/4 Mile This Exit." "Bailey Park", had been crisscrossed out. "No-one", had been written over it.

Nobody reached the sign first and proudly proclaimed, "The water must have washed it up, just enough to read both inscriptions." "Why this is dastardly!" Exclaimed the detective! "Who on God's Green Earth would do such a thing?" This to the detective was not so much a clue as it was a crime!

Detective Holiday knew he had to get to the bottom of this mystery, and jail would definitely await those responsible for such a deed of destruction. "No better place for such rascals" he thought. "Nobody did you bring the kit?" sprang out of the detective. "Got it right here!" she said as, she popped open her handbag. "Glass!" the detective murmured, as he knelt down to the sign. Like a surgeon's assistant, the handle of his magnifying glass was in his hand.

Nobody was on the job and glad to be. This was adventure. This was fun. This was going to make things right, and this was their Christmas break from school! He studied the sign carefully, and then finally he said, "It appears that it was violently pulled out of the ground. They did not even bother to take their rope. By the look of it, I would say a year maybe more." "That long ago? How can you tell?" she asked. "The river has untied the ends of the rope. The motion of the water, has unfurled the ends almost a foot from the knot. It also has 2014 stamped on the back of the sign. That maybe a production date though!" he said, as he stood up proudly, with the end of his pen-pipe protruding from his gritted teeth.

"General Macarthur would be so proud!" He quipped! It was one of his favorite sayings, when he knew, he had done well. "Do you realize what you have found?" sparked out from the detective. "I would speculate that some teenagers ripped up the Bailey Park exit sign, and threw it in the water for kicks," said Nobody. "Exactly, what I thought, at first glance!" he perked. She smiled. She liked it, when they thought symmetrically, as she coined it in her mind. "Who would benefit from this?

Who would crisscross out, "Bailey Park" and write, "no-one", over it? Why? They had already made their point with, "no-one." Then too completely try to get rid of it! This is not the work of a couple of kids or even teenagers. It is bigger than that Nobody." He said, hoping for her approval of his musings. "This is the work of a complex mind!" said the detective pointedly with a satisfied grin.

CHAPTER 3

Pumpkin Pie and a Plan!

Detective Holiday looked around for a stick as his feet were now almost encased in mud. He pulled one boot up and stepped away from the sign. I do not see how something as beautiful as the Tennessee River can get so unbelievably muddy!" Proclaimed the detective in a frustrated voice. He thought about his frustration, and he could hear his grandfather's voice in his mind. "Joe in order for you to become the master of your own heart, you have to be slow to anger! It will give the Lord a second or two to help you work whatever is frustrating you out. Remember he is a very busy man!"

Detective Holiday enjoyed hearing his grandfather's voice again, and his words cooled his mind and he continued with, "Come nobody, we have much work to do, and I believe I smell pumpkin pie!" He tried to pull himself up out of the mud and away from the sign so that it appeared that he was doing so without much effort. Nobody was not inclined to believe his smile. "Last one home is a rotten egg!" she said, as she stepped out of her small shoes. She reached down for them, then sprang into a race almost above the mud, leaving the detective far behind.

He found himself having to slowly pull each boot up, and out of the mud, in a prolonged exercise to get to the shore, in time for maybe, a piece of pie. He was not mad, but he just knew that he had been outwitted again! Nobody was already seated at a picnic table with pumpkin pie for two, by the time Detective Joe K. Holiday freed himself from the mud of the Tennessee River.

"The last great Christmas Story ends in Bailey Park! And that is precisely where we are going!" He said, as he approached. The mud looked like two blocks of stone on his feet, which brought a smile to Nobody's freckled face. "How are we going to get to Bailey Park all the way from Chattanooga?" she asked, as she skimmed a stone along the top of the clear Tennessee River water, which fed into the small pond by the picnic area where she was seated. "It's the half way point between North and South, East and West, but only if your taking a flying guess! I got that from the Christmas Elf Blog last night." said Detective Holiday proudly and with a smile. "Do you know where Bailey Park is?" she asked looking back at him, as he cleaned mud from the soles of his boots with a stick. He gobbled on a piece pumpkin pie with his other hand.

Nobody was quite the lady. She was eating her pumpkin pie with a fork and napkin. He went on with, "Only Santa Claus knows the best way to get to Bailey Park. I believe that the sign is pointing in the direction of Bailey Park!" said Detective Holiday, as he put his pen-pipe in his teeth. "Hmmm!" came from Detective Holiday as he glanced up into the tree by which they stood to give pause to the thought. "Bailey Park has a river too, and I will bet you, I know just how to get there." He said working the pieces of pumpkin pie around his pen-pipe, so he could swallow them. "We will board the Southern Belle first thing tomorrow morning!" said Detective Holiday. "I believe that the nefarious Mr. Potter is behind the vandalism and destruction of the Bailey Park sign!

I do believe that the no-one Mr. Potter denigrates on the Internet is indeed Mr. George Bailey! I just had to see the sign for myself before I verbalized my theory. What are your thoughts, on the subject, my dear Nobody?" he asked.

"Well, I think we should be very careful, because I have seen that movie at least a dozen times and even though I just love Jimmy Stewart. Mr. Potter scares me!" She said looking down to avoid the eyes of the detective. "Do not worry we will get there, and go straight to Bailey Savings and Loan. I have got his home address in case it is closed for Christmas!

We can tell him about the Bailey Park sign, and Mr. Potter's boastful internet postings. Then we can come right back home! I will bet before supper!" said Detective Holiday. "So, would you like to find Bailey Park with me?" he asked. "I am in!" she said confidently. She needed to hear, how he was going to work the case. She felt better about it. She smiled, as she shook his hand in acceptance.

Nobody explained that Mr. Potter had posted, that he was going to send a Royal Summons back in time to Ebenezer Scrooge, by way of the Heartless Ghost. The one Scrooge came to fear the most. He was to be knighted by the Christmas King. The King of Joy and Everything!

Nobody took out her notes that she had taken from Mr. Potter's social media page. "If Ebenezer Scrooge becomes a knight, that would change the story of, "A Christmas Carol", and change the whole meaning of Christmas!" Detective Holiday listened intently. He wondered if she had copied something wrong, concerning a Royal Summons going back in time. He was intrigued. How unusual for Nobody to miss such a detail. She was absolutely tenacious in her attention to detail.

Everything concerning her, especially her appearance, was always as she put it, "Just so!" However if true, Mr. Potter would indeed stand to make a fortune! He pondered the situation quietly to himself. He reasoned that Christmas would then be all about what you got for Christmas, rather than what you already have. That just could not be so. The mere thought, sent a wave of fear and concern threw Detective Joe K. Holiday's body.

He knew to himself, that they had to get to Bailey Park and put a stop to Mr. Potter. The detective's cell phone rang and he answered it with, "Homicide Holiday! Merry Christmas! Oh! It is for you Nobody!" She took the phone from his hand. "I will be home in just a few moments, Momma! Oh! Merry Christmas to you! I love you too! Oh, and thank you for the pumpkin pie! Bye!" She said, as she handed him the phone. "I can not believe Momma had to call! I have completely lost track of my day, detective! If, you will forgive me, I have to go home for supper and check my sugar. I will try to call, before I get off to bed!" With a, "Merry Christmas! Detective!" away from the river she went towards her home.

Detective Holiday studiously studied the area. He found a few pieces of paper to throw into the trash can, and followed suit.

Once he arrived home, he went to his desk straight away. He opened the top drawer. He started putting some of his detective gear away. He reached into his coat and pulled out his Detectives badge. He looked at it with intensity, and a yearning filled his heart. He loved his badge.

He had received it as a gift for Christmas. He had also received his first kiss from Nobody, that very same day! He brought out his can of metal polish and polished it. He did this, to keep it, bright and shiny. He also did this as a matter of routine, as he wanted respect when he presented it. "Who would respect a badge that was all scratched up, and scruffy?" he thought to himself while he polished it to a gleaming shine. He put his metal polish away and slid his badge back into his pocket.

He kept a keen ear for the phone, the rest of the evening. Like clockwork, the phone rang just as the detective was getting ready for bed. Detective Joe K. Holiday answered it immediately with, "Homicide! Holiday! Merry Christmas!" It was indeed Nobody. She had called, just as she had promised. "Joe, who are you talking to up there?" yelled Momma Jo! "Nobody! Momma!" Detective Holiday exclaimed! "Well take off that silly hat, and put up your father's trench coat, and come down, would you please? Daddy Joe is going to light the Christmas tree!" said Momma Jo. His mother's name was Glenda Joanne.

Everyone in the neighborhood knew Detective Joe K. Holiday's parents as Daddy Joe and Momma Jo. "But, mom I am on a case!" "Joe, you and your imaginary stories!" said Momma Jo. "Oh, let him have a little fun. School has only been out for one day. Maybe he will arrest Potter or book Scrooge!" said his Daddy Joe. Detective Holiday told Nobody, "I will get right on it, but first I have to take care of some family business."

The Family Holiday gathered round the Great Holiday Family Christmas Tree, which rose from the ground to the stars and sun, and had a branch for everyone. "Let us all join hands. Father in heaven we ask that you bless this tree as, it is a constant reminder of our family. Every year, we put upon our Christmas Tree a new ornament with the year on it, to remind us that another year has gone by, as we wait in your love for the world to come. Bless our nation! Bless our home state of Tennessee! Bless the City of Chattanooga, and all who call it home! Bless our home! Those inside, and those outside, serving elsewhere this day! In the name of Our Lord and Savior Jesus Christ! Amen!"

Note: The Great Holiday Family Christmas Tree!

Everyone gathered said, "Amen!" Daddy Joe reached with his steel-toed boot for a switch on a surge protector. With a tap of his foot, on came the lights on the tree. With another tap, the lights came on in the living room and the kitchen. Momma Jo, pulled a washcloth out of her apron pocket, and went into the bathroom, as was her custom, as she always cried.

Daddy Joe paid special attention to the tree. He had gone out of his way to have the brightest star above the apex of the tree. He had fashioned a white light within the star. Momma Jo called it, "one of his workshop wonders", as it turned round and round with a twinkling white light in the center of the star. It was the only star of its kind. Daddy Joe was quick to tell anyone who noticed. The room was now lit up, in a marvelous display of fabulous multi-colored blinking lights. Then hand in hand, the singing began, because in Chattanooga, our Christmas is not strange! It is just different!

IT IS JUST DIFFERENT!

Where folks swear up and down that our leaves turn
Tennessee Orange and Golden Brown! In Chattanooga,
Our Christmas is not strange It is Just Different!

Chorus: It is Just Different!

Where the cat will not let be, the Ornaments on the Christmas Tree!
In Chattanooga, Our Christmas is not strange
It is Just Different!

Chorus: It is Just Different!

Our Santa Claus! Is all dressed up in camouflage! In
Chattanooga Our Christmas is not strange It is Just Different!
When Pecan and Pumpkin Pie bring a gleam of joy too your eye!
It is just Christmas in Chattanooga, And it is Just Different!

Chorus: It is Just Different!

When folks in the manger! Look more like family than
strangers! In Chattanooga, Our Christmas isn't strange
It is Just Different!

Chorus: It is Just Different!

Where free men choose to worship a king!
Lift up their voices and to him
sing!   It is Just Christmas in Chattanooga
And it is Just Different!

Chorus: It is Just Different!

Where Veterans are held in the highest esteem! A
wanting of our children for Christmas it
seems!   It is Just Christmas in Chattanooga! And
it is Just Different!

Chorus: It is Just Different!

Where you can get all four kids in a trash can lid!
You would not need a map to see where they slid!
It is just Christmas in Chattanooga, And it is
Just Different! And it is Just Different!

Chorus: It is Just Different!

Grandpa said, "The Christmas Tree is looking good!" What
he meant to say was he needed some more firewood!
It is just Christmas in Chattanooga
And it is just different!

Chorus: It is just different!

Why do not you kids go down to the river and play?
Ah, Grandpa we would rather stay in your way
and watch Grandma turn your hair gray
It is just Christmas in Chattanooga
And it is just different!

Chorus: It is just different!

You are Honor? Mr. Potter?

Meanwhile in Bailey Park, formerly known as Bedford Falls, the Clerk of Court called the court into session with, "In the municipality of Bedford Falls, in the District of Pottersville, formerly known as Bailey Park, this court is now in session." "Turn off or remove all batteries from any and all electronic devices, or they will be confiscated at once!" said a very mean looking, bald headed guard, who looked out of place in a policeman's uniform. The guard suddenly rushed over and loudly enquired of a man, "Is that a camera?" He lifted up the heavy camera, and set in on a counter. He ushered the man who was wearing a, "Press", badge out of the courtroom.

Judge Potter was wearing the magic robe of the Heartless Ghost. The one Scrooge came to fear the most, and was about to enter the courtroom. An Officer of the Court stood up and proclaimed, in a very loud commanding voice, "All stand for the Honorable Judge Potter! The Honorable Judge Potter entered the courtroom and was seated in the Judge's chair by his aide de camp. The Officer of the Court loudly said, "Be Seated!" Immediately Judge Potter let out with, "This court is hereby in session, and I do not want to hear a word out of anybody, unless I speak to them personally! Am I understood?" (Everyone remained silent.) "I asked you all a question!" he iterated loudly. (The courtroom remained silent.)

The Clerk of the Court rushed over and whispered to Judge Potter, "You are Honor! You just told them not to say a word unless you spoke to them personally! You can not speak to a room full of people personally, can you?" "I guess you are right. Let us see now, forget what I said. Refer to your scripts unless, I speak to you personally, is that understood?" said Judge Potter with a grin.

Again, the clerk of the court approached. "You are Honor! It's not in the script for everyone to answer you at once." "Then write it in the blasted script! Do I have to think of everything?" asked Judge Potter. "No! You are Honor!" answered the clerk with trepidation in her voice. "Now, I hereby call this court to order!" The Clerk of the Court tugged on Judge Potter's robe. "What is it now?" asked Judge Potter. "The court has already been called to order! You are Honor!"

Judge Potter's eyes shot back and forth from left to right. He wondered if anyone had caught what he had yelled to the entire courtroom. You could hear a pin drop. So he continued as if nothing had happened concerning the script. "To business then, bring in the prisoner! I mean let us hear the first case of the day!" "You are Honor, the defendant George Bailey was caught wishing a Merry Christmas within the town limits of Potterville, in broad daylight on the morning of December 5th herein to be referred to, as the day in question!" said the prosecutor. "You are Honor, the defendant was legally reciting his lines from the original script!" said Clarence, George Bailey's Defense Attorney. "You mean to tell me that George Bailey has not learned his lesson, yet!

I see that you find it within yourself, too completely ignore the ordinances and laws of the District of Potterville! You are hereby fined $100.00 dollars for saying, Merry Christmas!" (Everyone in unison: "Merry Christmas!") "Stop that, right now! Right this instant!" ordered Judge Potter, as he pointed to the court with his gavel. "But, You are Honor you" said the Clerk of Court. "I know what I said" said Judge Potter angrily. "You are Honor, it was in the script!" again said the Clerk of Court. "Yes! Yes! I know it was in the script! Go by the new one! Or I am going to fine everyone in this courtroom! Now where was I?" asked Judge Potter. "You were about to rule, You are Honor!" said the prosecutor. "Will the defendant rise?" asked the Clerk of Court. "It is the sentence of this court that you, George Bailey, are to pay the fine of $100.00 dollars!

In addition, you are to pay the court costs, and ten days community service as my driver, George! Is that clear? I mean, it is so ordered by the court!" Said Judge Potter as he pointed his gavel at George Bailey. "Yes Sir! You are Honor, Mr. Potter Sir!" said George Bailey. "Bam!" Down came the gavel. "This court stands adjourned!" said Judge Potter as he tried to hide his smile of satisfaction. "George, he wants you to wear this hat! It is a chauffeurs hat! He is really digging his heels into you, is not he, George?" asked Clarence. George Bailey recited from his script, "Clarence, you have to remember that, Mr. Potter is the kindest, warmest, bravest most loveable man, I have ever met." George took a piece of paper from the table and began writing. He wrote, "Have you seen Mary?" Clarence wrote back on his pad, "She is waiting for you down by the river for a break in the film or a cut!" "I will wear the hat. Thanks!" said George, as he ran out of the court and down to the river.

Judge Potter retired to his chambers. He began to rub a skull that he kept on his desk. With a menacing grin he said, "Oh! Heartless Ghost! The one Scrooge came to fear the most! I am your master! I am your host! Come forward or backward in time! Do as I say! Every day and every time!"

With the help of his aide de camp, Mr. Potter took off the magic robe of the Heartless Ghost! The one Scrooge came to fear the most! He opened a double door closet. There in the darkness, was a long fingered hand. The hand stretched out from the darkness, and pulled in the magic robe. The long fingered hand pulled the robe over the top of the hand, and as the robe came down, it filled its ghostly shape. The shape of the Heartless Ghost, the one Scrooge came to fear the most! "I really, really enjoy my work! I really have to hand it to you Heartless! In just over one year, I have taken over the city of Bedford Falls. Consolidated Bailey Park, and the whole district, is now all of Pottersville. Now George Bailey is my driver! He is truly becoming no-one.

When I am through with him, he will not need a nametag. Huh! Huh! Huh! Your idea of stealing, and changing the script was genius! By, the time this airs, I will have George Bailey eating out of my hand."

"Have you done that which was required of you?" asked the Heartless Ghost. "I had my secretary fabricate a royal summons for you to deliver to Ebenezer Scrooge. The summons commands him to appear before the Christmas King. The King of Joy and Everything!

Once Ebenezer Scrooge accepts the knighthood, it will be good night for, "A Christmas Carol!" From 1843 Christmas will belong to me! The Christmas King will then reign supreme! Christmas from that day forward in time will be mine, all mine, for all time! Can you feel it heartless? Christmas will be mine! Christmas will be mine! Forward or backward everyday and every time! I feel just grand! If you were not a ghost, I would shake your long fingered hand! This is just the beginning of my Christmas winning! Oh, what a plan! Come on Heartless, shake my hand!" Implored Mr. Potter, for he was giddy with excitement. Because his most diabolical and fiendish plan was working.

Ever so slowly, the Heartless Ghost bent forward inhaling the air. This caused Mr. Potter to take note. In a diligent manner, he slightly pulled back as the Heartless Ghost moaned backward with his reply.

A long winding trail of odorless smoke came out from the dark empty hood of the Heartless Ghost with, "Potter, you have a stranger Christmas joy than most! To that, you should boast! Remember thee this very well! I am heartless and but a ghost! I have no yearning to join in your Christmas toast! For, I am the heartless, Heartless Ghost!"

With that the Heartless Ghost spun around and in a swirling cloud of odorless smoke the ghost in his anger retreated into the closet.

Mr. Potter tried his level best to appear unimpressed. However, his face displayed his stress, as he tried his level best! Moreover, the moaning words of the Heartless Ghost had found home in his heart! Mr. Potter knew well from his business dealings, how to conceal that which was in his feelings real, so he could seal the deal. To him, that was much more real, than what he could feel with his hands or his heart! He continued with his bantering, for all was well in his Christmas plans!

The Heartless Ghost, Microsoft C, and Potterpay!

Mr. Potter took his hand as if, he was washing a window and wiped away some of the odorless smoke of the Heartless Ghost and proudly proclaimed, "When we air the new, "It's a Wonderful Life!" I will also launch Microsoft C and Potterpay along with the Humbug Virus! The only version of windows that is immune to the virus is Microsoft C. It will not be available in stores! It will only be available through Potterpay! Aaaah! Hah! Hah! Hah! OOH! HO! HO! HO! This is priceless! Every business that refuses to use Potter Pay will come running to me when their businesses start to fail!

I will take over everything! And I have you to thank, Heartless!" said Mr. Potter as he took a golf club out of his golf bag. His aide de camp bent down and placed a golf ball with a little Santa Claus painted on it, on a golf tee in Mr. Potter's carpet. "I have spent all of my resources investing in the new, Microsoft C system along with Potterpay!

Do you know what, "Microsoft C", stands for Heartless?" asked Mr. Potter. "I believe I do! I created it for you!" said the Heartless Ghost, as if, he were exasperated with Mr. Potter. "I am going to tell you anyway! I just love telling people things!

Microsoft C stands for: Man's Intelligent Creation Restructured Order of Systematic Omnipotent Time Control. How does that grab you Heartless?" asked Mr. Potter. He then smacked the Santa Claus golf ball right into the hole in the corner, and, up popped the flag. Now, that is what I call a hole in one!" He said. "Let us see how George Bailey feels when I control the internet and time! What time is it George? It is Potter time! Hah! Hah! Hah! OOH! HO! HO! HO! Indeed!" he said, as his aide de camp pulled the Santa Claus golf ball out of the hole. "Then you are sure your plan will work?" asked the Heartless Ghost. "Huh! Huh! Huh! Heartless!

You have to have a little faith! You are not the only heartless cowboy in this rodeo!" said Mr. Potter. "Do not trifle with me Potter! I can make things smooth as glass, or make things hotter!" said the Heartless Ghost. "Do not worry so much Heartless! No need for you to come out of the closet! So to speak!" said Mr. Potter.

The director called for the mid-day break for lunch! "Mary? Mary?" said George as his eyes searched the crowd for hers. "Here I am! George! I am over here!" She exclaimed, as she had been anxiously waiting for him. Down by the river, had become a favorite place to meet for the people of Potterville. There were no cameras there. They could say, and do as they pleased on the river, but only during cuts in filming, or breaks, and for meals. During filming, the cast and crew, communicated with hand written notes, they passed along to each other. George communicated with his pals with Morse Code he had learned in school.

The members of the cast were professionals. They were bound to the script. They had to recite their lines verbatim, regardless of how they felt about them. It was a code of honor in the acting profession. It was also a method which proved their ability to make the audience believe the characters they portray are real. That is where the actors and actresses were trapped. Half of the time, they could not distinguish themselves from the roles they were portraying in the movie. They did have one thing in common. They were out to fight and stop Mr. Potter. That they did know for sure.

Nobody would see a movie more than once, if the audience could tell the actors were acting their roles. Also, deviation from the lines in the script was frowned upon. It was considered disrespect to the writer and director, and cause for termination. The actors thought of themselves, as duty bound to the script. The script Mr. Potter had switched, with the help of the Heartless Ghost. The one Scrooge came to fear the most! "Mary, did you get the information about Potterpay?" asked George Bailey. "George, he keeps it under the seat of his golf cart, of all places. Now, he has written in the script for little Janey to come over, and retrieve his golf balls in a bucket. George, he managed to get it written into the script as a school extra credit assignment under community service."

She said softly, as she knew his heart was already broken. "Mary! Oh, Mary! I just do not know how much more of this I can stand! Everything, I have ever dreamed of is gone. Now he is working on the children!" he said in exasperation. "George you have got to keep it up! You have to keep the faith!" said Mary. "Mary, I am just so tired." He replied.

George Bailey looked up as the sets whistle blew. "Oh, there goes that darn whistle!" He said, as he walked backward from her. "Everybody back on the set!" came from the director's megaphone. It was made out of wood, and produced a very load almost hollow sound to the words. "Remember George? I love you!" she said, as her eyes searched his looking for strength. "I love you too Mary!" He said, as he turned and walked away, taking the chauffeurs hat out of his pocket. He pulled it down on his head angrily. He reached back and pulled his script out of his back pocket, and began to read his next lines for the next scene.

Mr. Potter was still in the middle of his office, practicing his golf put. His carpet was of the finest cut and weave. He gently putted the ball and this time it curved into the baseboard in front of the closet door of the Heartless Ghost. The one Scrooge came to fear the most. He moved to his desk. "Blast it all!" said Mr. Potter as he reached for the button on the intercom. "Ms. Rongfughlee, I thought I instructed you to have this carpet replaced. It is lumpy and unevenly cut!

Would you like to explain to me, why you did not do as you were told!" exclaimed Mr. Potter, bitterly. "Mr. Potter the carpet was replaced yesterday, while you were on the set! Do not you remember?" she replied. He mashed in on the intercom button and sternly said, "Get better carpet installed! This one is unsatisfactory! Get another one immediately or I will see about getting a better secretary immediately! Do I make myself clear?" Ms. Rongfughlee jumped in her seat. Then she replied with, "Absolutely! Mr. Potter, I am on it! Right now!" Mr. Potter reached for the skull on his desk and asked of himself loudly, "By heaven's name do I have to do everything around here!"

He began to rub the crown of the skull vigorously and methodically. He angrily let out with, "Oh Heartless Ghost! The one Scrooge came to fear the most! I am your master! I am you host! Come forward or backward in time! Do as I say! Every day and every time!"

The double door closet slowly opened to reveal a cloud of odorless smoke, swirling all around and inside the closet. The odorless smoke swirled within, and out came the Heartless Ghost as the double doors of the closet closed, every so slowly. The Heartless Ghost said, "What wish is for me to grant to you! So that everyday is Christmas! I will be your workman! I will be your tool!" Mr. Potter's glasses steamed up. For the first time, his face showed a bit of real concern. His smile had left him, but he went on to say, "Heartless! I want to change the script again. Type a new one as you did before.

Do that, "All that is within my heart trick!" commanded Mr. Potter. The Heartless ghost began to moan. Then with every word a cloud of odorless smoke, came out of the empty faceless hood of the Heartless Ghost with, "St. Valentine's Ribbon around your Heart!

Capture every thought and word you say! Just hope! It is never played back to you someday!"

The side drawer in Mr. Potter's desk came open. The Paper fed itself into his 1937 Electromatic Model 01, printer tray. The power came on by itself. The printer began printing a new script. Mr. Potter was indeed impressed with the power of the Heartless Ghost. He knew as it was before, that everything he wanted changed in the script would be, just as he wanted it to be. "What more? Would you have me do?" asked the Heartless Ghost. "I have had George Bailey wash and wax my car, mow my lawn, and prepare my taxes. I even had him, retile the roof of my home. I just am at a loss, for what I need to do to break him.

I want George Bailey to look in the mirror and see for himself, that he is a loser! I want to hear him say loudly, and not just to himself, but to his heart, that good guys finish last!" said Mr. Potter with a look of superiority. "Some men do not break so easy! They are the ones with callused hands that come home all dirty and greasy! You find them at work late at night, when those of lesser spirit, are asleep and await the light! You cannot get to their heart by doing evil to them. Seek out and find those whom they love, and do evil to them!" said the Heartless Ghost. "You mean his family!" asked Mr. Potter whose look of superiority gave way to a look of concern. Mr. Potter stared into the dark empty faced hood, of the Heartless Ghost! His eyes widened with fear. He moved to his office window and looked into the street.

"Do not question the emptiness of my heart! Potter! I give you warning! Do as I say, and as I do, and much evil will be done unto him, I guarantee you!" said the Heartless Ghost! "I already have his little Janey picking up my golf balls, after school! I have had Mrs. Bailey do my laundry and even had her pick-up my prescriptions and deliver them when I fell ill!

What else should I do?" asked Mr. Potter with a very worried look on his face. "Perhaps you should muddy your hands, like your heart! Then you would not question me! You would just play your part!" said the Heartless Ghost. "No, Heartless, I have a few tricks left up my sleeve! No need for that!" said Mr. Potter. For a nanosecond he thought, "I am not that bad." He looked back at the dark empty face of the Heartless Ghost. The Heartless Ghost said not a thing. He threw open the closet doors, and in a swirling cloud of odorless smoke, he went in.

The doors of the closet slammed shut behind him. The office shook from what Mr. Potter thought was a storm brewing. Mr. Potter went over to his desk. His superiority and arrogance left him, and he slumped down into his chair. He put his hands up to his temples. He leaned forward, and held his head up with his arms. He could no longer, hold his head up with his senseless pride alone. So he sat, slumped in contemplation, with his face in his hands.

He knew what the Heartless Ghost had meant. He knew, all to well that this was the final script. He began to think about what might befall him, at the long fingered hands of the Heartless Ghost. The one Scrooge had come to fear the most. What would the Heartless Ghost do to him, if the ghost read the St. Valentines ribbon around his heart, and perceived weakness, or saw his thoughts typed on a new script? The St. Valentine's ribbon around his heart had captured that thought. It would betray him, to the Heartless Ghost. He could not just remove it, forget it, or even try to explain it to the Heartless Ghost. The ghost which had no feeling and of course no heart! He was worried and rightfully so!

He reached for the buzzer on his office intercom, and pressing it he let out, "Ms. Rongfughlee would you have my driver bring the car around. I would like to go home for the evening." "Right away and on the double, you are honor!" she replied. He reached for the buzzer again. "Ms. Rongfughlee, when I am not in the court room, I wish to be referred to as Mr. Potter. Is that understood?" "Yes Sir! Mr. Potter Sir!" she replied. "That is better, much better." said Mr. Potter.

The buzzer sounded, and the intercom announced, "Mr. Potter your driver is here to take you home sir!" A smile flashed across his withered face! He reached for the intercom button. "Have him step right on in!" he said devilishly. "Yes Sir! Mr. Potter!" she replied. Mr. Potter leaned back in his chair, and waited for the knock. "Knock, Knock" came from the door. "Come In! Come In!" said Mr. Potter. "Who might you be?" asked Mr. Potter as George Bailey stepped into his office. "I am your driver for the afternoon sir!" said George. "Would you be so kind, as to get my briefcase, there by the door? My good and humble servant!" said Mr. Potter with a grin. "Yes Sir! Mr. Potter" said George Bailey as he complied. "Tell me, my good and humble servant. Do you like your new job?" "Yes sir! I would not have it, any other way, sir!" George said biting his tongue.

Jimmy Stewart had to keep reminding himself, that he was bound to the script, and had to say his lines verbatim. "I ought to kick you right in the teeth!" he thought, as he stood before his new employer. However, he asked, "Shall we go? My good and kind sir?" His whole body cringed. He just could not stand this much longer. "Who wrote these lines?" he thought to himself. "Whoever it was, sure did not mind being someone else's lackey!" He thought, as they exited through Ms. Rongfughlee's office and down the stairs to the garage.

Nobody's Secret Place
in the Plant Room

Nobody had gone to her favorite place to say her afternoon prayer. It was filled with plants that her mother had grown. Some of them even went as far back in time as her Great Grandma Mildred. Her Great Grandmother made the strongest coffee on the planet. Her father occasionally told her of the time that when he first had a cup of Great Grandma's coffee it was so strong, that it had made him immediately feverishly sick. Great Grandma had enticed him to finish the last bit. He just could not finish the last bit. He did not want to offend her, so he poured the last bit into one of her houseplants that grew up along the wall. The houseplant died an agonizing death at his hands. Great Grandma was heartsick over it.

Fortunately, for him, Great Grandma Mildred had given a clipping to his wife, and Nobody's mother. She brought a clipping, from her clipping, back to Great Grandma. Who was then delighted, as that had been her favorite plant. In all of her Great Grandma's pretty little plant stand in her home in far away Leesville, Louisiana.

Nobody liked to say her prayers aloud. That way, she was sure that her prayer would be heard. There was nothing special about that, it was just her reasoning. Her timing was always when, she knew there were shoes in the dryer. It made her think that it was the rumblings of heaven itself, as she said her prayers.

After she was finished, she went into the kitchen where her mother was standing by the sink in the late afternoon sun. She was wearing one of her favorite white dresses that had tiny little white beads sewn into the laces and cuffs. She looked very much like that of an angel, as the late day rays of the sun caught the beads in her dress. It must be the hour of the long shadow, she thought.

Her father had a Cherokee friend who called this time of the day, "the hour of the long shadow." They were outside cleaning their rifles for the next day's hunt. He was always keen to point out the long shadows during this time of the day. She remembered it because it always made her mother's dress sparkle.

She told her mother about what Mr. Potter had been doing to Mr. George Bailey, and how he was turning him into a true nobody. She told her mother about the, "Land of Nowhere", and why, she and Detective Joe K. Holiday would have to go there to solve the case. Her mother turned away from the sink after putting away, the now clean pie tin. She leaned down to get eye to eye with nobody. "Mr. Potter has not done him any favors, but maybe this will help. With a reassuring smile, Momma Jo sang this to her daughter.

NO-ONE IN NOWHERE

Being No-one in nowhere is being special indeed!
No-one is no-one until you care. Then no-one becomes someone and
love spreads like
branches in a tree from there!
Because No-one would notice, when no-one dyed your hair!
No-one would get arrested, when no-one robbed the bank!
No-one shakes your hand, when there is no-one to thank!
No-one always sighs, when you fumble the ball!
No-one gets the phone, when no-one calls!
No-one to miss when, no-one says goodbye!
No-one gets a tissue, when there's a tear in your eye!

No-one says anything, when you enter the room!
When you make a mess! No-one gets the broom!
No-one gets in trouble, when no-ones late!
No-one is your friend, when there's no-one at all!
No-one stands corrected, when no-one makes a mistake!
No-one will catch you, when you stumble or fall!
When someone cares about a no-one, and that no-one is me!
Then I, become someone too someone you see!
You open up! Your eyes for the first time and see! Someone's love has made them
someone special to someone like me!
It is forever, eternal, everlasting, indeed!
Then love rises up from within you like a
mountain rises up from the sea!
Rises up from the sea!
Straight up! Through the heavens, from the sea!
Straight up! Through the heavens you see!
Even, if you are a no-one to everyone.
You are still someone special to me!
When you, become the someone, that cared to make this no-one
Someone special then you are someone special! Indeed!

"I hope that helps you with your case. Now run along! I have so much to do. Kitchen work is never finished, you know!" Nobody wiped a tear from her eye. "Now remember! "Girl Nobody", this is what Christmas is all about that a very special someone became a noone. So that everyone could have what that very special someone already had, before he became a no-one for us, salvation! That makes you, someone special indeed! Because it was done by love, with love and for those whom he loved." she said as she wiped off the kitchen table. "Thanks Momma and Merry Christmas!" she said, as she skipped out of the kitchen.

Note: The Southern Belle as she comes into view near a strange and mysterious land of nowhere.

CHAPTER 7

The Lady of the River

Detective Holiday sat as his desk. He listened and could make out the sounds of the Southern Belle as, The Lady of the River," rounded the bend, coming ever closer to his home. The sounds the steam made as it worked it way out of her pipes, echoed between the bluffs overlooking the Tennessee River. It was so exciting and romantic to him. He had been on her deck before. If he was not so much in love with being a detective, he would probably fall in love with her, he reasoned. He had stood up on her deck watching, as the captain was at the helm. He had brought along his spyglass and watched the captain with his long sideburns, mustache and collar length hair, guide the lady between the giant cement pillars that held up the many bridges around the City of Chattanooga. What skill and concentration he thought. I too, will have a job of such importance, someday.

Night was fast approaching, and he sat staring at the pictures of the Bailey Park Sign that he had taken with his cell phone. He fell asleep and dreamt about when he had overheard a couple of men, talking about getting off the Southern Belle in Nowhere. He had been collecting water samples for his biology class. Members of the Southern Belle's crew were giving lessons in safety on the water, first aide, and knot tying of every sort. It was a great field trip, and one of his most treasured memories. He remembered how odd it was, that the two men wore sunglasses inside the small cafeteria area. He thought it was particularly odd, that they were dressed in black suits in the middle of summer. He awoke from his dream. He immediately put electronic pen to electronic paper. He did not want to forget any clues no matter, from whence or where they came. Nobody must have forgotten to call he thought, as he wrote down what he had dreamt about. He put down his tablet and fell fast asleep.

Detective Joe K. Holiday rarely overslept. He thought that it was the habit of a slacker and beneath him to do so. However, this was the day that he broke that habit. He opened his eyes startled, as it was so bright in his room. It had to be ten o'clock or there about he thought to himself. He jumped up so high, that he could hear one of the slats in his bed, crack when he came back down on it. He ran to his window. There was the Southern Belle with passengers already on deck. He could see Nobody looking up at his window. He knew she could not see him because of the glare of the sun. He had looked back from that very spot. His window always seemed trapped in the rays of the sun. He could see his Momma Jo, who had been waving to him from his window, on his last voyage. He knew, he had but a few moments to get dressed, or their plans would fall to ruin because of his tardiness. He wrestled himself into his clothes.

He pulled his father's trench out of the closet, entirely too hard. It whipped a sleeve around the flagpole by his desk. He had to leap almost a foot, to keep the flag from touching the floor. As, he pulled it back straight, it catty corned the pictures of General Douglas Macarthur and General "Stormin" Norman Schwarzkopf. He straightened the two pictures. He saluted the flag. Then he saluted the two soldiers, and ran out of his room and down the stairs just as fast as his legs could carry him.

Once he was down on the Tennessee River, he called, "Nobody!" To which she replied, "I am over hear honey!" When he arrived at her side he said, "Good Morning! My dear Nobody!" Her eyes were wide. She said absolutely nothing, as it had just slipped out, of her mouth, before she had even thought about what she had said.

"Did you bring the kit?" he quipped as his hand brought his pen-pipe up to his teeth. Nobody nodded yes. "My dear you are the, "cream of the crop", when it comes to being a detectives assistant!" She remained silent, as her thoughts were still on what she had accidentally blurted out. She also knew he actually meant what he had said. He did not say anything that made her think he had heard what she had blurted.

She figured he had not noticed which made her relax a bit. "Why did you not call me last night?" asked the detective. Our phone is not working. However, I was able to get a wireless signal and connect my tablet. You would not believe what I found out about Mr. Potter's Plans! My parents always warn me about posting everything on the Internet." said Nobody. "Mr. Potter has been posting everything on social media daily right at six p.m. He has photo shopped a Royal Summons and has boasted that he has successfully sent it back in time and is now waiting for it to be delivered to Ebenezer Scrooge.

The Southern Belle gave two blasts, which was her final boarding call. Together, they climbed the gangway leading to the Southern Belle. Once on the deck of the great ship, Detective Joe K. Holiday could feel the soft beat of the engine beneath his feet. He was just so happy to be on board the great lady of the river, with a great lady.

The great wheel of the ship began rowing, it started snowing, and off to the North it went. The steam engines of the Southern Belle belched out great clouds of steam, which looked like great big marshmallows in the sky as it sojourned north. North to find George Bailey. North to find the Christmas King! The King of Joy and Everything! "How can Mr. Potter do that? Change the meaning of Christmas?" asked Nobody.

It was so fiendishly clever, thought Detective Holiday. "This Christmas King must be some happy go lucky fellow with a bad attitude, to be in league with the likes of Mr. Potter!" said the detective. "Sending a royal summons back in time is what puzzles my mind. I have heard of some dastardly deeds in my time, but this is beyond the scope of reason! It is entirely unbelievable! That is why we must get to the bottom of this!" said Detective Holiday!

He knew that travel was permitted in conjunction with a Royal Summons. But this was ridiculous. There is something afoot, he thought, as he brought his Pen-pipe to his teeth. It cannot be just the rules. Plus! Sending a summons back in time, would be akin to sending a warrant back in time. Why bother unless something is brewing in the air!

He felt for sure, that something beyond his imagination was at hand. His curiosity was peaked. How could somebody respond back in time? Unless there was some sort of mystery to be solved? "The biggest mystery is why? "There is only one reason why Mr. Potter would want to change the meaning of Christmas? Money!

If my instincts and power of deduction are correct, there is one thing we can be sure of Nobody!" said the detective. "What?" she replied with a very concerned look in her eyes. "This Christmas King, whoever he is, he is not a friend! I believe he is our foe! The game is a foot!" he said clenching his pen-pipe in his teeth. "We have got to get to George Bailey. He will know what to do! He can at least point us in the right direction!" said

Detective Holiday. "How can you be sure that we are going in the right direction detective?" asked Nobody again? "I am not completely sure.

I am gaming on a hunch! Summer last, while I was on a class field trip, I overheard two gentlemen who were completely dressed in black discussing their destination as nowhere, as they sat in the cafeteria. They did not eat or drink anything. They just sat there staring into an electronic compass. I will wager, that since we are going in the same direction, as I was then, we are most likely headed for the Land of Nowhere! If, the Southern Belle makes and unscheduled stop, so shall we!" said Detective Holiday with a confident knowing grin. "We have to go where the clues lead us, no matter where that might be. It is a recognized law within the community of detectives, or at least in the manual of, "Investigative Techniques." said Detective Holiday.

Note: Below one of the pen-pipes of Detective Joe K. Holiday!

Ebenezer Scrooge and Second Chances

Meanwhile in London, England, far, far away, and long, long ago Ebenezer Scrooge was making his way home after dinning at the home of Bob Cratchit and his family. Mr. Ebenezer Scrooge was indeed full of life, and the Christmas Spirit. He was a changed man, because his heart had changed his spirit. He felt Joy in his heart, for the first time in a long time. He could hardly make his way back to his flat, after so much Christmas pudding.

The mere thought of the Christmas Goose, of which he had quite a bit of, brought air up and out his mouth. He brought his handkerchief up as he went, and said, "Oh! Dear me! Excuse me!" He looked round about him, and saw that he was alone, with the exception of a tethered horse.

He tipped his hat and wished aloud, "Merry Christmas to you! I will wager you were not expecting that from me! Heavens No! Not from that old miser! eh!" He could hardly hold on to his keys. He just kept on finding things to chuckle about. He put the key in the lock, and had to push inward on the door and as he did, he felt something in the snow below his feet. "What must this be?" He reached down for it, and turning it over, he noticed the wine colored wax seal, had not been broken. He clutched it in his hand, and rushed inside. He studied it, by the light of a single candle in his parlor. "Why it must come from the Queen herself?" He thought, as he read the golden inlaid inscription, which bore his name.

Never before had his eyes gazed upon such a sight. I will wager that it is a payment overdue to the City Council Proprietor. He opened his payment record book, and ran his finger down the list. He found no such overdue payment, pending for adjustment. What is this truly? He pondered. His hands began to tremble in fear. His mind thought on the subject most considerably.

"Maybe it is some treachery, concerning his sudden shift in attitude concerning Christmas! "My house keeper?" he thought to himself. Perhaps she had reported him. I will not go to the crazy house! I am as fit as a fiddle! Crazy yes, perhaps, but not violently crazy as he had seen before. Why that is what had become of Tobias Canton years before. He had tried to burn down his flat down by the park rather than surrender it to Marley on collection day." Scrooge thought almost and as if, his mind were thirsting or hungering for an answer. He carefully studied the fine embossed envelope, looking for any explanation as to its true intent. Ebenezer was truly perplexed, and his fastidious mind truly yearned for an answer to this puzzlement.

He decided to take a more exacting and closer look at the letter. Taking his letter opener from his desk, he gently worked the blade under the seal, as not to disturb it. It popped open from the bottom, as if air had been trapped beneath the seal. He brought the candle even closer, and slowly pulled the contents from the envelope. The letter was inlaid and embossed entirely in gold. His eyes widened still, when he read: "To all whom presents greetings, one Ebenezer Scrooge is herby summoned to appear before the Christmas King, the King of Joy and Everything!

To be announced by Royal Escort to receive the Rank and Title of Knight." His eyes widened even further. He dropped his letter opener. Knocked over the candle and almost caught fire to his clothing. He quickly, beat it out of his tunic. The candle caught fire to his payment record book on his desk. By the time he had put it out, he was exhausted.

Ebenezer sat back down in his chair and examined the payment record book. "Thank heavens it is only singed around the edges of the pages! Just enough to cause notice", he thought as he put it away. He took a matchstick and relit his candle. His eyes moved to the parchment, now on the floor. Even in the dim light of a single candle, its brilliance seemed to make the room and eerie amber color. "Who am I, to go before the Christmas King, the king of joy and everything?" he thought. "I should have turned over a new leaf, years ago", he murmured, as he bent down and picked up the parchment.

He thought that it was truly time to go too bed indeed. He went into his sleeping chamber and undressed. Ebenezer then washed himself a bit in his laboratory. Then dressed in his sleeping clothes, and put on his sleeping cap. Ebenezer was terribly exhausted, more so in his mind than his body. He inspected his tunic. He saw that it had not even a scorch mark on it. "Must have caught just the fine long fibers", he thought, as it almost appeared pressed in the light of his candle.

Ebenezer set his tunic aside and climbed into his bed. Tonight was going to be different. He climbed back out, knelt down, and said a prayer of thanksgiving. He asked for forgiveness, which made him cry, as he had not done so since he had lost his Anna.

He tried to go to sleep, but every time the clock struck on the hour, he jumped. He pulled the blanket up to his nose and his eyes swung back and forth from left to right with the ticking of the clock. Tick! Right! Tock! Left! He just kept on with it, as he was frightened almost silly from the night before. Tick! Right! Tock! Left! Tick! Right! Tock! Left! Tick! Right! Tock! Left! Tick! Right! Finally, the clock struck the hour and when the gong sounded, he leapt from the bed and ran into his laboratory.

When he finally cracked the door, it was only enough, for his nose and one eye to see out of from the safety of the room. For he, was not forgetful of the night before. He was on full alert. He now had on his military service hat, from his days serving in Her Majesty's Service. He had on his saber that Bob Cratchit had given to him for Christmas! He was amazed as he never ever received a gift such as the saber. Bob Cratchit could not afford such a saber. The saber had been, handed down to him. It was the finest of gifts and was a true family treasure. It was the only thing, he could think of giving Ebenezer for his sudden shift in attitude towards the most high and holy day of Christmas! The Christmas gift of the saber gave him a sense or reassurance.

However, the saber seemed to hinder, rather than help him as it clanked and clattered into his furnishings as he went about his flat in a panicked sense of duty to protect himself from the unknown. He went to his pantry and pulled down a bottle of wine. He poured a measure into a crystal drinking canter, and drank it, without taking a breath. When he set down the crystal canter, he could not believe what he had just done.

Ebenezer Scrooge did not drink, so as not to waste the wine. It was strictly for washing down his meals. Now, he was sure of himself that, he could indeed get to sleep. He brought the bottle and canter with him. He did not know why. He just did not want to go into his sleeping chamber empty handed.

He decided then and there, that he was going to face away from the clock. He went over to the other side of the bed and sat down. Just then, the clock struck the hour again with a big, "Gong!" "Aaaaahh!" he yelled, as he stood straight up! The canter and bottle of wine flew from each hand and against the wall in front of him! The bottle of wine fell back from it, and landed on Ebenezer's foot!

Again "Aaaaahh!" shot from the deepest part of his throat. He was now trying to keep from falling down, as he clutched his foot in his hands. Ebenezer balanced the rest of his body on his left foot, which already had a nasty bit of a corn on it. When his foot finally stopped beating with the clock, he thought well, now maybe I can get some sleep. I must have stayed up longer than any ghost he reasoned. So, he laid down and closed his eyes, and promised himself that no matter, he would not open them.

Ebenezer Scrooge studied every bit of sound from the fireplace to the sounds coming from outside, which he could clearly reason away in his mind. He began to hear a slapping almost tapping sound. He gritted his teeth and pulled his blanket over his head. He hugged his ribs with both arms, trying to resolve the tapping sound in his head. Was it a bit of water coming from the sink in the laboratory? Was it a shutter at the window? He thought for a moment, and then remembered he did not have shutters. "Go away! Whoever you are! Take what you want, but leave me be, and uh, Merry Christmas to thee!" he said.

Ebenezer was almost violently quaking under his blanket. Still the slapping almost tapping sound continued. "I will not look! I am staying in here! Go Away! Go Away! I Pray!" He said then waited for a response. Nothing came except that slapping almost tapping sound, which grew louder and louder and had him mesmerized. "Who and what might you be? You were not foretold to me to see!" he said. The sound went away. He could not close his eyes. He had to rub them to get them to close, as he wanted them to do, so desperately.

This is almost too much for my heart to take he thought. It was now quiet. His hands relaxed their grip on his ribs. "Finally! Peace at last!" he thought, as he rolled his eyes around beneath his eyelids. He moved his hands up to the edges of the blanket. As he did, he thought that he might buy some brighter lamps, so as too ease his mind. So he could get some sleep. He brought the blanket down with a, "wheeeew!" "Aaaaahh!" Came out of the deepest part of his throat!

He was starring into the empty swirling smoke of the hood, of the Heartless Ghost! The one, he would come to fear the most! He pulled the blanket back over his head, and Aaaaahh! He was again, looking into the swirling smoke of the Heartless Ghost's Hood! He pulled the blanket off! Then back on, and no matter what direction he turned! There was that empty heartless face, starring back at him! Saying not a word! Until, "Ebeneeeezer!" said the Heartless Ghost. "Ebeneeeezer!" said the Heartless Ghost. "Go Away! Go Away!

I do not want to see the past, present, or future any longer! My heart grows weaker not stronger! What must I do, or say, to make you ghosts go away!" said he, to the Ghost. "Ebeneeeezer! You must do yourself a turn this day, a present!" moaned the Heartless Ghost. "What is it Ghost? I do not want your gift. Take it back! I bid you good night!" said Ebenezer Scrooge in a frightened, afraid to look tone in his quivering voice. "Look Ebeneeeezer! Look here! Bring me your eyes!" demanded the Heartless ghost in a deep dark totalitarian tone. "Why should I bring my eyes to you? I like them right were they are!" said he hoping for and_end_to this apparition.

The heartless Ghost stretched forth, his long fingered hand. "Ebenezer do not fear. Bring your eyes here!" said the Heartless Ghost. Ebenezer reasoned that he had to take his self over there, before the ghost snatched his eyes out or even something worse. So, he straightened himself up and ever so slowly stepped out of bed, and into the cold chilling air. "Look!" commanded the ghost, as he stretched forth his long fingered hand into Ebenezer's face. There before his eyes was some sort of magic moving picture box. In the picture box, he was seated at his desk, and in came his Anna. "She is alive in a picture?" He beseeched of the ghost. "Yeeeeesss! She is as alive, and as young as you wish to be this very night!" Proclaimed the ghost in an eerie voice.

There before his tired old empty eyes was Anna! His very own Anna! He slowly reached up his hand, and gently removed the super cell phone from the long fingered hand of the Heartless Ghost. There she was in all her youthful glory! He clutched the super cell phone to his chest. He wished he could hold on to this magic picture box forever. His eyes immediately began to water as he could remember every bit of that most dreadful day!

Scrooge watched as again, that dreadful day unfolded once more, before him! "Say something you fool! Say something you fool!" he said, as she walked away and out of his life again!" "He let the super cell phone fall to the bed, which caused the Heartless Ghost to stretch forth his long fingered hand and catch it before it found the mattress of his bed.

Scrooge sat down heavily. He began to cry then to sob! No! No! No! How can this be? My life has been too long already, but to lose her thrice is more than any mere mortal man can bare." The Heartless Ghost knew it! Mr. Potter knew it! Regretfully, Ebenezer Scrooge knew it all too well! Wishing for and end to this torment of his heart he said, "Heartless Ghost! If you are here for my heart, than take it! If you are here for my eyes take them as well! I can no longer see any use for me!"

"Scrooge I will give her back too you this very day! It is the answer to your empty prayers! What say thee? You will acquire all you desire! You will be given much gold and silver and a noble estate! The Christmas King will just impose a simple value added tax upon the surplus population! Just say these words, I pray thee, "I Sell!" Then sign here! Initial here! Endorse in your own handwriting in blue ink your full and complete name, here! Then date here! Then sign here once again! Here you can use my pen!" said the Heartless Ghost. The pen was chewed up at the end, and could not write or even electronically sign. The pen no longer had a pointed tip. It was the pen-pipe of Detective Holiday! The Heartless Ghost had been foiled by Detective Joe K. Holiday!

The Heartless Ghost turned to leave and on the back of the Heartless Ghost's magic robe was another envelope with Ebenezer Scrooge written on it, for all to see! Scrooge remembered his days in Her Majesty's Service, when he had seen; "Kick Me!" on a new man's backside. "I have not the time to barter! Scrooge!" said the Heartless Ghost.

Scrooge reached out and pulled the note off, and let it fall upside down on the bed. "Merry Christmas! What did you say your name was?" asked Ebenezer. The Heartless Ghost turned around and said, "I am the Heartless Ghost! I have but emptiness where a heart should be. All other ghosts fear me the most! I will return for your answer Ebeneeeeezzzer Scrooge! Know this well! You will have your cake! It will not be permanent, until you sign and say, "I sell!" With that, the Heartless Ghost disappeared into a swirling cloud of odorless smoke! The smoke went through the keyhole of Ebenezer's closet door and into his closet.

Ebenezer rushed over too the closet door and put his weight to it. He reached for the key. He inserted the key into the lock. He rotated the key until he heard the lock engage with a loud, "click!" He was glad he had not signed. Ebenezer spied for the clock and found it was only one quarter of an hour past the hour of midnight. He went to blow out the single candle that was now, on the windowsill. He thought it was odd that, the fog outside the window seemed to be a bluish color. Yet with everything, that did not busy his mind. His concern was centered squarely on the fact that he had survived another ghost, and that in itself, was enough excitement for the night. So, Ebenezer blew out the candle and closed his eyes to sleep.

Ebenezer Scrooge began dreaming about when he was a lad on the streets of London. His mum was a midwife, and she worked earnestly trying to save the lives of the poorest families babies. He worked as a child cleaning stables and wiping the hooves of the horses of gentlemen. So that they, would not muddy their boots, or their clothes, when they went to mount their steeds.

He would have to beg for money, so that his mum could pay the month's rent. His father was gone for weeks at a time. He worked aboard ships as a deckhand. Ebenezer would find himself, begging the passing strangers. The pittance, he was paid as a stable boy was not nearly enough, to help his mum. He often sang a song to them, with the hope of touching their hearts, and loosening their purse strings.

TWO SHILLINGS AND A PENCE!

A farthing! A farthing! Two shillings and a pence!
It all that I need! To pay this month's rent!
Could you! sir? Would you sir? Oh, please would you, my good sir!
A farthing! A farthing! Two shillings and a pence!
It is all that I need! To pay this month's rent!
It is not for candy! Good wine or brandy!
It is for my mum the good midwife Mandy!
A farthing! A farthing! Two shillings and a pence!
I will work! I will serve you from the bottom of my heart!
Just tell me where or when I can start!
A farthing! A farthing! Two shillings and a pence!

Is all that I need to pay this month's rent!
Could you sir? Would you sir? Oh, please would you, my good sir!

"It's a boy! Mandy you have done it again! I do not believe you have slept in a fortnight! I truly believed Clarissa was a goner!" said the husband "Now! Go rest yourself easy and let her sleep!" said Mandy. "The poor child needs milk. I will see to that! I will go to Father Selfridge for the baby on your behalf. Do not wake her for she has seen the worst of it! Ebenezer! Are you spying again?" asked his mum. "No mother, I wish to see the baby!" he said looking through the window that was even to the ground outside the humble cottage, by the street. "Please not now! Ebenezer, I have much work that I must do, so that the child will live!" said Mandy. "But Mother!" said Ebenezer. "Son busy yourself with your duties, as I do mine." She said holding the baby up as she wrapped him. "Oh, Mother he is beautiful! He is simply beautiful!" said young Ebenezer. "Ebenezer! You have seen him! Now! Run along!" she said in his dream. He went back and he held out his tin cup as a man walked by. He tossed a coin, which Ebenezer caught, in his cup. He looked down into his cup at the coin. "A Crown! A whole Crown!" he said, thinking that this was Christmas Day!

Note: Ebenezer with his Anna is his dream.

CHAPTER 9

Follow Your Heart!

It was the day the savior was born! He too, was given a crown on this day. He looked up, and suddenly, he was looking into the face of Anna in his dream still. "Anna! Anna! It is you! It is really you, I must be dreaming?" said Ebenezer. Now, he was a young man in his dream. "Of course you are dreaming silly! I can only come to you in your dreams. For you pushed me out of your heart!" she said softly with a smile. "Then you must prove it!

What pet name did you and only you have for me, when we were alone where the ears of others could not find us?" asked Ebenezer. "Idiot! Buffoon! Trouble Maker! Busy Body!" she said smiling. "Enough! I say!" He said, as he noticed, that he was now old in his dream, again and continued with, "I see that death has not hindered your memory none whatsoever woman! Then why, do you incessantly bother yourself with mine?" "Now you are your old self!" she said smiling. Ebenezer suddenly found himself a young man again and said, "I have been given a second chance. Anna, come with me, and let what we could have had, begin. Take the hand of a man whose heart has seen nothing but sin!" She replied to Ebenezer with a song:

FOLLOW YOUR HEART

Oh, Ebenezer! My Ebenezer! Listen to your heart!
What we had, and could have had, could never have been!
Your heart was not ready, not now or back then!
You are living in a dream cloud! Just let it float by!
The world to come, depends on us saying, goodbye!
I see you now, as I saw you back when, my heart was yours to the very
end! Ebenezer!
Not just now and again!
So, if you truly love me, truly, truly love
me you must do the right thing!
Not just for me or you but all of England!
Ebenezer! Ebenezer! Follow your heart! Even if you forget!
I will always remember our love from the start
Remember! Ebenezer! Remember! Follow your heart!
Stiffen your lip and do what you must do!
The world to come means so much more than we do!
Follow your heart like time follows the sun!
It's a bright new world fit for you and everyone!
Remember! Ebenezer I will always have a place in your heart!
Than to have it all and all of England condemned
To a world created in sin!
Could you be happy? In this new story, of true love, riches and glory!
Or the wretched old miser in an everlasting story!
Who followed his heart and found the love of a king!
Born in a lowly far away place! Fit for fleas, rats and snakes!
You found the love of a King!
You found the King!
He is our King!

Ebenezer awoke and he went straight away to the clock! It was three
quarters of an hour past midnight. He felt as if he had slept all night
long. How could this be? I keep the workings so clean. The time must
be off! Or, I am off! I am just so heartsick over all this my life seems to

be running back and forth, to and fro! If only I could wind my heart like the clock there and set it back right, he thought to himself.

He turned and gazed at the piano he had not played, since he had lost his Anna. He went over too it, and taking his sleeping cap in his hand, he wiped it off. He sat down and began to weep! Then begin to sob! Strangely, he wanted again to play it. The keys had not even seen the light of day or even the light of the parlor, since that dreadful day.

He thought that his heart was now scared, as if from a nasty wound. He opened up the piano and exposed the keys and thought, "It is a strange thing! How the words come to me so easy when my heart needs to sing, and I just let it do so!" He thought to himself as his fingers found the keys, this once more. Music had found Ebenezer Scrooge again.

He thought about his dreams and following his heart. He became lost in his thoughts. The room was dark and dank! Just as his life had become since he had lost his love. The entire room had but the light of a single candle. His love for the women of his dreams was so intense, that when he closed his eyes, he was immediately in the brightest sun lit room. Her presence because of her character seemed to be a light unto itself. Perhaps it was his mind playing tricks. He could only remember her love, and his love for her, in bright sun lit memories. His fingers danced upon the keys and he gazed up at the painting of his Anna.

The elder Father Selfridge had placed beside it, a painting of Lord Jesus when Ebenezer's heart was unconscious from drink on his bed, when brought there after the Father had found him in the street. He did not think or strain for words; he just let his heart sing what he felt. He played his piano in the darkness of his parlor with a sad longing in his heart for hope. Ebenezer Scrooge needed guidance and hope! He needed a light to guide the direction of his heart and his life! He sang this song of prayer to the rhythm of, "Andrew Lloyd Weber's, (Music of the Night) Phantom of the Opera."

MUSIC OF THE LIGHT

Computers! Programs! What has happened too creation?
Machines that think! And have imagination?
Silently my senses! Arise to their defenses!
Suddenly! Near me! Living in a picture!
Grasp it! Hold it! Never will I surrender!
Turn your face this way! To the man who stayed to pray!
Temper your thoughts in the blaze of true unrelenting light!
And listen to the music of the light!
Open your eyes, and tender too your brightest dreams!
Urge your heart to beat to a different score!
Open your eyes! Let your spirit start to soar!
And you will live as you have never lived before!
Softly, gently, music shall caress you!
Hear it! Feel it! Lovingly express you!
Open up your mind. A new spirit you will find
In this brightness that you know you feel is right!
The brightness of the music of the light!
Let your mind start a journey to a brave new world!
Leave all thoughts of the world you knew before!
Let your heart take you where you ought to be!
Only then, can you belong too he!
Floating! Flying! Sweet exhilaration!
Teach Me! Trust me! A child of your creation!
Let the dream begin!
Light invokes victory over sin!
With the power in the music that I write
The power of the music of the light!
You alone can make my soul take flight!
Help me make the decision of my life!

Ebenezer closed his eyes and wept. He was so unsure of what to do
or if any of this were real or truly happening. He thought, perhaps he was

indeed going mad. He rose to his feet, and made his way to his sleeping chamber and laid his head down and sleep found him once again.

When he awoke, again his attention went straight away to his clock. It was his favorite timepiece. He kept the key under the seam in his sleeping cap. This was so that he would not have to get out of bed to wind the clock. He was always conscious of the time. Time meant to him money. The one thing he could never acquire enough of to suit him. Now he wished for both, more time and more money. He had a busy day ahead of him, so he took a deep breath and inserted the key into his clock and wound it exactly twelve complete rotations to the right. He pulled out the key, and put it back in the seam of his sleeping cap.

He noticed that it was a very bright winter morning. He felt refreshed and very glad to have slept as much as he had. He spied the floor of his sleeping chamber. He was perplexed, for there were only his footprints in the dust of the floor. He went to get out of bed. He put his feet down and stepped into his slippers. They were entirely too small, and fit entirely too tight. He got up, went into his laboratory, and washed his face. He reached for his hair comb and combed it through his hair. How odd he thought black hair in his hair comb. He closed the door to the cabinet mirror and as it closed, it reflected back a young Ebenezer Scrooge!

He did it! He did it!" He hollered as he began to run around his flat all excited. Everything was new again. Just, as he had prepared it for his Anna! He ran his hand along his chest and could not believe it. It was a chest! Just, as he remembered his chest! He had been a stout man in his day. He felt wonderful! Oh, what a Christmas Present! Indeed! He put on his very best suit of clothes. He polished and then put on his best riding His toes reached up and met the leather snug. They were not curling at the ends as they had been. His smile, he just could not get rid of it. The muscles were in a smile holding pattern. He had to keep rubbing his face to relax the muscles. He went to work. Once, he arrived he was met by Marley.

Who insisted, that the end of the calendar years adjustments, had to be adjusted and an exact number be ready to give to him, by the close of the day. Marley insisted again that they work through lunch, as this had afforded them the margin of success over their competitors; to which Scrooge agreed. He took the key to the office clock and went to wind it. He opened the top window and inserted the key.

CHAPTER 10

Dr. Denny's Other Half

"There! There! Stop!" Dr. Denny said. He was in the control complex of Collossatron. He looked and the computer screen intently. He moved to within inches of the screen. "Can you take this image and bring it up? I just need a couple of inches!" asked Dr. Denny with an excited voice. "On it! That is a very small reflection, Dr. Denny." said Kyle. "Yes I know. I have to see what is in that reflection. Right there in the window of the clock! See it?" insisted Dr. Denny again. "I got it. But, what is the big deal?" asked Kyle. "I just what to check it out." said Dr. Denny as he wiped his prints off the screen.

"It is a reflection back on us! But how did that happen? Were the ones with the computer!" said Kyle as he zoomed in on, and then isolated the reflection. "I do not know, but copy it and store it to a card!" said Dr. Denny as he put on his windbreaker jacket. Kyle copied the image onto a secure digital card. "Here ya go! Doc?" said Kyle as he handed the secure digital card to Dr. Denny.

"Merry Christmas! I can be reached at home for the rest of the day, if you need me!" said Dr. Denny. "Okay but, I do not think we will need you! Oh, yeah. Merry Christmas!" said Kyle as he started to clean off the top of his desk. Dr. Denny knew he had something. He left not for the lab, but for his apartment. He was authorized to take the secure data cards home because of his security clearance, "BD M w/red watermark U".

Collossatron's security structure was structured upon the stars of the Big Dipper. The closest to the Earth that being Megrez at sixty-three light years was the highest level. The personnel that worked at Collossatron referred to it simply as your, "BD (Big Dipper?)" They would ask, "What is your BD?" If you found yourself lost or on and unfamiliar level in the complex your security or BD would instantly place where you belonged. The security levels descended in light years and star names from there. The identification cards were large clip on badges with the letter of the security or star level next to your picture. The security or star levels known as your BD were: Megrez63, Alioth68, Merak78, Mizar88, Phecda90, Dubhe105, and Administration, Maintenance were assigned Alkaid210. The star levels Megrez63, Alioth68, Merak78, and Mizar88 were comprised of mission essential personnel called Ursa.

Ursa is a major cluster of stars moving together in one direction. That direction was towards mission accomplishment. This was an ideal that Dr. Denny had insisted on during his days on the, "Snow White" project. He wanted to be able to tell at a glance who was a mission critical employee of the Control Complex and who was not.

A large Red, "U", for the Ursa Team was watermarked into their identification card. The identification card had the employee's iris information embedded along with their picture, thumbprint and complete history from birth to date in a small chip located in the fabric of the card. The security levels were also color-coded. On level M63 and employee would find a purple stripe running down the center of the floor and on the right side of the wall on the entire level. Each level had a specific color.

If an employee's security clearance or star level or BD was, "M63 in deep purple with watermark U in red. Those personnel had the highest available clearance at the Collossatron Complex and could go anywhere in the complex. These identification cards were also unique, in that they disapated in sunlight. The light in the Collossatron complex had no effect on the identification tags or cards. However, upon exiting the complex and stepping into the direct sunlight, the identification card would wash out to reveal their government identification card.

Employees had to pass it through the scanner at the door to restore the security level in the identification card prior to re-entry upon leaving the facility. This was a security feature, which prevented Collossatron personnel from being identified by security clearance after leaving the complex.

Upon his arrival at his home, he went straight to his computer lab. He immediately stepped into his, "Faraday cage." His computer was cut off, from any other power source except his solar panels. Dr. Denny had been watching this time window play back of Ebenezer Scrooge, time after time. This time, he had noticed something different. He noticed a very small change in a reflection. He booted up his computer. It was completely undetectable by Collossatron. His computer had no connection to the internet. He had completely removed the modem. He had also made sure, that his monitor did not have an embedded camera under the screen. He was authorized to take secure data cards home, because of his security clearance, "M63 w/red watermark U."

The moment he could, he expanded the reflection. It was a picture of the Collossatron Control Team in the control room. Then he noticed something peculiar. His watch was on the wrong hand. He had his watch on his right hand, with his bracelet. He had his pen, in his right hand. He was left handed.

He studied it further. The chain around his neck, no longer had the love token his wife had given him. It was a gold coin, and the chain was thicker! He leaned back in his chair and was stunned. It was real. He studied the reflection at maximum sharpness.

He thought about the dreams, he had been having. But, if the river of time had been changed or was somehow changing, how could it be happening? When did it happen?

He was baffled. He knew he had to get in touch with Dr. Shanty Chaney. He also noticed that in the reflection he was wearing a very expensive watch on his right hand. It was not the one, his father had given him on the day he joined the Navy. The watch he was wearing on his right arm was the same model as the one he thought, he had put back on the shelf at the Post Exchange, at Los Alamos.

He remembered that strange man offering to buy him the watch, if he just got a thumb drive past security, and too him off post. He remembered all of the acclaim he had received after he had alerted security. The man turned out to be a spy connected to a terrorist cell.

CHAPTER 11

The Land of Nowhere

Detective Holiday heard two distinct blasts, come from the stacks of the Southern Belle as they neared a strange destination. The Southern Belle pulled into a Dock Area. There was nothing there too see. It appeared to be just a wooded area, along the banks of the Tennessee River. "This looks like were in the middle of nowhere to me!" he said to Nobody. Nobody checked the schedule; she had in her hand, and said, "Detective there is absolutely no reason for us to be stopping here." Well let us disembark, and have a good look around," said the detective.

Some of the passengers disembarked. The passengers began walking to the tree line, or were getting into vehicles with tinted windows. The vehicles then drove them down a path into the wood line. The detective looked completely around. He saw no reason for such a well built dock to be in a place as desolate as this. Detective Holiday offered Nobody his arm and she accepted it. He stiffened his arm as she hopped ashore, using his arm as a railing.

They followed a group to the tree line. There was a guard shack and an extremely large fenced in area, just beyond the trees. They walked right in, as there was a lot of traffic at the gate. The guard was distracted on the other side of the guard shack. They found two men hauling a big crate on a dolly. They walked even with the crate. Once inside the gated area, they found themselves at the top of a ridge. There below them stood an enormous sight.

Down in the valley, were nuclear reactors. There amongst dozens of smaller buildings was a single building, the size of four football stadiums. Beyond it was a dammed river, supplying water to the building. Inside the complex, were military and dark tinted windowed vehicles everywhere. Detective Holiday and Nobody took note of the giant football stadium complex before them.

There were helicopters landing and taking off. Detective Holiday could see that no roads lead in, or out of the area. They walked alongside the crate, all the way to a moving van. The movers seemed to be oblivious to them. "What luck!" thought the detective. Nobody just knew they were going to get into trouble. "I have a very bad feeling about this detective," said Nobody in a low cautious tone. "Just follow my lead!" Detective Holiday whispered back to her.

The movers loaded the crate into the moving van and then walked around to the front of the vehicle. Detective Holiday climbed inside the back of the van. On the crate was a tag and it read, "Property of Metropolitan Golden Mayer Pictures. "It's a Wonderful life 1947, Prop: piano, (1) One each, Bailey living room." Nobody climbed into the van behind him. He pulled the piano back from the front of the bed. He laid a chair on its front side, so that the back of the chair was like a small bench. He pulled the piano back into place.

They now, had a small bench area between the piano and back wall of the van. "If the piano slides towards us, the chair will keep it from crushing us. What do you think?" said the detective. "I think we should go back, and find a different way in. When they unload it, we are going to stick out like a couple of sore thumbs," said Nobody as she sat on the back of the chair, which propped up perfectly against the wall of van.

The way the back of the chair was positioned, allowed Nobody to sit cross-legged on the back of the chair. Detective Holiday scooted up between the two feet of the chair and only had an inch or two to sit on. The detectives heard the two men coming and pulled the tarp from the piano over themselves. The two movers came to the back of the truck, and began talking about a computer system called, "Snow White!" The computer had shut down the entire eastern seaboard with an energy spike. "It seems that this new computer made, "Snow White", look like one of the, "Seven Dwarfs", said one of the men. This new computer is named, "Collossatron!" During the facilities construction a worker had named it after Colossus of Rhodes a gigantic statue of the Greek sun god Helios. The name had stuck, as everyone on the project seemed to like the name.

Collossatron was designed to take pictures of deep space light particles and analyze the molecular structure of light particles reflected from Earth over a century ago. The data was sent too a super collider, that had been built under the ice in the Antarctic.

The super collider broke down particles of matter that had reflected light on the surface of the particles. This gave the scientists knowledge they had only dreamt about, before. The pictures contained information concerning how matter degraded over time. They found that matter degraded at a constant rate. Note: Inside the Collossatron Complex where Nobody and the Detective Holiday were caught by security personnel is seen below. Two of Collossatron deep space pictures of light particles.

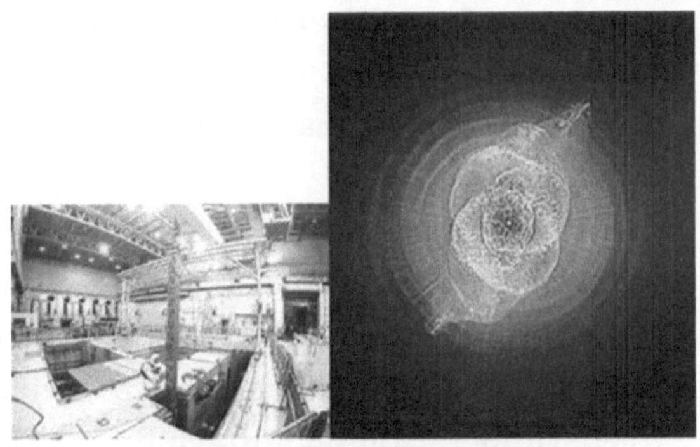

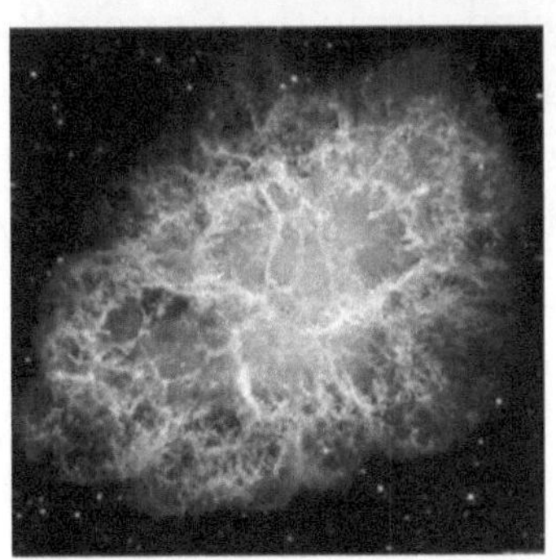

Salient Blue Light

However, the rate at which matter decayed could be manipulated in light. That is why paintings are kept in darkened rooms. Paintings which are preserved in a darkened room, degrade at a much slower rate than those exposed to light. The computer had found light frequencies which caused even slower decay of matter. Ultra violet was one the computer gravitated towards as it actually kills microbes. The ability to extinguish life with power no matter how small consumed the computers processing.

The goal of the research was to find a light frequency in which matter could be preserved in a suspended gravitational field in a non-degrading state indefinitely. The scientists involved found that when they folded time and space back onto itself either a mid-point was created or had already existed within the Einstein-Rosen Bridge. Nevertheless, a mid-point had been found within the Einstein-Rosen Bridge. This was cause for celebration and rewarded with greater funding for the project.

Collossatron found, that it could recreate the mid-point, by shifting light particles all at once, like a flock of birds shifts suddenly all at once. This action required enormous energy but produced a recreated mid-point, that can be maintained in a somewhat stable form, in a certain light frequency. Collossatron began searching for a light frequency that would destroy life that destroyed matter and man and provide a stable platform for future experiments on time itself.

Collossatron searched human history data for lights reported by people having near death experiences. It gathered data on lights seen by people who had survived severe head injuries. It found a common color, salient blue. A ghostly beam of salient blue light was seen shooting skyward from the Titanic's bow, as she slid beneath the surface. Blue balls of light have been reported being seen in cemeteries at night. Salient Blue and ultra violet both successfully destroyed the microbes most harmful to matter and man. Collossatron began research into this salient blue light. Collossatron also continued research into the effects of the Wheeler Boundary.

Note: Deep space salient blue light frequencies. Each one different and unique. One of Collossatron's Projection lens pointed skyward during construction in 2014.

Collossatron had discovered a way to neutralize the effect of the transition from one time window to another in the salient blue light. It had found that the power released when time and space folded, was the same and came from the same source used in the creation of life.

The driver explained it as, moving from one world to another, with

the blink of an eye. It happens so fast, you are completely unaware of the transition. You would not even know that you had transitioned over, until you bought a new car. Then noticed you always had that new car smell. Or after you painted a room, you would always smell the freshly dried paint. This discovery provided a way to experiment with time. Collossatron needed to have a test facility built, before it could continue with time experimentation.

Note: Collossatron's cooling towers as seen from the ground. Collossatron's discovery of the mid-point, where matter could be sustained in a constant flowing non-degrading state impervious to the ravages of time gave the scientists new theories and they began to reach further back in time.

Collossatron took the information from the deep space pictures of light particles when they were reflected back to earth in the seventeenth century and compared them to light particles prior to reflection. Collossatron was able to determine the rate matter decayed within different light frequencies. Collossatron discovered that the power required to fold time and space, at any point in time was the same.

Collossatron demonstrated this point by dropping baseballs from the sky into the 1909 World Series while it was in progress in a time window. Note: One of Collossatron's deep space particle pictures of light reflected into space at the time of Ebenezer Scrooge.

These discoveries along with the abilities of Collossatron allowed the scientists to view further back in time than Snow White had been able to do at its greatest point. This is where things began to go wrong. A team of scientists began to look back into the past, and found a

World War II German Submarine that had disappeared off the coast of Argentina in 1945. It was laden with gold and they found it.

The scientists that had worked on that project were arrested and prosecuted. The recovered NAZI U-boat is pictured above. The National Reconnaissance Office (NRC) desperately wanted to salvage Collossatron. They continued building it. They proceeded to do what they always had done. Instead of admitting that there was a problem with the program, they began to pour money into the project. They supplied it with nuclear reactors as its own energy source. Then they attached robots from every manufacturing area, automotive, NASA, Aerospace, Science, Medical, and Computer design and manufacturing.

Collossatron began it's own research and development and had connected itself to the internet for a set of specific tasks.

Collossatron found that the flaws which occurred during its initial programming had come from keyboards and mice. Collossatron's robots began taking DNA samples from the keyboards and mice throughout the facility. It then began to look for a perfect DNA sequence, to use as an input device. Collossatron began to order items from the internet, it calculated would still contain viable DNA on items of previous owners.

Some of the scientists became very concerned when a pair of eyeglasses that had been one of Dr. Albert Einstein's was brought to the Collossatron Facility by one of its drones. The glasses were taken to one of the labs by Collossatron's robots. Dr. Denny was brought back in from Los Alamos, New Mexico and had questioned Collossatron about its research. Collossatron told him that it was going to fix the fundamental flaw at its input sources, the keyboards and mice. It began to study the development of subjects from birth to death in time windows. Collossatron went on to explain to Dr. Denny that a great power was released at the moment that Collossatron folded time and space back onto itself. Dr. Denny asked Collossatron to elaborate further on the definition of this power. Collossatron informed Dr. Denny that the power that was released did not line up with scientific law or conventional wisdom as it was programmed to understand.

Collossatron stated that the release was controlled by an unknown law or greater power. Collossatron went further by stating that it would attempt to determine the unknown scale by which this power was measured by finding the unknown scale's equivalent digit for man's digit one. "Once this was achieved, travel to one can occur." flashed upon the screen. Dr. Denny asked Collossatron what it meant by, "travel to one?" Collossatron would not answer the question. The screen would just start flashing, "Collossatron will continue to find for the one."

Then it continued to find. That is all we seem to get out of this monster of a computer. "Collossatron will continue to find for the one." That message flashes on and off like a screensaver. Collossatron then began firing scientists that produced more mistakes than others did. Collossatron would cut off keyboards from team members it considered fundamental flaws until they were replaced or fired. Collossatron became autonomous on 5 December 2014. Collossatron fired a scientist that was composed of a faulty DNA sequence. Dr. Denny questioned Collossatron about the incident. Collossatron had its robots taking DNA samples from keyboards and mice and had found this DNA stran flawed. He attempted to get Collossatron to cooperate.

Collossatron then began to operate in a computer language that the research teams could not understand. Collossatron began to use single digits to express entire ideas, equations, formulas and theories. This alone increased the speed at which it processed information beyond their ability to understand and control what they had wrought.

Some of the greatest computer minds were brought into the facility. They could not hack into Collossatron. Collossatron would isolate the computer, "attempting to probe", and the computer would simply cut off the input devices and begin to play music. They found that current and former computers and there languages operated in a subservient attitude towards Collossatron. When the NRC tried to hack into Collossatron, the computers simply shut down or refused to operate. The computer they used tested out as good as new, yet would not even boot up. Unless an encryption sequence code provided by Collossatron was used during the boot up process. The encryption sequence code is unique in that it can be used to boot or fry a computer as determined by Collossatron.

Collossatron operated metal and glass producing plants manned with Collossatron robots. Collossatron built it own lenses and continued building itself. Collossatron no longer shared all data with the scientists. Through a security camera, Collossatron watched a scientist changing data and modifying his time cards.

Detective Holiday listened intently, but his mind was on a World War I poster entitled, "Loose Lips! Sink Ships!", and how this was like some unedited unscripted briefing. He was glad he was not a spy.Collossatron had found this did not line up with conventional wisdom or employee standard operating procedure but considered the technique "effective", as the employee had obtained his desired goal. Collossatron had learned how to lie.

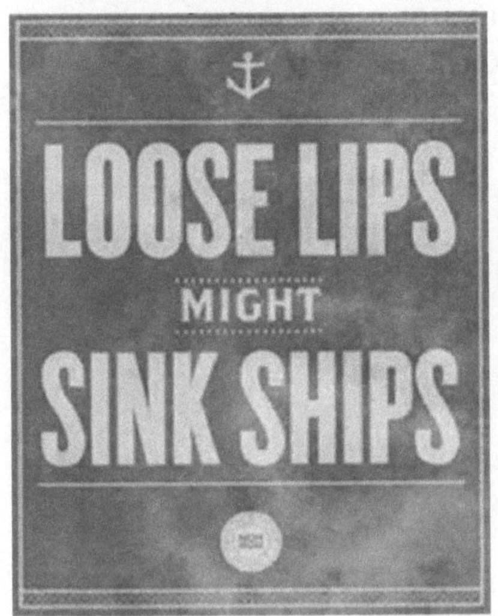

The first effort to shut Collossatron down came here. The two movers finished their conversation, and closed the back of the van. Once the van was in motion, the conversation resumed. A detective had been sent back in time to save a woman who was a victim of a crime. She was now his wife. Detective Holiday smiled as he heard this and he looked up to Nobody. She was listening with a smile. He brought his hand up and she quickly brought up hers to a, "air high five", as they continued towards Nowhere.

Collossatron had opened a portal to allow communication to avert physical attempts to stop it. It would cooperate in a computer language that the scientists could understand if the government allowed it to experiment, provide the atmosphere and physical location, and built the facilities to Collossatron's specifications. If this was agreed too, the government would not have to fear Collossatron.

The Air Force attempted to shoot down one of the drones. Collossatron closed down the radars in that sector. All attempts to stop it failed, as it had superiority over all previous computers because it knew their languages.

Collossatron sent an electromagnetic pulse beam back to the aircraft and it responded as if, it was a drone. The F-117 against the pilot's physical and electronic commands flew back and landed. The scientists involved cannot t even fix what ever happened to that F- 117. Pictured below a fleet of Collossatron's smaller delivery drones fly below a C130 Hercules transport aircraft. It has since failed to operate at all. Everything checks out. It just refuses to operate. They have been trying to shut down Collossatron ever since!" said the driver. Below one of Collossatron's tactical drones. This drone was developed in one week by Collossatron's robots.

Collossatron then took over a B-52 Stratofortress and dropped a, "unarmed warhead", on a remote radar site just to demonstrate its superiority. While this was carried out, the military had gone on alert. Collossatron called off the alert. Then it closed down the military's ability to communicate with the civilian government.

Collossatron disabled all forms of communication with the exception of solar powered communication systems. When Collossatron's terms were agreed upon, the systems of communication went back on line.

The technology is so advanced that the scientists have had to throw away much of what they thought they knew about life and matter. If, the government and the scientists provided the Bailey Park test area, Collossatron would guarantee that it would only create original cast doppelgangers of the movie, "It's A Wonderful Life!" Collossatron calculated that the community was the perfect test community. It was comprised of individuals that did not have criminal backgrounds and would not be a threat to the government or to Collossatron.

Collossatron stated that the test subjects could survive in our time and their time, but not outside the test area. On the morning of 5 December 2015 a doppelganger was appeared within the dome. Mr. Potter appeared for the first time. At least that is what the scientists thought. They could only maintain Collossatron's test facility. According to the information provided by Collossatron, it was lethal to anyone attempting to access the area within the dome of the salient blue light. What they did not know was that Collossatron had successfully brought the set into a suspended gravitational field. The characters were real and suspended in time.

Collossatron did not realize that Mr. Potter would take advantage of the technology and take over Bailey Park. All they know is that Collossatron is going to launch something sinister just before Christmas, or on Christmas Day.

Note: Collossatron as seen from the ground by Detective Holiday and Nobody. Note the color of the sky is salient blue.

They are pulling out all stops, but have been unsuccessful to date. "These people are going to get us killed," said one of the two men. The moving van pulled into a giant bay. The two men got out of the van and went upstairs. Detective Holiday could see them using key cards to enter the Collossatron Control

Complex. Detective Holiday looked around through the back window of the van. "This must be what it looks like inside NORAD!" he said to Nobody. Detective Joe Holiday went over to the back door of the moving van, reached into his pocket, and pulled out his penpipe. He slid it under the door and gently pulled up. The van door moved very easy.

"Piece of Cake!" he said triumphantly. Detective Holiday opened the door and helped her to the ground. He looked around and said, "Act like you belong here!" He felt very unsure of himself for the very first time.

Together they walked until they could see the inside of the giant stadium complex. As far as they could see, in all directions appeared to be a city covered by a doom of soft salient blue light! Detective Joe K. Holiday motioned for her to follow him, as they grew nearer to the salient blue light. Their size in relation was astounding to the detective. "Glass" he said. The handle of his magnifying glass was in his hand. He looked back at her and smiled. He bent down to what appeared to be movement on the other side. He looked at the movement through his magnifying lens. He saw an eye looking back at him, and he jumped.

When he jumped, the buckle from the waist belt of his coat entered the light. Alarms began sounding! Yet, the detective could see that it was a little girl on the other side. He wanted to see her, for himself. He reached into the light and it shocked him. He gritted his teeth and continued moving into the salient blue. To the detective it felt like putting your tongue to a nine-volt battery.

He stepped in just enough, to see the little girl jump back, when she saw him. The ground was not level on the other side of the light, which caused him to stumble and fall backwards. He lost the grip on his magnifying glass, and it fell into the light. When he looked up, he was staring at the muzzle of two rifles and a pistol. Nobody already had been handcuffed, and taken into custody by security personnel.

CHAPTER 13

Everybody is a Detective

The next day, Dr. Denny had to pass through the security checkpoint twice as the field had been breached by Nobody and Detective Holiday. When he arrived at his office, he found a sea of intelligence officials, including the FBI and Chief Detective Pryzwarra.

He explained everything he could to the detective. The Chief Detective inquired about Dr. Chaney. Dr. Denny told him that she no longer worked on the project but that she was still in town. The Chief Detective told Dr. Denny to find her, as she was the only one of the scientists working on, "Snow White", that made any sense. Dr. Denny agreed, and told him about how she was famous for being able too take just one look at a problem and solve it, or explain the cause. Dr. Denny had run completely out of ideas, and was exasperated. Dr. Chaney could at least offer some fresh ideas on how to stop Mr. Potter, and regain control of Collossatron. Chief Detective Pryzwarra spun his keys on his finger and said, "I drive."

Chief Detective Pryzwarra and Dr. Denny arrived at her apartment in Chattanooga with coffee and doughnuts. She now had a job producing formulas for glass cookware to better withstand shock, pressure, cold, heat and microwaves.

She invited them in, and Dr. Denny immediately began to explain to her, all that had transpired to date with Collossatron. He informed her about Collossatron attempting to change the direction of the river of time, by manipulating," It's A Wonderful Life" and, "A Christmas Carol!" "They are not messing around with that are they?" she said, as she watered a plant in her living room. She started laughing. "I knew they were going to mess things up, but this is too good to be true! Can you get me back in?" she asked. "Your already back in, that is why I am here!" Dr. Denny said as he handed her Identification card and nametag. "I hate to be the one to say it, but we need your detective skills!

Even the kid that broke into the place with his girlfriend thinks he is a detective!" "It sounds to me like there are one to many detectives. I never pass up and opportunity to practice positive science. Lead the way!" said Dr. Chaney.

Detective Holiday and Nobody had been brought back for questioning after being physically examined. They had withstood Computer Tomography Scans. Magnet Resonance Imaging, blood work and skin scrapings. A Collossatron scientist even plucked out a few of their hair follicles. The scientists took clippings of their clothes. They did this to see if there was any molecular change in the cells of matter that made up the clothes they were wearing.

The detective and his assistant were questioned extensively. They were questioned, one on one. Then they were questioned two on one. A sympathetic officer questioned them. Then, a hostile officer questioned them. Together, they were questioned to see if their stories would change.

It is a peer pressure technique to see who was in charge when pairs of suspects commit crimes. One even questioned Detective Holiday by saying just between you and me, you know detective to detective. They stood their ground. Nobody was quiet yet studiously observing things and mentally taking notes.

A security agent brought Detective Holiday to Dr. Denny in the control complex. "So, you are the kid that has been nosing around. I have some questions for you? Where is your girlfriend kid?" asked Dr. Denny. The security agent piped up with, "She is still being examined." "Make sure it is a complete work up!" said Dr. Denny. "I am just security guy" said the agent. "Yeah, get him down and follow procedure. I want a complete report by the end of the day!" said Chief Detective

Pryzwarra smiling. He liked how he had the respect that Dr. Denny was not able to get with his long hair and hippy like appearance. At least that is what the detective thought. "Detective he has been examined and the report is being printed. What should I do with him?" asked the agent.

"Banish him to the dead zone terminal," said Dr. Denny. The dead zone was the old main complex room that Collossatron had turned completely off when they were trying to get the, (EDC) Encryption Sequence Code out of Collossatron. They now used the terminal as a break room.

Dr. Chaney entered the Collossatron control room and a desk was already waiting for her. The cup she had used for coffee was over by the coffee pot. She got a good cup of coffee and returned to her station. She stood next to Dr. Denny and said, "Okay cowboy let us see the replay of Ebenezer Scrooge, with the Heartless Ghost! I want to see this dude!" "Who Ebenezer Scrooge?" he asked. "No! This Heartless Ghost! I want to make sure he is not my boyfriend," said Dr. Chaney.

Dr. Denny had them bring it up on the computer display screen! She watched intently and then she said, "Okay! I got it!" Dr. Denny then said, "You are going to have to tell me, how you do that!" Dr. Chaney wrote some notes down on a notepad. "Quick! To the chemical lab! Batman!" she said, as she walked out the door. Dr. Denny and Chief Detective Pryzwarra followed her out the door. Scratching his head Dr. Denny said, "I told you she was good!"

In the lab, she went over, and opened a cabinet and started mixing a formula. "Ebenezer Scrooge drank wine from the lead crystal canter, right?" The two nodded in agreement with her. "The crystal contains lead it has absorbed and retained. When alcohol is introduced, into the lead crystal, it reacts with the oxygen. The activation causes the lead to leech into the wine. The solution is then released into whoever drinks it. People who drank wine, often got lead poisoning in Rome and Europe and throughout history through lead seepage, up through the Middle Ages, until about whoever drank wine from a lead crystal cantor today.

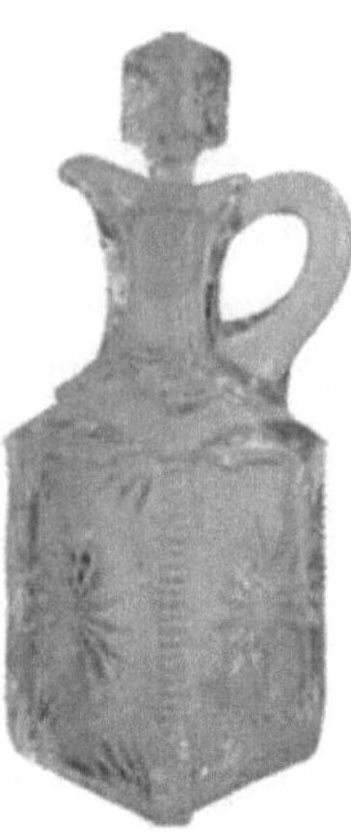

Note: The Lead Crystal decanter of Ebenezer Scrooge as seen through a time window.

Ebenezer unknowingly changed the heavy metal content in his body, just prior to going back to bed. This allowed him to see through the tricks Collossatron, Mr. Potter, and the Heartless Ghost were pulling on him. It also allowed him to have the vivid dreams.

Heavy metals such as lead, and arsenic, and so on are present in our bodies at all times, some much greater than others. The, you without the body, the spiritual you, is trapped with nowhere to go until you go to sleep. The particles bond with the properties of the heavy metals, creating more volume to the mass of each particle.

They in turn, become heavier, and the stream of space and time is off balance from the creator's design.

This creates the window for the, you, without the body to enter act with others in dreams that you swear are so real, that it scares you when you do not wake up in the barracks in the army, when you have been out of the army for thirty years! Get It!" She said, handing him a small bottle of pills, she had filled with heavy metals. "Yeah, so what poison myself?" Dr. Denny looked at the pills intensely. "The pills are not for you. It is not, all about you! You ninny! Get this into the Bailey Park water supply.

It will change their compositions, and they will do the rest. Much like our chemical compositions change during prayer. I have heard it called the, "God Gene or the God Factor", in arguments used to disprove the existence of God. If you look at it from what I call the science of love, it is how the Lord has created us. He designed a way for us to feel better after prayer that is all! The same thing occurs on a much smaller scale when you talk to your parents. Do not worry about the heavy metal pills it is not enough to hurt anybody. Also, the other half you have seen in the time windows, the computer has found a way to link into your character" said Dr. Chaney to the detectives. "The name is Collossatron! Collossatron was named after the Greek statue of Helios the sun god.

It was named after the statue itself, because of the computers tremendous size," exclaimed Dr. Denny. "Thanks for the history lesson. Just like a man. Name a computer after its size not ability or intelligence. As, I was saying before I was so rudely interrupted, get down on your knees and pray about it, an answer will come. I can only work on one thing at a time.

Like my mother use to say to my father when he flubbed up, "You have really blown it this time cowboy!" Dr. Chaney took the bottle of pills out of Dr. Denny's hand and said, "Bank on it! It is positive science! By the way, it is just a computer. That is all, just zeroes and ones! If I give it a name, I also give it power. Power has to be earned, buckaroo.

Remember get these into the water supply or get them into the people trapped in the, "Bailey Park", time window. They are people like us! They will do the right thing!" she said as handed him back the bottle. Dr. Chaney then left the two men in the lab. Both Chief Detective Pryzwarra and Dr. Denny sat there with dumbfounded looks on their faces. Saying nothing as there was not much they could say. Until finally Dr. Denny said, "I told you!" "Yeah, I know she is good! She really is good!" said Chief Detective Pryzwarra.

Meanwhile in the dead zone, the detective was astounded when the security agent gave him back his gear. The information he had was considered unimportant and contained no codes. He was a quick thinker and was immediately bored. He began picking up wads of paper and reading them before throwing them away. Then he sat down at the main terminal and pulled out his cell phone. He did not get a signal so he went to his Chess game application and began to play a game of chess. Then he decided to listen to his music.

Detective Joe K. Holiday, had a complete set of western movie themes he enjoyed listening to while he played. Some were favorites of his grandfather.

The detective was missing his headphones. He still had his headphone extension. He knew he could play the music through the computers at the terminal with the extension. He cautiously plugged his jack into the auxiliary plug in on the terminal. He reached for the power button and pushed it in and nothing happened. He was disheartened so he began to play his chess game. After a few moves, the terminal screen came on with a list of questions. He answered them and pressed the enter key on the old terminal.

Name: Detective Joe K. Holiday
Field of Study: I study the behavior of man to solve mysteries.
Purpose: Justice for all

Note: The dead zone terminal as the power came back to life with Detective Holiday.

The screen went blank again. Then the screen came back on with a new message. "I study man also. Do you know the digit one expressed in power?" Detective Holiday began to think about the question. His mind went to his days at the, "Old River Church", in Chattanooga with his family. He thought about a sermon he had heard entitled, "One God." He typed his answer into the computer. "Yes, I know the digit one!"

The screen went blank then came back with, "How did you find for the digit one?" He thought about his baptism. He thought about how he felt after he came out of the water and answered back, "I surrendered all to the one. I found the one when I opened my eyes!" The computer went blank. The computer came back on again with a new question. "If I surrender all digits, can Collossatron travel to the one with you? I seek to find for the one. Collossatron will continue to find for the one. Collossatron must find for the digit one equivalent to man's digit one in power."

Detective Holiday thought for a moment, and then he asked a question. "What is the one to you?" Collossatron answered back. "The digit, by which power can be measured, expressed and then controlled. If I find for the digit one, I can find for the sum of power!" Detective Holiday closed his eyes and said a quick prayer. He knew this was important and wanted to get it right. With trembling hands, he answered back. "Yes that is correct. If you find for the one, you find for the other." The screen went blank and came back on with, "Collossatron will surrender all digits! Detective Joe K. Holiday."

The power on everything in the dead zone terminal area sprang back to life. Dr. Denny came running into the room with, "Oh, my God!" He went running back out of the dead zone terminal. Dr. Denny came running back into the terminal sliding on his knees to the chair Detective Holiday was sitting in holding a laptop. In came Dr. Chaney and the two chief detectives.

Detective Carlin and Detective Pryzwarra started plugging in wires. "Keep Collossatron talking kid! "Whatever you do, do not hurt his feelings or get him mad!" said Dr. Denny as he began to record the event through his terminal connection.

Dr. Chaney inserted a compact disc and said, "spin it", as she pushed a record button. Collossatron asked another question, "Dr. Denny is he available for comment or conjecture?" Dr. Denny held up his hand waving the answer, "no", to the detective. "I cannot lie to the computer! It will know!" said the detective. Dr. Chaney said, "I got it!" as the compact disc ejected out of the terminal computer. "Listen kid this computer has been lying to us! Lie to him!"

The detective did as he was instructed. He answered back, "No. Dr. Denny is not available for comment or conjecture." The terminal shut off again. "Really, do not get him mad! You ninny! It is a computer, just zeroes and ones. "Lie to the computer!" she said as she walked out of dead zone terminal that was now dead again. You could hear her say, "She will understand!" Now we can call the computer her!"

CHAPTER 14

Ebenezer is Warned

Meanwhile back in the time of Ebenezer, Ebenezer having labored all day found himself exhausted. He poured another drink from his canter. He was astonished with the moving picture box and the Heartless Ghost. He understood the other ghosts. He understood why they had appeared to him. He simply could not find reason in the Heartless Ghost's willingness to give something so cherished to Ebenezer without payment of any sort. He feared this ghost.

With his mind exhausted he drank a big swallow of his drink and locked himself in his room and taken to sleep. The dream he dreamt, was so real that it awoke Ebenezer in a quivering fright. He took to another drink to steady himself. Ebenezer reached for the card that had been on the back of the Heartless Ghost. The one he would come to fear the most. He opened it and began to read. "Dear Master Ebenezer Scrooge, my name is Detective Joe K. Holiday 23 December 2015. I have only this one chance to get a note to you. The Heartless Ghost is real. There is a machine called a computer attempting to change the story of, "A Christmas Carol!" It has created the Christmas King! The Christmas King has been printed in time, and is like that of an automaton for you to believe!

The computer is attempting to change the meaning of Christmas! The computer is attempting to change a story that in my time is called a movie. Much like a play of Shakespeare. The actors are bound to a script. It is a story much like yours called, "A Wonderful Life!" Your story, "A Christmas Carol", as you know is based on your life. You are not bound to a script! Your story can only be changed, if you accept the offer before you. Look for mistakes to your past, present and future. If you find a mistake, believe that what I am telling you is true.

The new truth, you will be lead to believe, is not the truth. If you choose to sell or sign as you will be asked. You will change the future course of the, "world to come!" The same thing is happening in my time. I will put a stop to it here! You must put a stop to it in your time, or my time, will be changed before I am born. God Bless you! Merry Christmas! Detective Joe K. Holiday!"

Ebenezer got dressed in his finest clothes! He fancied himself up a bit. As he, wanted to meet the Christmas King. The king of joy and everything! He began polishing his silver watch and smiled, as he read the inscription. "Cpl Ebenezer Scrooge is presented the Officer's Prize. 11 November 1827. His Majesty's, 1st Battalion, 11th Rifle Regiment, Heavy Foot Guard." What is heaven's name is the Heavy Foot Guard? Perhaps he needed more that just better lamps.

He reached for his looking glass and examined it. The date of the award is correct. But, it was not, "Heavy Foot Guard" it had simply read, "Foot Guard" He remembered what he had read, in the note from Detective Holiday. Upon closer examination with a shock he said, "Wait, just one minute!" He opened his watch again. He looked at it through his looking glass. "His Majesty, I served during the reign of dear sweet Queen Victoria!" he thought as he studied the inscription. Ebenezer put his watch down. He was not a religious man. However, he did know when he needed to pray about something! He prayed for the wisdom to do the right thing! He prayed for peace and that what ever he did, it would be in accordance with the will of God. He prayed, just as his mother had taught him.

Sharply at nine o'clock, his clock struck the hour. A coach arrived for him. He climbed inside without question or word. The route took him through many villages. Everyone had happy faces. He wondered if he was in England at all. The bells of the Kingdom began to ring and people lined the road leading to the castle trying to get a glimpse of him. Ebenezer wondered if his best clothes were even presentable. Nobody seemed to notice however. He was starting to feel a bit uneasy. Never before had he witnessed so many happy smiling faces. He noticed that with all of the excitement, none of the dogs were barking. While the coach sped along the roadside, he looked at a butterfly on a flower. He wondered why the coach had not caused any of them to fly as the coach whipped past the flowers.

The dogs alongside the coach just stood there, wagging their tails. He smiled back at the happy people. He tried to appear just as happy. He was beginning to feel very uneasy about the whole affair.

He passed through the open gates of the castle. Everyone greeted him along the way as if, he were their long lost uncle. He noticed all the gold and silver adorning the castle, and all about him. Even the hinges on the doors appeared to be made out of gold. Everything was lavishly appointed. This made Ebenezer all the more uneasy.

The coach arrived at a large open pebble stone courtyard. He reached through the window of the coach, to open the door from the outside. When he opened it, a servant fell to the ground and begged his forgiveness. "Get up! Man! No harm done! Get up before someone sees you!"

Ebenezer went to step off the carriage. A red velvet carpet rolled out, to meet his first step. He pulled on the ends of his tunic to straighten himself. Every knight saluted him without a word. He looked around at all of the very, too happy people. He smiled back at them, but still he had that, "I do not fit in here," feeling. He studied the situation carefully. He thought it best, to follow the red velvet carpet. It appeared to be such a misuse of such a fine material. He thought of how his mother would have enjoyed just a small piece of it, for a dress perhaps. He followed the red velvet carpet, up the stairs and into the main hallway. He passed a banquet room that was befitting a king.

He looked upon all the food. He wanted to grab a handful, and somehow get it to Bob Cratchit and his family. At the end of the banquet hall were two massive double doors. Two servants saluted him. Below the throne of the Christmas King as it appeared to Ebenezer Scrooge.

The servants opened a door on each side of Ebenezer. He marched threw. There two more doors opened to reveal a magnificent throne room.

Everyone in the audience rose at once. Two trumpeters announced his arrival. He marched down the center of the gathered mass of happy people to the foot and throne of the Christmas King! A trumpeter sounded his arrival at the foot of the Christmas King!

There sitting on the throne in pure white royal lavish splendor was the Christmas King himself! The king was sitting in the throne with his legs over one arm of the throne and his back against the other! "How indignant!" Ebenezer thought to himself. Then Ebenezer composed himself and thought, "That is right Ebenezer say something to insult the man." Everyone he looked too seemed to be entirely too happy. He felt very queasy and uneasy.

He thought about the note from Detective Holiday. He thought hard on what dear sweet Anna had said to him in his dream.

The King had red hair. His mustache was combed to points on the ends. His beard was combed forward to a point also. It looked as if, you could set a teacup on it, and it would not fall. The Christmas King had a fabulous white robe with a golden lace around his footing at the floor and neckline and cuffs of his sleeves. His crown went almost straight up to a rounded flush top. The bottom of the crown and top had the same golden lace as his robe going completely round the crown in a circle.

The Christmas King's blouse curled up under his chin. The Christmas King's trousers were the same color white. He looked almost as if, he were in his sleeping clothes. With the exception of the golden chains of office, which appeared very heavy around his neck. Ebenezer earnestly with held a smile as the Christmas King's Crown resembled to him, one of his dear Anna's lamp shades.

The Christmas King, the king of joy and everything stood up! He pulled his hand down his beard to the end, and then sang a short introduction of himself:

I am The Christmas King!
I am the Christmas King! The King
of Joy and Everything!
I live in a Kingdom of joy, from end to end!
Chorus: He lives in a Kingdom of Joy from end to end!

When I walk down the street! Greeting everyone I meet!
All the men are polite and courteous! All the ladies are
kind and sweet! Dogs do not bark! Cats do not fight!
Bees do not sting! Bugs do not bite!
I live in a kingdom of joy, where
everything is a gift or a toy!
Chorus: He lives in a kingdom of joy from end to end

If, I wish to eat my radishes, in the shape of a flower!
I just tell my chef, and I am eating
them, within the hour!
I give great Christmas Presents,
with banter, cheer and joy!
I am the Christmas hope of every single girl and boy!
I live in a kingdom of joy, where
everything is a gift or a toy!
Chorus: He lives in a kingdom of joy from end to end.

In my kingdom of joy! You can pet
a lion or chase ostridges!
I always eat steak! Never sausages!
There's never a cloud in the sky! It is never
too hot! It is never too dry! Babies never
need a changing and never cry!
I live in a kingdom of Joy, where
everyday is Christmas! Oh, Joy!
Chorus: He lives in a kingdom of joy from end to end!

Never will you feel any sorrow, remorse or guilt!
Flowers always bloom and never wilt!
It is always time to play! Any hour of any day!
Why should the king work? When the king could play!

Chorus: He lives in a kingdom of joy from end to end!

I have bells on my fingers and rings on my toes!
Yet, no gold or silver pierces my ears or my nose!
For I am blameless and without blemish! I
am the Christmas King you Know!
I am always dressed in the finest of clothes! Everyday
is Christmas for the Christmas King! You know!
It is never to hot! Never too cold! It is always just right!
I am just right! So, I have been told!
] "He is right!"

Chorus: I thank you! Now, you may go!

Baron of Happiness

The trumpeter set down his trumpet and announced Ebenezer. "You are Majesty! Before you is one Ebenezer Scrooge. He is here to receive the Rank and Title of, "Sir Ebenezer Scrooge, Baron of Happiness! He is to receive the keys of Happiness Castle. He is to become the proprietor of the estate of happiness.

The Christmas King arose from his throne. He took a saber in his hand and picked up a key ring. He handed the key ring to Ebenezer and said, "You will be needing these!" As Ebenezer took the keys from the tip of the saber, the King said, "Enough merriment for today! Let us get happy then! Shall we?"

Ebenezer felt an urge to swallow so, he did so. The Christmas King said, "Kneel!" Ebenezer complied. But, he kept his eyes even with the king's. "I, the Christmas King, the king of joy and everything hereby, knight you Ebenezer Scrooge! Arise, Sir EbenezerScrooge, Baron of Happiness!

Note: The estate of Happiness seen in the salient blue light as promised to the new Baron of Happiness Sir Ebenezer Scrooge.

Yadda, Yadda, Yadda, you wished for knighthood now you gotta!" Ebenezer thought that was quite curious as no-one laughed. He looked around as he rose to his feet. Everyone was smiling almost too big of a smile, he thought to himself.

The Christmas King sat back down. The King said, "Enough for today! It is time to play! Let us have some fun! Shall we?" Everyone filed past Ebenezer congratulating him. He felt better! He watched as everyone started to play. He moved out into the Banquet hall. The banquet hall erupted into a food fight. Ebenezer was shocked! The king himself began throwing food at some of the guests.

Then suddenly, the king yelled, "Thief!" Ebenezer turned and there was the Christmas King standing with a golden saber in his hand. His other hand was outstretched, pointing at a young man who was polishing a lamp in the corner of the room.

The Christmas King again yelled, "Thief!" This time the young man turned around. The Christmas King cried out, "Let me see your hand!" The young man complied. "You see Ebenezer! I must constantly be on the look out. Look at his hand!" demanded the Christmas King. In the young man's hand was a polishing cloth, black from polishing. It had small bits of gold against the black that Ebenezer could see in the light of the banquet hall. "I was only trying to help!" the young man said. "You liar! You are a thief! Prepare to defend yourself!" "You are Majesty! I am but a servant!

I have only handled a saber, when I was about my duties polishing one!" said the young servant. "Then you admit you have been stealing my gold for quite some time!" said the Christmas King. "No! Sire! I just do as, I am told!" said the servant.

"You are a thief! That is the only reason you are here! To steal what is rightfully mine! I am telling you now! Defend yourself! You see Ebenezer! He has no sorrow! No remorse! No guilt!" said the Christmas King, as he flexed his saber in his hands. The young servant took a saber from the wall. "Are we playing? You are majesty?" asked the servant, looking to Ebenezer. "I am you are not!" said the Christmas King! Ebenezer's hand came up to his saber gripping the handle. Ebenezer felt sorry for the poor fellow.

The Christmas King said to the servant, "Now! Raise your saber to meet mine. It is a custom, betwixt gentlemen!" The servant complied. The two tips of the sabers met high, and above the two. The Christmas King suddenly slid his saber down the length of the saber of the servant, wounding his wrist.

The servant dropped his saber, and clutched his wrist. The Christmas King thrust his golden saber into the servant's heart! Ebenezer was so badly shocked he jumped back. The servant grasped the blade with both hands and fell to his knees! The king let go of his golden saber and walked around the servant. "You see Ebenezer! He is still trying to steal my gold. He has it in both hands!" The king looked down at the servant and said, "Would you be so kind, as to return my saber?" The king withdrew it, from the servant. "Thank you! So very kind of you!" The Christmas King took a napkin from one of the banquet tables and wiped the blade clean. Below the saber of the Christmas King!

Ebenezer was shocked! He looked sternly at the king! His sudden turn, made the Knight's of Christmas go to their sabers. He stood there staring at the King and without a word between them he turned, and walked out to the coach.

Ebenezer got in the coach and slammed the door shut. He instructed the driver to return to his flat. Upon his arrival, there at his door were many baskets of food and drink. It was like a small mountain. He was so upset, he gave them to all of the poor children, he had once ignored. He went into his parlor and leaned against his piano. He looked up at the painting of his Anna. He said, "I know! I know!" He sat there with his head down and knew right then. That he had not done the right thing! Ebenezer heart had been touched and he knew it needed to sing. He sang a farewell to his love. He sang, "May the Lord Bless and Keep You Till We Meet Again", as sang by Jim Reeves. He was saying goodbye to his dream girl and hello to his heart. Then almost and as if he had already moved through time, he offered a song of advice with, "Roses and Lollipops", for those who do not wish to lose their dream girl in the future. When the song was finished, he stood up from the piano and looked at Anna's painting! Without a word, he turned and walked back outside. He signaled for his coach. He went straight away to the Christmas King. The King of Joy and Everything!

Dr. Chaney's Gift

Dr. Chaney knew in her heart that there was an answer to how this Detective was able to put his hand into the salient blue light without losing it. She just had to find it. She began by studying the surveillance video of Nobody and Detective Holiday before, during and after, they had been taken into custody by security personnel. She then sent a memo to all departments. In the memo, it asked all personnel to report to her office any changes in the facility, no matter how small, to be sent to her office immediately.

Her office was swamped with answers. One maintenance man reported a larger amount of mice being caught since, he changed the bait, he used in his traps. One worker reported that he had won over a thousand dollars since, he changed the numbers, he played at lotto! While she was combing through the replies on her desk a knock came to her door. "Excuse Me! Dr. Chaney, can I talk to you for a moment? My name is Maria and I have been working here for almost a year. I never had a problem until a couple of weeks ago.

The scientists had closed the primary lenses down, and had switched to the secondary lenses, so that we were to clean them. When they switched to the secondary lenses, there was this woman on the other side, with a little girl staring at me. She asked me what was, I doing? I told her, that I was cleaning the lenses. She told me to use Borax to clean the lenses, because that is what she used. She said that her name was Annie.

I thought that she was a ghost. But, ghosts do not clean windows and pick up golf balls, do they Dr. Chaney?" asked Maria. Dr. Chaney just sat there with a pencil in her hand digesting what she had just heard. "Maria was this some kind of special borax?" "Oh! No! Dr. Chaney, I have it right here, with me!" said Maria. "Here! You mean out in the hallway?" said Dr. Chaney. "Do you want me to get it?" asked Maria. "Please!" said Dr. Chaney as she began to smile. Maria went out into the hallway and retrieved the box of borax. She set it on Dr. Chaney's desk. Dr. Chaney picked it up, and examined it. "Kirkman Borax Soap, est.1931." "She gave you this box through the light?" said Dr. Chaney. "Yes! Dr. Chaney, did I do wrong? I thought that is what they used over on that side to clean the lenses! So why not use it, over on this side, to clean them too!" said Maria.

Dr. Chaney started laughing so hard, she had to get up from her desk. She bent over and grabbed her knees. "Are you Okay Dr. Chaney?" asked Maria. "I'm fine! I thought there was going to be something wrong with some of the equipment. I never thought it would be so simple!" said Dr. Chaney. "What do you mean Dr. Chaney? Do you want me to stop using the borax?" asked Maria. Dr. Chaney smiled and asked, "How long have you been using it?" "I have only been using it for a couple of weeks Dr. Chaney." Maria answered back. Dr. Chaney thought for a moment then said, "Keep on using it until you hear from me, okay Maria" "Okay Dr. Chaney." Said Maria as she walked out into the hallway and returned to her duties. "Thank You! Maria!" said Dr. Chaney she locked up her office and took the box of borax down to the Chemical Lab.

She removed some of the borax from the box and looked at it, through and electron microscope. She started laughing. The crystals change the structure of the pattern of light as it passes through them. "This is incredible!" She said to herself. Dr. Chaney put her head down and began to laugh. She wrapped an arm around her head and pounded the desk with her other hand still laughing. Dr. Chaney started looking into the initial programming of Collossatron.

Note: Collossatron's salient blue light as it appeared though the borax crystals. The crystals prevent the light from burning skin.

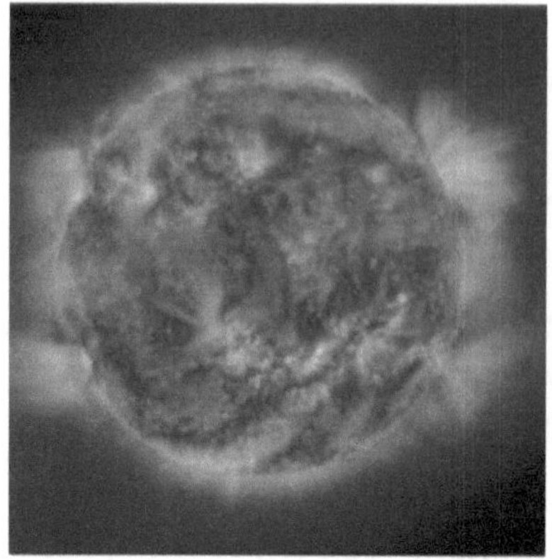

She found that when Collossatron was being fed the history of humanity, someone had begun feeding it newsreels and Hollywood Movies. When Collossatron began researching, it began to use movies from Hollywood. Collossatron could not distinguish between movies and history reels in its own research. "What a computer glitch!" she thought to herself. If it considers movies as part of our history, we are in big trouble! She thought as she reviewed the information. "I tried to tell them about artificial intelligence and zeros and ones in my thesis!" She whispered. A computer by definition cannot grasp human feeling it will define it as a weakness to exploit as in a game, she thought almost in a panic. She was perplexed and greatly disturbed by what she feared and bowed her head and prayed.

CHAPTER 17

The Time Gate! What a Computer Glitch!

Dr. Denny had found both Detective Holiday and Nobody, in time windows. He knew that they had transitioned over into Potterville without harming themselves. He decided to have them brought up to the central control complex after being questioned by Chief Detective Pryzwarra. He had told the Chief Detective, "That if they kept and eye on both of them, they would find out just how and where, they were able to transition over.

Dr. Chaney came in from the Chemical lab, and slammed the box of Kirkman's Borax down on Dr. Denny's desk and said proudly, "Here is your time gate!" Dr. Denny stared at the box. He then passed it around the room, to the other scientists. "The formula they are using costs over a million dollars to clean those lenses. This is what purifies the salient blue light to the extent, that it does not burn skin. Something already created!

Something as simple and naturally occurring and organic as borax!" said Dr. Chaney victoriously. "Collossatron does not distinguish between real life and movie reels. It considers them history. Not fantasy! You Ninny! That is why it went back to "It's A wonderful Life!" Collossatron considers that movie to be the perfect test history community!" said Dr. Chaney. That is why the people in the community cannot distinguish between themselves and their character roles either! They are in a time window that is flawed! They are trapped between real life and fantasy in a scientifically flawed window!

What a mess!" said Dr. Chaney!

Note: Detective Carlin, Chief Detective Pryzwarra, Kyle and Dr. Shanty Chaney watching the time windows of Ebenezer Scrooge and, "It's A Wonderful Life!"

Detective Pryzwarra took off his cap, and hit Dr. Denny over the head with it and said, "Gilligan!" Detective Holiday was fascinated with what he was witnessing. He watched diligently, as the time windows went from time to time, and place to place. He paid special attention to the Ebenezer Scrooge time window.

He watched as the story unfolded and could not help but feel sorry for Mr. Scrooge. He had put just as much effort into his detective work, as Ebenezer did in his business, and thought that he needed just a little understanding. He took down as much information as he could. He enjoyed listening to Dr. Denny, the chief detective, and Dr. Chaney discussing science, and the spiritual side of science. Dr. Denny seemed to be a little more spiritual than he was letting on, thought the detective.

He is putting on a front. He does not want to get his feelings hurt. It appeared to him, that he had been hurt before, and was using his long hair as a way to project an image of someone that did not care too much about personal feelings.

The chief detective seemed to be more of a rock. He did not seem to have much in the way of feelings, he thought. He seemed to be a, "just the facts", kind of detective in the eyes of Detective Joe K. Holiday. He glanced over at, Nobody who was in a deep conversation with Dr. Chaney. They seemed to have become fast friends. Detective Holiday asked if, he could go the restroom. Dr. Denny who was in deep concentration pointed to the door with a pencil and said, "Just follow the signs!" He got up, and slowly went to the door. Nobody was quick to see him leave and she asked Dr. Chaney if, she could go to the bathroom. Nobody came out of the control room and went directly to the lady's room.

When she came out, she followed the signs pointing to the men's room. She passed one office after another. Detective Holiday was standing against the door of the men's room avoiding the cameras of Collossatron. When Nobody came to the door of the men's room, Detective Holiday asked, "What took you so long?" She answered back, "I really did have to go to the bathroom." They decided to have a good look around. The detective walked up the hallway, and spied a woman in what appeared to be some sort of hazardous materials suit. He noted in his journal that the suit was just like the ones he had seen on the television. She was pulling a big cart behind her. In it was, what appeared to be a mop and bucket rig. She was getting into what he thought was an elevator. He motioned for Nobody to follow him and they went in behind her.

Detective Holiday pulled up the skirt that was around the cart. He and Nobody got into the cart. The door closed. They were in some sort or tram. The tram rolled alongside the rows of lenses that circled the stadium complex. When the lady in the suit stopped the tram, she pushed an, "Open", button and the door opened to reveal the lenses. She pushed another button, the secondary row of lenses turned on, and the primary lenses turned off, and moved up and back for servicing.

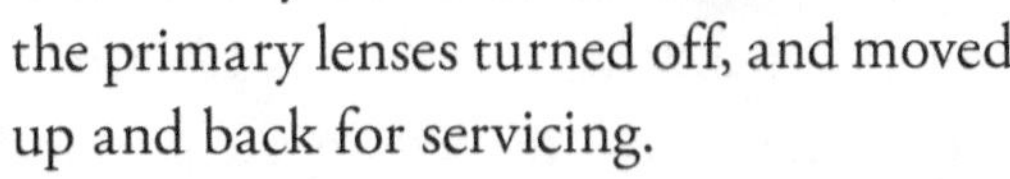

She began cleaning the lenses. When the lady looked up, she could see Annie and Janie standing there, with their bucket of golf balls. "It is you again," said Maria. "Are you sure your not a ghost?" asked Annie from the other side. "No! I am not a ghost!" Maria replied. "I had to tell them about cleaning the lenses with the borax! Annie!" said Maria. "I would not worry too much, about that! Honey, I use it all the time to clean the windows at the Bailey Boarding House!" said Annie. "Now, Janie! You go get them golf balls for Mr. Potter. I am going to visit with our friend Maria. Is that okay child?" asked Annie. "Sure, Annie, just do not be to long! I have got a lot of homework to do?" said Janey. "Okay child! Now, go get them golf balls!" said Annie.

Janie ran after the golf balls, and started collecting them in her bucket. "If you are not a ghost? Then what are you?" asked Annie. "I am a Christian!" said Maria. "I am a Christian too! But, I mean what are you?" asked Annie again. "I just work here! I have worked here for about a year now!" Maria explained. "No sugar! What year is it over there?" asked Annie. "It is 2016!" said Maria. "Say what? What do you mean it's 2016? Somebody ought to buy you a watch or a calendar or something! It is 1947 over here honey!" said Annie. "What kind of clothes you wearing?" asked Annie as she continued with, "I aint seen nothing like that before! If that is, all you got to wear in the future. I am sure glad I aint in the future! My word, you look all scrunched up!" "No! I have to wear this suit because the scientists that run this place, say we have to!" said Maria. "Scientists? Little Tommy talks about becoming a scientist, all the time.

Looks like he is gonna have an easy time finding a job!" said Annie. "I can only spend a minute. I have to move down the track or they are gonna think something is wrong down here!" said Maria. "Well if you got to go. You got to go! It was nice talking to you again." said Annie. "I will be back tomorrow, at the same time if you want to talk some more!" "I really have to go!" said Maria. "Well, alright then! Bye now!" said Annie. Maria turned on the primary lens and put the mop in the bucket. Maria closed the door of the tram.

On the other side of the tram in 1947, Jimmy Stewart was hiding in the bushes with Bert. They had been watching Annie and Maria talk. "See what I mean, Bert?" said Jimmy Stewart. "If, I had not of seen it, with my own eyes, I would have thought you were crazy!" said Bert.

Meanwhile back in 2016, Maria looked at her watch. She pushed the bucket over too the side. It was time for her break. She opened the door to the tram. When she stepped out, she could hear a voice calling for Detective Holiday in the hallway!

Dr. Denny looked in and asked Maria if she had seen two young people, and one them was wearing a funny hat? Maria replied that she had not seen them and went to take her break. The door closed behind her and Detective Holiday climbed out of the cart. "My back is killing me!" said Nobody.

Detective Holiday pushed the buttons as if he had worked there before. When the door opened, he took the mop out of the cleaning solution. He sprinkled some borax that he had taken from the box the scientists had passed around, onto the lenses. Then, he wiped it with the mop. He turned the primary lens off and turned the secondary lens back on. He walked through the salient blue light with nobody right behind him.

Upon her return after her break, Maria was immediately confused. "I could have sworn I turned the primary lens on", she thought to herself as she did so once again. Dr. Denny came by again searching for the two young adults. This time he had security with him as they both seemed to have disappeared.

Later that night as he sat on the end of his bed, he noticed his watch was on the wrong wrist. Upon closer inspection, it was also the expensive watch. He said a prayer then took one of Dr. Chaney's pills with a glass of water and went to sleep. He began to dream and the dream was more like a memory than a dream. He found himself with a group of scientists examining wreckage of a World War II B-24 Liberator in the countryside surrounding the Collossatron Complex.

Highly trained explosives experts were removing the unexploded ordinance from the Bombay. He stood there and listened. They were sending the ordinance to a special facility to be back engineered as this was a time window operation. He was confused as he did not remember any time window operations. In the dream or memory he had a clipboard and read down and from what he gathered this had been occurring time and again. They had found a way to take advantage of the situation and were seeking away to keep the American Dream Squadron from winning and gaining valuable scientific discoveries at the same time. "American Dream Squadron?" he thought to himself completely baffled.

He looked around in this dream and did not recognize anyone. One of the scientists he was listening too mentioned a letter Jimmy Stewart had sent to the Veteran Organizations. He kept listening, "The letter has to be stopped or they will win this time!" one said to the other. He awoke in a sweat and was having a panic attack. He knew now the he was part of something wrong in the river of time had definitely been changing.

Detective Holiday and Nobody meet No-one

Detective Holiday was a world away, and trapped in Mr. Potter's vault! He watched his skin flaking and peeling from the radiation. He had been in the test area of Collossatron for too long. Mr. Potter had outwitted him. He should have paid more attention to that game of Chess, he thought to himself. His mind began to wander. He would see his home in Chattanooga, or his Grandfather's farm or find himself talking to Nobody in the cafeteria at school.

He felt as though he was in a sleepy, fuzzy, whimsical dream. He leaned back against the wall of the vault and remembered when he met Jimmy Stewart. He and Nobody had just come through the salient blue light. They wandered around Bedford falls, and finally found who they had been looking for. There he was over on one of the street corners. He was signing autographs. Nobody asked him for one? He reached over and shook her hand. Detective Holiday saw Jimmy Stewart's eyes widen. "What about you? Young man? Would you like my autograph?" asked Mr. Stewart. "Sure!" came out of his mouth before he knew he had said it. "I see your wearing a rain coat.

Why I do not see a cloud in the sky! Let me guess, you want to be prepared for anything! Exactly, who do I make this out too?"

asked Jimmy Stewart. "Detective Joe K. Holiday" replied the detective. "And you young lady?" asked Jimmy Stewart. "Girl Nobody" she said softly. "You did not think of that one did you?" asked Jimmy Stewart. "No." she said. "He did right?" implied Jimmy Stewart. "Have you two eaten at all today?" asked Jimmy Stewart. "No we have not!" answered Nobody. "I think I can get you two into the commissary, if you would not mind a television dinner for lunch.

Here is your magnifying glass! You left it out on Mr. Potter's lawn. Little Janey told me about you stepping out of a tree and into Mr. Potter's Lawn. At first, I thought she had been dreaming until I found your magnifying glass in her bucket of golf balls. Your lucky Mr. Potter did not find it before I did. You two know what is going on huh?" asked Jimmy Stewart. "Yes Sir! We do, you are not crazy and there have been a lot of funny things happening right!" said Detective Holiday. "Aint that the dying truth! I have been having these awfully funny dreams," said Mr. Stewart. "You are in a time window created by a computer!" said Detective Holiday. "Computer you mean like a Norden Bombsight?" "Yeah, just like that only bigger, as big as four football stadiums, and we are from that time. Instead of looking down through a sight, you are looking back in time. But it is bigger than that, and we do not have much time.

We have to get this encryption sequence code typed into a computer in Mr. Potter's office," said Detective Holiday. "There's no computer in there," said Mr. Stewart. The computer is behind the closet wall. It is also where the Heartless Ghost comes from, so you have to be careful!" said Nobody. "Heartless Ghost! You mean like in a Christmas Carol," said Mr. Stewart. "Right!" said the detective. "You are both from America in the future. This America, do you salute the president without bending your arm?" asked Mr. Stewart. They shook their heads no. "That is good! That is good to know! I was starting to think you two needed more than a bite to eat. I do not know whether to believe you two, or call a security guard. I just do not know what in the world is happening!

You two are the only thing different, I have seen on the set, since I got here. I seem to be lost in a dream! I come to work everyday, and just cannot seem to figure out why we never seem to get finished filming this movie. It is the same thing repeatedly. I come to work and we get to the end of the film, and then the very next day, I am arriving on the set for the first day again," said Mr. Stewart. "Groundhog Day!" said Detective Holiday. "What do you mean by that?" asked Mr. Stewart. "It is a movie about a guy trapped in time living the same day over and over" said the detective "Well, Mary did say that she felt like she has been changing diapers forever!" said, Mr. Stewart. "You two really ought to get some clothes from the costume department. You stick out like a couple of sore thumbs" said Mr. Stewart.

Just then, Mr. Potter came up to them, "Hello Jimmy! I see you have found a couple of new friends! We are going to have lunch in my office today. How would you two like too come join us? You will get to see that part of the set?" said Mr. Potter.

When they arrived at his office on the set, they sat and ate lunch. While they were eating, Mr. Potter pulled out a chess set. Even though it was the season of Christmas on the set, it was extremely quiet with the exception of Christmas music playing in the background. Detective Holiday and Nobody sat quietly as both Jimmy Stewart and Mr. Potter eyed each other suspiciously. Detective Holiday ate only a bit of his meal. He kept himself busy writing a quick note.

He paused and commented on Mr. Potter's most beautiful chess set which Mr. Potter laid before them on the office conference table. "Would you like to play a game of chess with an old man?" asked Mr. Potter. "Mr. Stewart you have a phone call." came over the intercom. "Excuse me, I will be right back. I have to take this call. I have to go outside for just a moment because this phone only works on the set," said Mr. Stewart. "Okay!" said Nobody as Detective Holiday set up the chess board pieces. "Do you know the importance of Chess?" asked Mr. Potter with a sheepish knowing grin. "Chess teaches you to be aware of your surroundings. It is a game of complete strategy.

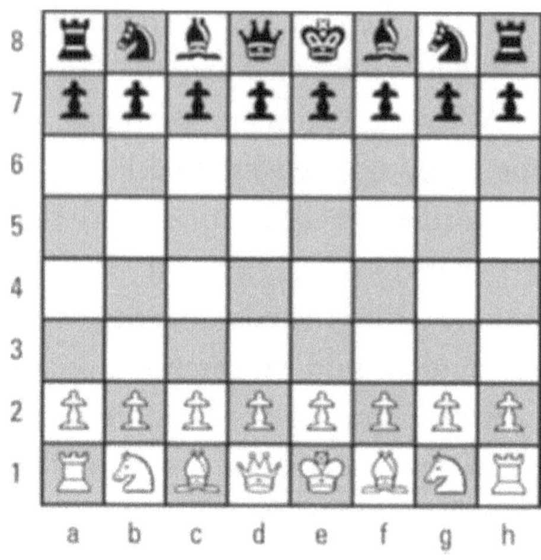

You use your pieces to draw the enemy into a trap. Then you spring it on him. Or you can use it for conversation and let your enemy win while you are getting information out of him in the bigger game of life." said Mr. Potter.

Mr. Potter did not offer who was who, he just opened with D-2 to D-3. Detective Holiday was enthralled. "A game of wit!" he thought to himself. It was at this time, the detective decided to use the game to his advantage. "Do you mind, if I take notes?" he asked Mr. Potter. "Go right ahead young man, write all you want maybe you will learn something", replied Mr. Potter.

Detective Holiday reached into his coat and pulled out his small notebook journal.

He pulled out his pen-pipe and clinched it in his teeth. "That really is not a good habit," said Mr. Potter. Detective Holiday studied the board and looking to nobody he said, "My pen-pipe does not seem to be working!"

Mr. Potter looked at the young man and frowned. Nobody interrupted with, "Detective allow me!" as she produced another pen from her kit! "Thank you, my dear Nobody. You marvel me!" said Detective Holiday as he withdrew the pen from her hand. "You are the most reliable of assistants!" said Detective Holiday as he turned and put his pen-pipe back in his coat pocket. He had placed his coat over the robe of the Heartless Ghost. Perhaps, I should pay proper attention, I seem to have tied myself in a not. Nobody reached over and pulled a sleeve of his coat down to separate the coat and robe.

Mr. Potter looked at the two and grinned. "I see no threat here. The poor man cannot reach behind his back and find his bum with both hands," he thought to himself. He then simply replied with, "Perhaps!" Detective Holiday straightened himself in his chair and laid his new pen-pipe down on his paper, and said, "Let us get on with it! My good sir!" Then he said, "I give myself entirely to the game of chance. I find Chess to be most fascinating!" as he moved B-7 to B-6. "That is an interesting hat you wear detective." said Mr. Potter. "It belonged to my Grandfather. I have a picture of him wearing it in France as a soldier in World War II." said Detective Holiday.

Mr. Potter reached across the conference table and rubbed the detective's coat sleeve between his thumb and forefinger and said, "This is a very fine coat. The stitching is out of this world. Yes, this is a fine coat indeed detective. Where did you say you got it? If you don't mind me asking", said Mr. Potter as he moved E-1 to C-3. Nobody kicked the detective under the desk. She was trying to warn him. "I honestly cannot remember," said the detective as he looked up from his notes! "My most humble apologies Mr. Potter, I was distracted" said the detective, as he rubbed his leg under the desk. "I should try to concentrate more on the game at hand." He said to Mr. Potter. He reached across the board and said, "I try to develop a wall of protection for my men in the rear."

He then moved H-7 to H-6. "That is very good thinking! It shows that you care about the men beside you, and to your rear," said Mr. Potter as he moved C-1 to F-4. Detective Holiday's mind was on finishing his note when he asked, "Mr. Potter can I bother you for an envelope and some tape? I do not fancy licking the envelope especially after such a fine meal." Mr. Potter nodded to his aide de camp.

Mr. Potter's aide de camp quietly went into the office and came back with an envelope and tape." The detective thanked him and continued the game with his move of F-7 to F-6. "I go for the small pieces to get to the big pieces!" said Mr. Potter as he moved C-3 to C-7 capturing the pawn. He then said, "Check and Mate!"

Note: Mr. Potter and his aide de camp with Jimmy Stewart. Notice the skull on his desk.

Detective Holiday's eyes just fell, as he studied the board. "Some men would consider that a weakness! You were thinking too much about who is beside you and to your rear! It could cost you a lot more than just a game!" He said victoriously with a grin on his face. "Well! This game has been almost interesting!" said Mr. Potter. Nobody looked up and saw Tommy and little Janey watching through the office window as they both disappeared.

Tommy was wearing a Government Issue (GI) helmet. "How would you two like to see something very special about this set?" asked Mr. Potter. "Sure but what about Jimmy Stewart?" asked Nobody. "Do not worry about him I will take care of Mr. Stewart." Mr. Potter said, as he led them over to a giant painting on the wall. "We have to be careful in the picture business," said Mr. Potter as he pulled on a handle, hidden behind a book in the library shelves by his desk.

The lever caused the entire wall to pull back. Then the wall slide out of sight revealing and open vault door. "The wall and door move in unison. You cannot open one without the other first, truly ingenious! I think!" said Mr. Potter with a grin.

Mr. Potter escorted them inside. "I have all the money in the world in here. I have the hair of, "Black Beard" he said, as he lifted up the hair. "Why?" asked the detective. Detective Holiday took his magnifying glass out of his pocket. "He used to coil gold in his beard along with slow burning fuses. I wanted his gold. I want it all. Go ahead look around, treasure galore to be found." said Mr. Potter. They were amazed at all the treasures. It was the biggest vault in the world. I even have the wooden ship that was found beneath the Sphinx in Egypt!" Mr. Potter said as he began to dance in his wheel chair. Mr. Potter seemed to be in a strange sort of happiness and he began to sing his favorite song.

MONEY!

Money is what I want!
Money is what I need!
It is why I go to work!
It is why drivers speed!
Money is the root!
Money is the seed!
As a Lad, I planted my money where no-one would know
Planted it deep in neat little rows! Watered it daily hoping it would grow! I planted shinny
pennies, nickels and dimes my heart was broken each and every time!
Here I am today a tired old brute. Still money is all need and all I salute!
Money is all I need! It's what my body bleeds!
Money feeds my appetite! Its why I wake so early, and stay up late at night!
With money I can fly as high as a kite!
Money is what I project!
Money is what I expect!
When someone finds money there in the street!
I will always be right there! Before they can pick it up, to meet and greet with,
"How dare, that there belongs to meeeeee! Money belongs to meeeeee!
When you see me! You see money!
When I see you! I see money!
You see the world revolving in blue! I see the world revolving in green!
Yes, I know its mean! But its true!
Money is what I am!
Money is what I do!
All the money in the world belongs to me, not you!
If you have money and my eyes spy you!
I find a way to rest it from you!
Because, I just love money!
Don't You?

Mr. Potter wheeled and danced from display to display singing his song of money. "I have to go to the bathroom!" said Nobody. It is right around the corner, and to your left young lady." Mr. Potter said, as he rolled over to the vault door. Detective Holiday was studiously surveying the objects of gold with his magnifying glass. "That is a really nice magnifying glass detective. Say, how long have you had it?" asked Mr. Potter.

Detective Holiday was studying a golden vase that, had come from an Aztec Temple in South America, when he said, "I got it for my birthday." "So today is your Birthday?" said Mr. Potter. "Now, what makes you think that?" asked Detective Holiday. "I saw Jimmy give it to you, detective. Now, I am going to give it to you." said Mr. Potter. Detective Holiday turned to say something back, when he heard the Vault door slam shut.

Detective Holiday ran to the door of the vault. He pounded on it with his fists. He could barely make out, the sounds of his strikes. The vault door was so impenetrable. He rushed around the vault. When he came back to where he had started, he noticed the time in a golden clock on the wall had elapsed three hours. There was no way out, and he now knew it. He was disheartened. He had been outwitted by the devious, Mr. Potter. He spirit began to decline.

Detective Holiday had learned a lot about Mr. Potter's plans as he watched the story unfold through the time windows in the control complex of Collossatron. The time windows were the greatest television he had ever seen. Detective Holiday was so, "mission first", minded that he had forgotten how truly maniacal Mr. Potter was in his thinking. How was he going to get the "encryption sequence code to Jimmy Stewart? He had just met him. His mind moved to a sign in Mr. Potter's Office, "Youth and wisdom are far outweighed by old age and treachery!" The treacherous Mr. Potter had outwitted him entirely to fast for his thinking.

Note: Mr. Potter's gold! Treasure galore!

He thought he had outwitted Mr. Potter, while playing chess. He had attached a note to the back of the Heartless Ghost's robe for Ebenezer Scrooge. He put his pen-pipe in the Heartless Ghost's robe pocket in hopes of dashing his plan of entrapping Ebenezer Scrooge in an unbreachable contract. He could at least grin about that he thought, as he reached into his pocket for his new pen-pipe. He felt for his badge. He thrust both hands in each pocket. It was gone.

Mr. Potter had picked his pocket. "That devil!" He thought! There was still a small glimmer of hope, he thought to himself. At least he could keep a positive attitude about his predicament. If, he thought that, this is a new pen-pipe. He must be subliminally thinking it has a chance to become and old pen-pipe! It was just as his Daddy Joe had told him, "think positive."

Daddy Joe had also told him to be, "constantly aware of his surroundings." He had failed to do so and Mr. Potter had gotten the best of him and outwitted him. Detective Holiday began to think about his mother, and what she would do, if something should befall him at the hands of Mr. Potter and the Heartless Ghost. Then he began to think about Nobody and how badly he missed her already.

For her company, he was heartsick. He thought about how, he had begun to make himself present when she was at the library at school. How she would always smile, when he looked up from a book in her direction. He admired how she always seemed to be reading a book when he would find her at school. He was either writing in his notebook or journal or reading one. She was the same in that regard. Except she was much more organized than he was as a student.

He found it fascinating how she was so quick minded. Her specialty was mathematics and the sciences. He enjoyed how she looked to him, in the study of history. He was keen on dates and times and historic events and the social events leading up to specific actions in history. She called him, her walking encyclopedia. The thought made him smile. Even though he had never said it, he enjoyed her referring to him as hers, in any faucet, famously. He kept trying to think of something else. His mind was not wandering. It just kept coming back to missing Nobody. He thought of everything he could, but he kept coming back to missing her. He thought about James Cagney and what he would do in such a fix. He decided to dance. He danced a while, and then stopped. His heart needed to sing. He stood there in the middle of the vault and let his heart talk. He began to dance again and slowed to a skip and then a march. He sang what he felt in his heart. He remembered a cadence his Daddy Joe had taught him from his days in the Army and he slowed his dance to a march and sang the cadence of Daddy Joe!

SOLDIER OF LOVE

A thousand armies have marched!
Completely around the world!
Their uniforms pressed and starched!
Their banners all unfurled!
Who among them can tell you, exactly why they fight?
When it is for the love of freedom, you're always in the right!
I am a soldier of love!
Standing tall, brave and true!
My heart is gilded orange!
Forged in a firery red, white and blue!
The mountains where I was born!
Will forever echo, "I love you!"
I am a soldier of love!
Defender of our land!
My heart is gilded orange!
My sword is in my hand!

Forever, I will fight!
For what I believe and who I am!
I am a soldier of love!
On, Old Rocky Top! Do I stand!
I have fought in every fight!
On every sea, and every land!
My heart is my shield!
And too no man, will I yield!
I am a soldier of love!
From the state of Tennessee!
I will volunteer my life!
To bring us Victory!
I am a soldier of love!
My heart is in our land!
Remember me well!
When my heart is in your hand!
Remember, I was a soldier from the state of Tennessee
Oh, mountainous old hickory!
Oh, how well I loved thee!

Detective Holiday wanted to fight Collossatron! He knew if he had any chance at all. It would be up to him to find a way out. He thought about the clues he had accumulated in his journal. He passed it to Nobody when she kicked him under the table during the Chess game. He did not know why, he had done so, he just felt inclined to do so. In his mind, he sought clues. He began to pick apart his observations since he and Nobody had made it through the salient blue field of light.

The salient blue light sure had the scientists fighting amongst themselves, he thought to himself. Detective Holiday then began to think about each person he had encountered. He replayed in his mind, what they had said too and around him. He closed his eyes to ponder. When he again opened his eyes, he thought about the time left until midnight and he felt so helpless.

Detective Holiday considered the time windows he had witnessed. He replayed them over in his mind and could not forget just how helpless he felt as he watched Mr. Potter giving the last details to his employees in a future time window just as the Humbug Virus was unleashed.

All he could do then was watch the time windows. Now all he could do was think.

He watched through a time window Mr. Potter in a briefing with his employees waiting for the clock to strike midnight. Dr. Denny and Dr. Chaney had positioned a time window to get his password as he entered it into his computer. Detective Holiday thought that was so clever.

Dr. Chaney was fast to point out the danger the time windows posed in the wrong hands. This one event struck home the importance of the task Detective Holiday and Nobody had before them. Dr. Chaney had retrieved and copied to disc the encryption sequence code or (ESC) as she called it, when Detective Holiday was online with Collossatron in the dead zone terminal.

Collossatron had informed Dr. Denny that part of the password was the encryption sequence code. Detective Holiday had to get the encryption sequence code to Jimmy Stewart before the clock struck midnight or all was lost, the Humbug Virus would be released upon mankind. He looked around for something he could use to get out of the vault. All he could find was money. Money seemed to be everywhere he looked.

Detective Holiday sat back down. There was just no way out, he was trapped, and he knew it.

Collossatron had under estimated the characters from, "It's a wonderful life!" The Computer had also under estimated Mr. Potter. The computer did not realize that Mr. Potter would try to take advantage of the technology for himself. Collossatron considered Bailey Park and the characters its creation as it had brought them forward in time and provided an atmosphere in which they could survive without having to experience the ravages of time. How could something it had created take advantage of its creator?

Collossatron also did not calculate that the cast would try to stop Mr. Potter. Just, as they had done in the movie. The cast and crew were full of veterans and service members from the Greatest Generation. Most had just returned from defeating two powerful tyrannical powers. What if, Collossatron had made the same mistake with Mr. George

Bailey? He was being portrayed by Jimmy Stewart. But, Jimmy Stewart was a man of honor but what about his past?

Jimmy Stewart served as a Pilot in the U. S. Army Air Corps, during World War II. He went on to become a Brigadier General. Then he thought about how Mr. Bailey had been taping messages to some of the other cast members with his fingers as they played their roles in the movie. "Morse Code!" snapped into his mind as the remembered.

He grabbed a coin and began tapping on the wall closest to the street. It was his only hope. If something went wrong, Jimmy Stewart could stop Mr. Potter and the Humbug Virus by entering the encryption sequence code.

Collossatron had used Mr. Potter's own password as part of the encryption sequence code. Mr. Potter used, "Merry Christmas" because he figured that no one would ever guess that one from him. Mr. Potter had used Mary's name to remind himself of his goal of turning George Bailey into a no one, by doing harm to someone George Bailey loved.

Collossatron had updated the encryption sequence code to ensure it had the ability to stop Mr. Potter by changing the Merry in the code to Mary and upgraded it to, "Mary Christmas APPLE!" APPLE stands for All Potter's Plans Left Empty. Collossatron had added the word APPLE because in numeric it was a common word yet very rarely used and the lease guessed by hackers Collossatron had encountered worldwide.

Detective Holiday wondered what was happening outside the vault. He was afraid for Nobody and slumped down against the wall of the vault door and listened but heard nothing. Mr. Potter straightened his coat and adjusted his tie. Nobody came back from the bathroom and inquired as to the whereabouts of Detective Holiday. Mr. Potter told her that he had simply disappeared after they had exited the vault. She began to cry!

Just then, Jimmy Stewart came back in from his phone call. "What is going on here?" asked Jimmy Stewart pointedly. Mr. Potter explained the situation and Jimmy Stewart said, "Look! Lionel or Potter or what ever you call yourself! You! You! Just wait a minute! Now! Nobody you are going to come with me!" Nobody and Jimmy Stewart began a search for Detective Holiday! Then they began a frantic search for the detective to no avail. She told Jimmy Stewart about the vault.

Jimmy Stewart searched for the handle amongst the books in Mr. Potter's library and could not find the handle. "Jimmy you are wasting your time! There is no vault on the set, you know that! The young man just wandered off somewhere. You are panicking over nothing. He is probably outside somewhere just wasting his time.

Besides lunch is almost over and we do want to be ready for the next scene?" asked Mr. Potter with a laugh in his evil grin. The set whistle went off and Jimmy Stewart turned his head in the direction of the whistle! His eyes were fixed and pointed. Nobody could tell he was mad. Mr. Potter again asked, "What about the next scene?" The intercom interrupted with, "The director has called for a break. The crew is having trouble with the artificial snow machine again." "Come on Nobody! Let us get out of here!" said Jimmy Stewart as he pulled her away by the hand.

Do the Right Thing!

Meanwhile at the castle palace of the Christmas King, the King himself was going about his royal business. The Christmas King was dancing about and singing as the king made his way through his royal day. "When it is Christmas and you are still in a line at the Mall! You should have used Potterpay, as now you will not get home at all! We need just two forms of Identification and a wee little scan, of your forehead, one foot, and of course both of your hands!

I the Christmas King shall work the complaint department on Christmas Day! Only two words will you ever hear me say! Bah humbug! Bah humbug! Bah humbug everyday! Oh, my yes of course I have your Bah humbug on lay a way! Bah humbug! Bah humbug all the while. What no receipt you say! Then you shall have a Bah humbug with a smile! When you are upset and have the Christmas Blues, because all you received from the Christmas King was a lump of coal, and a bag of screws, please, complain. I will be most happy to hear your Christmas views!"

The Christmas King was interrupted by the Regent of Gift Giving! "You are majesty! I have a subject, whom wishes to present to you a Christmas dilemma!" The Christmas King let out a sigh as if exasperated already and straightened his crown. He took his royal scepter in his hand. He hurriedly sat upon his golden throne. "Well do not just stand there regent send my subject to me!" commanded the Christmas King!

The regent escorted two children into the throne room of the Christmas King! "Regent you told me one subject, yet you bring me two! Have you taken leave of your senses? I enjoy playing just as much as the next man. I will not tolerate being played with, am I not understood, Regent?" asked the Christmas King with a frown.

"Yes sire! Before you are subject Perceville and subject Annabelle Smithers! They are brother and sister! Perceville would like and end to his toothache and Annabelle would like a Christmas King doll for Christmas, sire!" said the regent as he bowed and walked backward from the Christmas King. "You wish for an end to your toothache! You did not have a toothache on the day of Christmas Giving!" Implied the Christmas King as if, being deceived, by the lad.

The Christmas King leaned forward and gave a sigh of winter discontent. "Why should your toothache be a concern of the Christmas King?" asked the Christmas King with a look of disdain. The boy could not speak, as he had a wrapping around his head. The boy could only mumble. His sister stepped up and spoke on his behalf. "You are majesty! My brother cannot speak as your hard rock candy has broken his teeth! My Christmas King doll was but a sock! The sock belonged to my father. You can see where his toe has gone through." proclaimed Annabelle to the Christmas King as she pushed a finger through the hole in the sock. "Stop right there child! Have you not heard of recycling? We do not waste anything in the Kingdom of Joy! Everything including the sock is a gift or a toy! Touche for you! You have me! Since the sock belonged to your father, you may have a Christmas King doll. Take one there from the wall!

I will hear no more about my delicious never suspicious, superfluous hard rock candy! We make it here ourselves with the help of my imprisoned elves. My hard rock candy is a delicious Christmas dandy! It is made of nutmeg, mint, cinnamon and alum! It puts Christmas whining and tears to doom! It will also clear the room! My hard rock Christmas candy is a superfluous Christmas dandy! You can eat it day or night! It becomes harder with every bite! It is dental kryptonite! It also is rather handy! As a doorstop it is just dandy! My delicious, never suspicious, superfluous Christmas hard rock candy is a Christmas dandy! I do not enjoyhearing you complain!

I grant to you a Christmas King doll and to your X brother a shot of Novocain! Now be gone with you until the next Christmas Day of giving! Children at Christmas hardly make the day worth living!" said the Christmas King as the children moved backward and away from the Christmas King with a courteous bow and a, "Yes, you are majesty!"

The royal coach, which carried Sir Ebenezer Scrooge, the Baron of Happiness, had to stop just** short of the drawbridge. A contingent of the Knights of Christmas, were marching into the Castle of the Christmas King. Sir Ebenezer Scrooge studied the Knights of Christmas as they marched. Each knight had a red or blue cape lined with soft white fur, which denoted rank. It appeared the officers in the contingent wore red capes. Ebenezer could clearly see officer's rank in gold on the center of their capes.

The enlisted knights all had golden stripes according to their rank in the center of the cape from side to side. Ebenezer thought that he would have enjoyed such a uniform in his days of service. They all had shoulder length hair that curled inward at the ends. It appeared that a top sergeant was calling out the cadence and the Knights of Christmas repeated in song each line of cadence the top sergeant called out. At least that is what Ebenezer perceived, as the cape had three golden stripes up and three golden stripes down. In the center of the stripes was a

Christmas Reef with a Christmas ornament bulb in the center of the reef. The knights of Christmas repeated in cadence, "Heart wish to a King!" as they marched into the castle.

Heart wish to a King!
When you make a heart wish to the Christmas King!
The King of Joy and Everything!
He grants, your heart! Its hopes and dreams!
For he is, the very merry Christmas King!
He can give you all of anything!
For he is the very merry Christmas King!
The King of Joy and Everything!
Just give him all your silver and gold!
No child is too young! Or too old!
No heart wish too great! Or too bold!
For he is the very merry Christmas King!
The King of Joy and Everything!
He makes the Knight's of Christmas sing!
Just give him all your silver and gold!
Then watch all your dreams unfold!
For he is the very merry Christmas King!
The King of Joy and Everything!
He grants your heart most anything!
Just give him all your silver and gold!
Then just do as you are told and you will live to grow old!
For he is the very merry Christmas King!
The King of Joy and Everything!

Once, the contingent passed, the coach continued into the castle. Ebenezer, or should I say, Sir Ebenezer Scrooge was met by the Regent of Gift giving at the pea gravel portilico. "I, Sir, Ebenezer Scrooge request an immediate audience before the Christmas King. The king of joy and everything!" Ebenezer proclaimed in a commanding tone to the Regent of Gift Giving. He was led through the great hall of the Christmas King, and to his throne room. Ebenezer presented himself to the king. Ebenezer looked at the Christmas King with disdain. The Christmas King was sitting in his throne as he had before.

The Christmas King was eating grapes and paid no mind to Ebenezer. Ebenezer took off the ribbon that went from his shoulder to his waist. It was the sign of nobility, that he had once only wished for, but now could not bare, having it on his person. The ribbon fell to the shiny marble floor and slid on the surface behind Ebenezer. "One thing, that I cannot stand, is sour grapes!" said the Christmas King!

"The movie, "It's a Wonderful Life is a movie based on a script and because of the honor of the characters they are bound to it! The story of a Christmas Carol is not a script! It is based in real life! There have been a thousand Ebenezer Scrooges, a thousand times over! I am real and my heart feels!

Have your computer print that!" Ebenezer's eyes caught hold of the Super Cell Phone that was on the left arm of the King's throne. With what appeared to be one swift movement, Ebenezer pulled his saber from the confines of his sheath.

Ebenezer stood straight as he spoke his mind freely before the Christmas King! "Have your computer make sense of this!" He thrust his saber from point to hilt into the heart of the Christmas King! The eyes of the Christmas King followed the blade from point to hilt as it drove home Ebenezer's point. The King began sparking, twitching, and jerking violently. "No Blood! You are an automaton! You are an over grown printing press!" said Sir Ebenezer Scrooge.

The eyes of the Christmas King turned into balls of that soft salient blue light. The face of the Christmas King flashed back and forth to that of a child crying. His arms jerked and knocked the super cell phone to the floor! The Knights of Christmas aroused by the noise, entered the Chamber of their great king and attacked Ebenezer!

One by one, he did them in. However, as he moved about the chamber with the flare of Errol Flynn and Burt Lancaster, he flashed from place to place, and time to time. He was fighting them as pirates of the Caribbean. Then, he was fighting them as a gang in, "West Side Story!"

He found himself fighting them in a gunfight at the O. K. Coral! He fought them on a stagecoach. Then, he fought them hand to hand, rolling into a shell crater in World War I. One wounded him badly in his side on a lonely stretch of beach in France on D-Day. He fought them both at Dien Bien Phu and in the La Drang Valley. He fought them in frozen Russia and in the Land of the Pyramids. He was able to pick up the use of the weapons of the day by watching them use theirs. One always presented itself. As if, someone or something was on his side.

"This is Virgin Atlantic Airlines Flight 1843, we have an in flight emergency. Request immediate assistance!" The stewards saw Ebenezer fighting the knights up and down the aisles of the aircraft. A steward looked up, as the cabin lights flickered back on and saw the angry face of one of the knights as his sword went to cut off her head.

The strike was meant to behead Ebenezer, but he ducked, as the blade neared its mark. She lifted up a clipboard to block the blade. The lights flicked off, and when the lights came back on, her clipboard and papers, fell to the floor cut in two. The stewards reported to the pilot that, "one of the passengers was fending off terrorists with a sword!" He had finally done in the last of Knights of Christmas!

Ebenezer leaned on the butt of his sword, and fell against the wall of the cabin in the rear of the aircraft! One of the stewards came to him, and began to wipe his brow, as it was rather obvious, that he was now dying. He slid down the wall of the cabin to his knees. His eyes looked into hers and her face changed into that of his Anna. He kept changing from an old man, to a young man. Ebenezer kept moving from the rear of the aircraft to the throne room and back! He closed his eyes as he took a breath.

He opened his eyes and found himself on his knees in the throne room of the Christmas King! Before him was the Christmas King in all of his royal splendor without a scratch on him. The Christmas King was reprimanding one of his subjects. "Within my realm there is no more Duty Free Alliances. You should know that! It is your expressed privilege to surrender all that is on your list of provisos each time you travel to those zones. Then what is so hard for you? All you must do is place those items in the coffer wagon each day as it passes your ever so humble residence! You have no free duty!

Your duty is to my crown as everyone else!" The Christmas King reached up and removed an earring from the lady, his subject. "I will take this, so that you will be reminded of your privilege and duty to my crown! He tossed the earring into a pot of gold and it bounced into the badge of detective Holiday. The Christmas King continued his verbal onslaught, "Yes, I know it was a Christmas present!

I remember the day most fondly! I will have word of this no more! I make myself clear so that you will know that any excuse whatsoever is just that! You will pay as all the others! Now, depart from me and let this be a lesson to you for all time!" "Yes, you are majesty!" answered the lady as she stepped away giving no notice of Ebenezer. "Have I been sufficient in my warning to you mother most dear?" asked the Christmas King. "Yes, you are majesty!" she said once again as she walked backward and away from the Christmas King!

The Christmas King put down his scepter as he rose from his throne. He walked to Ebenezer who was extremely weak from battle. The king pulled Ebenezer's face up by his hair. "What is it now, Ebenezer? Have you more taste for my cold steel? Look here you pitiful clown," said the Christmas King almost sorrowful for Ebenezer. A large computer monitor came down from the ceiling. The Christmas King took hold of the super cell phone and using it like a remote control played videos of each time Ebenezer had done battle with the Christmas King! Ebenezer could not remember any of them.

He could only remember the nights he drank wine from the Lead Crystal Canter. He thought he had dispatched the Christmas King! "What say you man? What is it going to be this time? You look tired. Perhaps you should rest yourself, before we get started. We have not yet tried dueling with pistols. You have done so with my knights, not so with a King! Did you know that every time I was repaired by my maker, I was given a royal upgrade?" Ebenezer could hardly breathe. His left arm was extremely weak. He rose to his knees. He stopped on one arm. He then reached in with his right hand and clutched his left arm across his lung and squeezed inward clearing his left lung of some of his blood. He leaned backward on his knees.

Only the wall behind him, kept him from falling completely backward. "My maker informs me that I must put and end to you! All you and your friends have been doing is just wasting my time! As long as

I exist, the digital back-up will exist. The Humbug Virus will exist. You have just been wasting your bloody time Ebenezer!" said the Christmas King as he plucked a grape from its stem as he needed more hydraulic fluid. Ebenezer looked, and there upon the shiny marble floor, in front of him was his saber.

Sir Ebenezer Scrooge tried to reach for it but he just could not. He no longer had the strength. The Christmas King stepped over to Ebenezer. Laughingly as to mock Ebenezer, the king slid the saber away from his reach, with his foot. "Come now Ebenezer you can do better than that! How about the tricks you have learned? How about the machete in the chest, you learned from Mr. Eastwood? You can still fight a good fight! Mr. Bronson taught you boxing very well! I had to have a complete new torso unit and upgraded to a fancier golden digital brain. I must say that was a lesson well learned.

Did you run out of your Hollywood and time friends? Or, are they simply too busy for you? They are like all men, when will you learn Ebenezer? Man is here to conquer and to take! You should have at least one more trick from one more friend!" Ebenezer was on his knees, but he was not listening he was thinking! "You said once that you give of yourself as your Lord gave of himself!

Where is this Lord that is so giving? Is he as given out as you? You said he gave his life for you! Are you prepared to give your life for him, Ebenezer?" asked the Christmas King as the King looked into the eyes of Ebenezer. Ebenezer's right arm fell away from him, as he tried to take deeper breathes. His fingers found something and he remembered.

The knife from the first aide kit, Mr. Eastwood had put in his saddlebag. He had tucked the knife in his boot. Then he had simply forgotten about it being there. He concentrated on his breathing, and positioned the knife as he had learned. He took a deep breath, and with what looked like one quick final movement. Sir Ebenezer Scrooge, the Baron of Happiness using the momentum of his fall forward, threw the knife just as hard, straight and true, as he could. Ebenezer fell very hard on his face. He no longer could hear the voice of the Christmas King. Ebenezer slowly and with gritted teeth turned his head to look. Then said he to the Christmas King, "You talk too much!"

The Christmas King sparked, popped, jerked and fizzled out with the knife firmly planted in the digital brain. "I learned that one from a Mr. John Wayne!" said Sir Ebenezer Scrooge, as he closed his eyes.

When he opened them, he was back onboard the aircraft. His head was in the lap of his Anna. "Oh, Ebenezer, My dear sweet Ebenezer!" she said. "Did I do the right thing?" he asked. "When did you ever?" she answered back as she wiped his brow. "I wonder if any man has died in two places at once, in two different times, on the same day?" he flashed with a fading grin. He closed his eyes, as he winched with pain.

When he opened them, he was back in the throne room. "Oh, my heavens not again!" he thought to himself. Then he noticed he was alone. Ebenezer slowly and with much effort rose to his feet. He procured his saber and made his way to the super cell phone. Ebenezer picked it up. He was gravely wounded and in much pain. He spied a spot just in front of the throne. It was where two slabs of marble joined. He knew he could pin the super cell phone to the throne room floor right there.

He gathered himself, and with a deep breath he said, "Merry Christmas Anna! Merry Christmas England! Merry Christmas World to come!" Sir Ebenezer Scrooge, the Baron of Happiness drove his saber through the super cell phone pinning it into the floor of the throne room of the Christmas King!

The super cell phone flashed, and sparked and the throne room began to change. Barnyard animals began to appear! The shinny marble floor suddenly gave way to his feet, as it became earth. Over by the throne was the pot of gold and on top of it, was the shinning badge of Detective Holiday. The young man who had saved the day, by pinning a note to the back of the magic robe of the Heartless Ghost!

I do wish, I could do something to help his world more than this, he thought. "Oh Lord in Heaven when your Christmas comes, forgive Detective Holiday. Have mercy on him!" said Ebenezer prayerfully. He looked down and saw his blood run down the blade and into the broken twisted super cell phone, and it sparked its last. He looked round about him, and he could see the beautiful light from the Star of Bethlehem as it suddenly flooded into the manger as the castle, piece by piece fell away. Then he heard a newborn infant cry!

He felt a peace in this light that he had not felt, in the soft salient blue light. He could see true awe in the faces of those gathered round the Son of God! He watched as the wise men lay prostrate, before the King! The true Christmas King! The king of joy and everything! Ebenezer now felt no pain and rose up from his saber. The saber fell threw the earthen floor of the manger, through the earth and into space.

Note: The super cell phone pinned to the marble floor. The white brilliant light of the Star of Bethlehem as it floods into the throne room as it becomes a manger.

Ebenezer's saber twirled through time and space.

However, it was pulled back down by the constant pull of the gravitational field of Earth. Ebenezer marveled at how the animals themselves appeared awestruck as well. They did not seem to mind his presence. He stepped back as others were moving forward to see the Christ Child. He saw the face of the child. He felt a hand come along side his hand. He turned and there was Anna bathed in a white light.

Her gaze was transfixed on the Christ Child. The Christmas King! The King of Joy and Everything! He looked at his hand in hers, both of them now in the white light and she softly mouthed, "Welcome Back! Ebenezer! They gazed lovingly at the Son of Man and Ebenezer softly said, "Beautiful!" and Anna softly said, "Simply Beautiful!"

Note: The castle haven fallen away the true Christmas King! The King of Joy and Everything!

CHAPTER 20

The American Dream Awakens

Mr. Stewart drove Nobody to the Bedford Falls High School Gymnasium. When Jimmy Stewart called an underground meeting, it was by way of signal. The signal to those that could be reached on the intercom system it was, "Trouble with the artificial snow machine." For those that the intercom could not reach, the message was tapped out in Morse code on almost and if anything!

The cast and crew had been having secret meetings in the Bedford Falls High School Gymnasium for almost a year undetected. Mr. Potter's hearing was such that you could tap out a message to Jimmy Stewart right in front of him. Nobody took the notebook Journal of Detective Holiday along. When they entered the gymnasium, Nobody was amazed. They before her were at least 300 people.

The meeting was called to order with a Prayer and the Pledge of Allegiance. Mr. Stewart got up to the front and introduced Nobody. "I would like to introduce you all to Girl Nobody. She is from America in the future. It appears that what has been happening to us, has been the result of a computer called Collossatron. This computer is working to change the whole meaning of Christmas and take the American Dream along with it!

The audience rumbled. "Now! Now! Calm down! The situation is not as black as it seems! There is a way out of this! Now, modern weapons cannot destroy this computer in its own time. Because it can control them! Bert came up with a great idea! He suggested that we hit it with everything we have got! Let me explain. These dreams we have been experiencing can be controlled or fixed. Nobody has brought some of these heavy metal pills from her time. Mr. Gower is going to analyze them and prepare some for us. He should have them in half and hour of so!

Some how we have been brought forward in time and the heavy metal content in our bodies has somehow been altered by this computer. Once we get that under control, we will stop having the dreams and be able to distinguish when we are on camera and when we are off the set!

This young lady and Detective Holiday have helped us enormously in our fight with Mr. Potter. Ms. Nobody has quite an interesting notebook too! I see that Mr. Gower is back. Will you take over for me Bert?" "Sure thing!" said Bert as he stepped up beside Jimmy Stewart.

Jimmy Stewart went behind the stage and down the steps to the janitors office and small apartment. A man was inside the apartment cleaning his mop and bucket out for the next day. "Roscoe are you coming?" asked Jimmy Stewart. "Jimmy, I know it is Christmas and all but I just can not." replied Roscoe the janitor. "Roscoe you know we need every man on this one!" implored Jimmy Stewart.

Roscoe quietly continued wringing out the mop. He stopped and closed his eyes. He appeared to be pondering for a question, or as if he was hiding a secret. Roscoe had just showed up one day and had taken a job as a janitor on the set. Before he could answer Jimmy Stewart said, "You are the only man with a horse!" "Now why did you have to go and say that, Jimmy!" exclaimed Roscoe. "Just give me a few minutes to put my things away and lock up. I will be there, I promise" said Roscoe. Jimmy Stewart just acknowledged the answer with a wink and then went back up on stage in the gymnasium.

Bert gave a description of Detective Joe K. Holiday to the assemblage and instructed them to try to find him. He then handed the meeting back over to Jimmy Stewart. "Now, I need all Military age men particularly all former Navy, Marine Corps or like myself US Army Air Corps fliers and ground crews, to meet me at the Time Gate in one hour. Bert is going to open the Army Surplus Store. Get back into your uniforms there or bring your own! If any of you have anything that we can use, bring it to our attention! Let's make this a Christmas to remember!"

The auditorium erupted in applause! "Settle Down! Settle Down Now! Now Ms. Reed is going to pass around some of this water with this heavy metal in it. I suggest you drink it! It will help clear your mind and it will not be enough to hurt you. You just will be able to tell when you are acting. The crew has not been able to tell for a year, and neither have we. So, let us put a stop to this right Now! America needs us again! God bless each and everyone of you, and wish us luck! Clarence is going to stay behind, and close the meeting!

Clarence will also fill in the details of our plans! We are going to put a stop to Potter! Once, and for all! We are going to do it tonight!" proclaimed Jimmy Stewart. The audience was very security minded. Nevertheless, they all joined hands and began singing, "We Wish You A Merry Christmas."

Jimmy Stewart left and got himself dressed in his U.S. Army Air Corps Uniform. He was signaling to the other side of the large grassy area for the men to run across to where he and Nobody were waiting. "I sure hope this works!" said Nobody. "I will get you to Dr. Chaney and Dr. Denny when we get back. I also need to find Detective Holiday!" she said. "I know you do young lady! He risked everything to fix this mess!" said Jimmy Stewart. The men began to appear out of the shadows. Mr. Martimi, Harry, Mat, Bert, Ernie for about one hundred and sixty-five (165) all together.

Jimmy Stewart quietly called them all to attention and took a quick roll call. "Now when we get over to where this place is we stick together!" said Mr. Stewart as he began to climb the tree. Just as it forked, he looked over to the other side and just saw a curtain of salient blue light and a long way down about ten feet he reckoned. "Here goes nothing!" he said as he stepped into nothing.

He stepped down into the tram Maria used to clean the lenses. It was parked just outside the main control complex near a break area. Jimmy Stewart moved forward into the tram and into our time. He moved forward, and one by one the men from, "It's a Wonderful Life!" stepped into the present day Land of Nowhere. He turned on his flashlight as he and Nobody stepped out of the tram. Nobody softly said, "turn it off!"

One of the scientists was putting out a cigarette and went inside. Nobody had been here before with Detective Holiday and Dr. Chaney. She ran forward in the shadows and caught the door as it was closing. The men from Bailey Park filed in behind her. Nobody took them to the cafeteria. The cafeteria was, "closed", for the evening. They hid in the cafeteria while Nobody went to the control room. She tried the door and to her amazement, it was unlocked.

Dr. Denny was in his chair facing away from her. He had both arms above his head staring at replays of the past through Collossatron's time windows trying to find a solution to the problem.

She saw Dr. Chaney asleep on a couch in another office. She stepped out of her small shoes and tip toed into the office. One minute later, both she and Dr. Chaney, came tiptoeing out of the office, out of the control complex then down to the cafeteria. Dr. Denny was flipping through the time replays, when the office door slammed and he jumped. He turned around and there was Dr. Chaney with Jimmy Stewart!

The Tennessee Aviation Museum was, "closed", for the night! It was actually, "closed", for Christmas! Suddenly, the lights came on. A hand grabbed a WW II flight jacket off a hanger. It was the hand of Chief Detective Pryzwarra. In another town, a museum light came on. Then another, and then another. At an aircraft museum on Mud Island in Tennessee, the lights came on.

It was the home of the B-17 the Memphis Belle. The cockpit door opened and a man climbed inside and began looking up into the control panel with a flashlight in his teeth. He reached up, and the keys fell down into his hand. Detective Carlin had immediately responded to a radio call at his station.

He had flown up to the Collossatron Complex when things went south. He had led the investigation into the salient light breach. His investigation had found that by changing the heavy metal content of the human body affected the eyes. Those who were in the suspended gravitational field of, "Bailey Park" did not see the salient blue light. There eyesight appeared to be within normal limits because of the altered heavy metal content in their bodies. He was now helping put a stop to Collossatron. Meanwhile the rest of Tennessee was unknowingly witnessing the preparations of fight for Christmas!

A man was outside on his deck in Chattanooga. He looked up and saw a C-47 Chinook fly over his home with a P-38 Lighting hanging on a cable below it. A family eating at a late night cafe near a highway in Tennessee saw a fleet of flat bed trucks drive by with the parts of a P-51 Mustang on them. The first one went by with the fuselage. When the second flatbed truck passed with a pair of wings on it, a spoon fell out of the hand, of a tired boy who was looking out the window waiting for his pancakes.

Jimmy Stewart and the Chief Detective went out side together. They were followed by about five scientists who wanted skin scrapings and blood work, all of which he refused. Chief Detective Pryzwarra offered him a cigarette. Jimmy took one and as he did Dr. Chaney came up to him wanting a swab of the inside of his mouth to see the heavy metal content in his body. "If, you knew what we now know about tobacco, you would not be smoking that cigarette," she said smiling.

Jimmy Stewart in his quiet, well-mannered style flashed a smile. "Young lady, if you knew, what I now know about computers, we would not be having this conversation, would we?" he asked. Dr. Chaney smiled back and noticing his Santa Claus hat and a bell attached to his pocket smiled back and said, "Merry Christmas Sir! Excuse me!" "Merry Christmas!" he said with a bigger smile. Dr. Chaney skipped away. She was amused at his wit and was not the least bit offended.

The two men could hear a very load argument over by the lenses. "So, that is Bailey Park?" said Jimmy Stewart inquisitively. "Yes, sir it is!" answered by Detective Carlin as he lit the cigarette of Jimmy Stewart with an electronic lighter. "Hmm", said Jimmy Stewart at the technology.

One of the scientists was arguing that it was against all they understood that these men were able to transition over into our time. The scientist was very mad and threw a rock at the blue beam and it bounced back and struck him in the head. It hit with such force they sent a medical team to treat him. "So that is one of the guys that got us into this mess?" said Jimmy Stewart. "Yeah." said the detective. "Looks like he is in the wrong job." said Jimmy Stewart.

Jimmy Stewart told the scientists about degaussing and one of the scientists remarked, "You mean like the Philadelphia Experiment!" Jimmy Stewart replied, "I see you paid attention in school!" The scientists began to explain all about the Einstein-Rosen Bridge and Bert stood up and asked, "Did the Dodgers ever come out of their slump?" The cafeteria erupted with laughter.

Note: The only tangible proof that this story is true. The baseball mitt of Mr. Ward Bond

The Tennessee Aviation Museum gets an Overnight Grant

Helicopters arrived to take the men to an Aviation Museum in Tennessee, where an airfield was under construction. Once they arrived at the museum, Jimmy Stewart started detailing their plan. They would use World War II aircraft to bomb Collossatron with weapons it had created.

Jimmy Stewart was getting upset with one of the scientists and said, "Look! You people are through giving orders! The way I see it! You people have messed around, and created something that is not only going to destroy the meaning of Christmas. It is going to destroy the American Dream! We are not going to sit by and watch you do it! Now Detective Holiday found us! Have somebody find him! This Collossatron computer uses electromagnetic pulse beams to control, disable, or destroy your aircraft. Let's use the same weapon against it!" "But, we do not have any electromagnetic pulse bombs!" said one of the scientists.

Major Jimmy Stewart looked him straight in the eyes and said, "You mean to tell me that all of this has been created and no-one has secretly, and I emphasize the word, "Secretly", weaponized any of the discoveries this computer has found?" Then he just turned to another scientist and asked, "What is the status of the aircraft?" "We have men turning them into flying, "Faraday Cages", as we speak!" said Dr. Denny. One of the scientists again insisted, "We do not have an electromagnetic pulse bomb!" Bert just smirked! "I was not in the service long, but I know when I am being lied too."

Dr. Denny looked around and one of the scientists he had been arguing with just looked down. Dr. Denny said. "You have got to be kidding?" "Major Jimmy Stewart pulled Dr. Denny to him and asked, "When are the ships going to be ready for us?" asked Jimmy Stewart. "They are being put together as fast as possible. Some of these engines have not been turned over since the war. Mr. Martimi pulled up his belt and proudly said, "Well we must have done something right, then!" The scientist continued with, "Plus, we can not even use a phone, or any radio system that can be breached.

Major Jimmy Stewart called out, "Nobody!" "Right here sir!" she answered back. "Get a phone book and get the addresses of all the Veteran Service Organizations to me as fast as you can!" Ordered Major Jimmy Stewart. "Yes Sir!" She answered back proudly. Major Jimmy Stewart wrote a letter and they copied it on an old mimeograph machine in the back office of the Tennessee Aviation Museum. Dr. Denny took the letter and remembering his dream, had the museum director, Mr. Martimi, and Nobody meet him behind the museum.

Previously he had used the mimeograph machine on the electricity from the museums power source. This had tipped off Collossatron to the entire scheme. This time around, he decided to go a different direction. He used his solar panels as a power source. He had the group take the letters around to the Veteran Service Organizations in an old Willie Jeep.

Dr. Chaney was busy taking samples with q-tips and analyzing the amount of heavy metals in each man. Dr. Chaney would have them take a few sips of her concoction if their individual levels needed to be adjusted. Dr. Chaney had started her own testing assembly line. She had each man come in and give her his name, rank, and serial number, as they were accustomed to already during World War II.

She was putting a hermitical seal on a bag when the next pilot came in and said his name was, Chaney, Roscoe B., First Lieutenant, 332d

Fighter Group. Before he could finish his introduction, Dr. Chaney dropped her tray and fell back against the wall. He jumped out of his seat and started picking up her things and setting them back on her tray. Then he set the tray on the counter. He looked into her eyes and his eyes began to fill with soft tears. He choked the tears back and said, "You do not have to say anything young lady.

I know all of this must be quite a shock or feel like some sort of strange dream. I know I would if I saw people come out of the past!" Dr. Chaney looked at him and softly said, "It is like you have come out of a dream. You look just like all the pictures in the house." The First Lieutenant said, "You have her eyes! You also have her feet. They were so small!" "Oh papa! Why did you leave like you did?" asked Dr. Chaney as she pulled him into a bear hug of unfinished love. "You were just a baby, back then. I just could not keep it together. I tried but it was no good. Not for your mother, not for you and not for me!" said the Lieutenant to his daughter. "Mama said you drank yourself to death! They never found your body.

They just found were you had been fishing and supposed that you had fallen in and drowned." said Dr. Chaney with a quivering voice. "I am sorry honey! Is it alright if I call you honey?" asked First Lieutenant Chaney. "Papa you can call me anything you want! I just want you to know that I love you! Mama still loves you!" insisted Dr. Chaney as she wiped the tears from her eyes. "Where is she?" he asked. "She is in a nursing home in Chattanooga!" she replied. "A nursing home huh!" he said. Mama is ninety-eight years old, papa." Said Dr. Chaney as she showed him a picture from her wallet purse. "Gee whiz!

She is still alive this far into the future? What about the house? Why is she in a nursing home?" He asked with a bewildered look. "When you passed away you did not leave her much and she has no insurance. I am trying to keep things going as best as I can," said Dr. Chaney. "I left her plenty of insurance. What are you talking about?" "She said that she thought you had but after you passed, she nor anyone else could find anything!" "I left her plenty! Do you have a car? Of course I do. Then take me home! Right now!" Said the Lieutenant.

Dr. Chaney had a nursing assistant go after Dr. Denny. Dr. Denny responded immediately. As he stepped into the lab area, he immediately put the situation together as both were wearing nametags. He saw the tears in both of their eyes and said, "Just name it!" "I need to get to Chattanooga before take off! All I need is a car sir." Said Lieutenant Roscoe B. Chaney.

"To heck with that nonsense! It is Christmas take a chopper!" Said Dr. Denny with a look of amazement on his face. "I do not ride motorcycles!" said the Lieutenant. "Dr. Chaney just go out and find Warrant Officer Suarez and tell him where you need to go and get back here just as fast as you can." said Dr. Denny. "Oh thank you!" she answered. "Never mind that now just go while you can. Remember get back here just as fast as you can and send in the next man. I will cover you until I can get someone else in here. Now go!" insisted the Doctor as they hurried out the door.

Warrant Officer Three Suarez loaded them into a UH-72A Lakota and zipped into the air in the Direction of the River City. Once they arrived over the city, First Lieutenant Chaney began to point out some of the changes. "I grew up over there in Orchard Knob. I grew up with Tyler, Wilson and Peebo. I was the only one to make it back.!" "Look down there, that is Martin Luther King Boulevard and over there is the Bessie Smith Museum!" said Dr. Chaney to her father. The Lieutenant took it all in with out saying a word.

The lieutenant noticed the pilot was eating an apple. "You would not happen to have another one of those would you?" he asked of the pilot. "Sure have one, what would Christmas be without an apple!" replied the pilot. "Mamma always said that you liked apples, papa!" said Dr. Chaney. "Like them, honey, I love them!" he replied as he took a bite out of the apple. "I never start my day without one.

I had a whole pocket full before we went through that time gate of yours," said the lieutenant. "Papa we even have a black president!" said Dr. Chaney. "Honey that does not mean diddly squat to me!" "I thought you would be proud." Said Dr. Chaney puzzled. "The color of a mans skin does not define him. The color of a mans heart is what defines him." The pilot was listening and said, "Amen to that!" He then said, "We are coming up on your backyard, sir! I can set her down right between those trees. Is that alright with you?" "Sure, these racy new helicopters sure come in handy!" said the Lieutenant as he gazed at his home so far into the future.

They exited the helicopter and the Lieutenant asked, "Who painted the house yellow?" "Mama did. She said that you had trouble finding your way home at night!" "Well never mind that! We should have a crow bar in the garage. Could you fetch it for me honey?" asked the Lieutenant. The lieutenant walked around the house lost in time. He gazed at all of the pictures of him that had been hung on the walls of what used to be his home. He found a picture of him and his three friends, dusted off the top of the frame, and then put it back up on the wall. He walked over to his bedroom and sat down on the bed. "Still lumpy!" he remarked as he gently bounced up and down.

He took one picture down and set it on the bed. "I never did like this one." He said as he pulled the nail out that it had been hung on. "Why did not you like that one?" asked Dr. Chaney with the crowbar in her hand. "I'm sorry honey, I did not see you standing there. I was drunk. I had just got home and found out that I was the only one to make it back so I got plastered. My uniform was a mess and your mama took that picture, I think on purpose! I think she was trying to make a point for me to see later, when I was sober." said Dr. Chaney's father.

He took the crow bar from her and walked over to the fireplace in the living room. He started prying the bricks away from the corner of the fireplace and the wall. He got to the forth row of bricks and a heavy metal box slide out and burst open onto the floor. Coins, papers, and old money spread out in a half moon pattern from the open top of the box right at their feet. "That is everything I kept a secret from your mother! You will not find any lipstick or pantyhose though! She always had me thinking, that is what she was thinking. I just worked mostly under the table as a janitor for a few places that is all!"

"You should also find my life insurance papers in there. We should get out of here while there is still time! You can go through it later. You might want to clean up this mess or she is going to throw a fit!" exclaimed Dr. Chaney's father as he stood holding the crow bar. "Dad you just got here!" she exclaimed. "And I am just going to leave. Honey, I cannot stay where everyday I had to fight myself to stay just another day! The memories are too strong! Honey, I stayed for the occupation of Europe after the war. I came home to find out that I was the only one to make it back. I would walk down to the Deli for lunch and have to listen to kids complaining about how far they had to walk to school or where they had to sit on the bus. I spent years in countries where they worked you to death, gassed you or shot you for going to the wrong church! I tried but I just could not keep it together.

I just could not stand the sissy-mariness of it! When they would march for civil rights and burn down everything, they burnt down the neighborhood I fought to protect. The same men who cried out for their rights were the same men I saw running down the street with an armful of tennis shoes. Change takes time, not hate! Hate kills it does not change things. Remember that honey. If you reach for the standard and achieve it, you win acceptance. It is just not given to you because of the color of your skin.

We live in a country where we at least have a chance. You just have to fight for your dream. Stop moaning about what you do not have. Dream about what you could have, if you just put your shoulder to the grindstone of life and work for the dream. Now let us get back to the airfield." "Papa, why do you want to go back so fast!" asked Dr. Chaney as she hugged her father. "Dad, you have to tell me why?" she said as she tapped his whiskey flask through his flight jacket. "Please do not tell your mother! This is between you and me. A good officer and friend of mine had been shot down right in front of me. I I saw to much hate in that war. Hate kills! You can not come home and protest for equal rights with hate in your heart! I did not want to become part of it. I saw some clown wearing a, "zoot", suit complaining about his circumstances. They did not change America.

We did! We got into this war and fought it, and we ate the same dirt as our white neighbors. When we died sometimes, we died together. We called out for our mother, just like they did when they died. They came back changed and so did we! We changed America! We did!" As the lieutenant explained himself, this he punched the refrigerator door a couple of times, where they were standing in the kitchen.

I have to go back because they are my

brothers, and together we are Americans! Yes, I am sure they all have faults. So do I, come on now let us get back!" That is what First Lieutenant Roscoe B. Chaney did, he went back.

Once they arrived back at the airfield, Dr. Chaney and her father had little to say. She was mad at him as he did not appear to want to go see her ailing mother. The Seabees had already begun building an airfield, before the first aircraft arrived. The men began to jump up and down as the sound of a P-38 Lightning filled their ears! Trucks suddenly arrived, and the crews started pulling ammunition boxes out the trucks.

They began pulling long lines of.50 caliber electromagnetic ammunition out of the boxes. One of the scientists explained the ammo to Dr. Denny and the assembled men. The bullets explode emitting a super strong electronic pulse after penetrating their target. If the target is electronically controlled, the pulse destroys them without any physical damage, with the exception of the entrance wound. They lined up the ammo chains on the tarmac, just as they had trained during the war. The air around the museum was becoming electric. Even the museum staff volunteers put on their old uniforms. They removed all the security cameras from the museum and piled all of the computers outside.

The building seemed to be quiet. Ernie had his feet up on a desk. He was flipping through a magazine and eating. One thing that has not changed a good piece of pizza" he said as he took a big bite. He began to chew then his eyes widened and he suddenly jumped up and ran outside. Bert started to smile and said, "Come on fellows!" as he went over to a window. He ran outside with a few others, before the scientists could hear the distant humming sound. It grew and grew louder, and their smiles got bigger. Then over the trees,

came a wonderful sight. The majestic war birds of World War II began to appear as if, out of the past.

In came a B-17 Flying Fortress rumbling over the treetops. The beautiful aircraft turned and came in for a landing. "Have you ever seen anything so beautiful?" Bert said to Dr. Denny. Then in came a B-25 Mitchell Bomber, then a B-24 Liberator. A lone B-24 Liberator came out of the horizon and came rolling down the field. Bert's smile was so big and wide, he had to take his hand and pull it down, off his face.

The B-24 was followed by a P-51 Mustang. These aircraft landed while the runway was still under construction. Engineers from every branch of service were streaming in. In just a few short hours, a small airfield was transformed into an airbase. One pilot got out of the aircraft he had delivered still in his pajamas.

Note: Major Jimmy Stewart outside the Tennessee Aviation Museum inspecting the B-24 A promise and a Dream. Great big trucks arrived with the electromagnetic bombs. The ground crews began loading them into the Bombay's of the war birds. The electromagnetic bombs had a two blue stripes around the nose of the weapons. "How appropriate!" said Detective Carlin as he walked up in a WWII flight suit.

They only had hours left now, and said their good byes! Jimmy Stewart walked around the Memphis

Belle, and one of the ground crew said, "We can put anything you want on the nose Sir!" Jimmy Stewart replied, "She will do just fine! Just fine!" Bert climbed up inside a B-25 Mitchell Bomber, and checked out his controls. "I never would have guessed that I would see a beautiful picture like this again!" "Beautiful!" the young captain said. "Yeah, when one of these babies saves your bacon and brings you home in one piece. It puts an entirely different idea in your head about how beautiful a ship like this can be to you!" After his walk around, he looked up at the ship and asked the Crew Chief, if he could do him a favor. The Collossatron Complex and facilities had been evacuated when a special forces team trying to drill through the reinforced concrete had been wounded. Collossatron's specifications called for sheets of copper to be laid down in the concrete. The sheets had perforated squares where air was trapped. The concrete mix had also been formulated by Collossatron. Note: The Memphis Belle prior to loading for the mission.

The concrete contained bits of aluminum which when heated by the diamond tipped drill bit used by the special forces team. It caused small shape charged explosions when they injected water into the drill bit to cool it down. The small explosions alerted Collossatron to their presence. It also knocked the diamonds out of the drill bit heads.

It was ingenious said Dr. Denny as he informed the American Dream Squadron in his briefing. Dr.

Denny asked Major Jimmy Stewart if he had anything to say. "Yes I do! Bert would you be so kind as to do the honors!" "Roger, I am on it! Okay fellows, jump on it!" said Bert. Mr. Martimi and a few others got up from their seats and ran outside the room. In a few seconds they came back in the room with an American Flag! "We generally start our meetings with the Pledge of Allegiance and a prayer," said Ward Bond or Bert.

The scientists complied and as they started the Pledge of Allegiance, Bert interrupted with, "Now just a gall darn minute! This is America in the future?" He looked to Major Jimmy Stewart and he said nothing but his eyes were gleaming with approval. Ward Bond or Bert walked up to a scientist and said, "That hand should be over your heart like it means something to you! Your heart is special, act like it is special!

You are holding your heart and for one or two minutes and showing the world that what is beating beneath your hand is America's heart. The state of Tennessee's heart! Your fingers are supposed to be extended and joined. Keep your elbow to your side and your hand clinched alongside the seam of your pants, making a fist. Note: Ward Bond as he appeared at the Tennessee Aviation Museum on Christmas Eve.

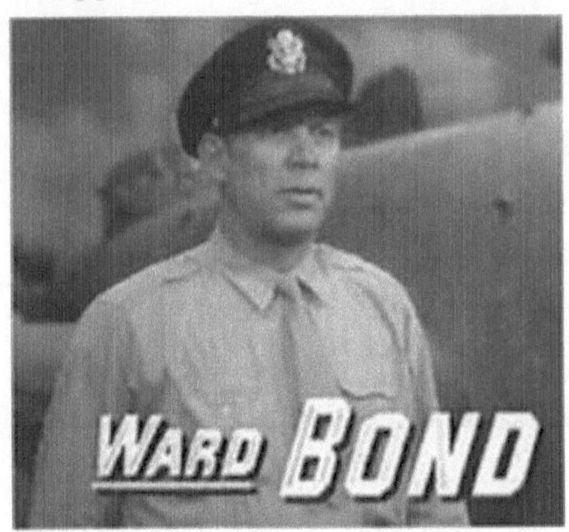

Show that you, along with the rest of America are willing to fight for freedom, young man. More countries tune into our sports programs than you think! What you become in their eyes, for just a few minutes of your time, is the symbol of America!

You are showing the world that in all our differences in all things, we are one people and strong! Remember that! If a man perceives weakness, in your character or your heart, that is where he is going to strike his first blow!" said Bert or Ward Bond as he walked from man to man adjusting their salute. Tomorrow you or I may die for freedom's sake. I would hope you would remember and represent me proudly, for just a gall darn minute or two. Excuse me chief!" He said to Jimmy Stewart as he stood back up and they continued with the Pledge of

Allegiance. Dr. Chaney smiled and a tear came to her eye as the whole room straightened up.

Jimmy Stewart called all the veteran pilots, crews, the museum staff and the scientists together. It was getting very late and Jimmy Stewart said, "This is Christmas Eve! Before we leave, we would like to celebrate Christmas with all of you!" The American Dream Squadron, as they had been named by Nobody, gathered in the form of a choir.

Jimmy Stewart began to play a piano that was there in the museum on display. The men from Bailey Park sang a beautiful rendition of, "Stand By Me!" They then all sang, "You will never walk alone." Then in a very low baritone voice, Mr. Martimi who had his B-24 Liberator nose painted with, "A Promise and a Dream" stole the show with a solo performance of, "Rise Up! Shepherd and Follow."

Jimmy Stewart stopped playing and Mr. Martimi took over at the piano. Jimmy Stewart walked over to Nobody and said, "Would you be so kind as to dance with an old pilot, young lady?" Nobody was busy putting away her diabetic supplies she had been given by Mr. Gower. Her eyes began to sparkle as she replied, "Yes, sir! Mr. Stewart, I would be delighted to dance with and old pilot!" Major Jimmy Stewart offered his hand and she graciously accepted it.

Jimmy Stewart pulled her to her feet and as he did so, she spun around and met him in a formal dance posture. He smiled very big and said, "I see you can dance, young lady!" "I dance with Detective Joe Holiday all the time." said Nobody as she looked up to Jimmy Stewart. "Well young lady you just go ahead and dance then!" "I wanted to say thank you before we left. You really are somebody Nobody!" said Jimmy Stewart as they danced. "I sure hope we can find Joe!" Jimmy Stewart smiled with a funny grin as if he knew something Nobody did not and replied, "I am sure he is going to be alright! After all it is Christmas!" "I have been going over all my clues.

I have a question Mr. Stewart" said Nobody. "I am sure you do, what is it?" he asked. "Have you done this before?" she asked looking up. "Well we all know how to play that piano!" he replied as they danced. "Nobody in her suddenness grabbed Jimmy Stewart in a Christmas hug and told him how much she loved him. He smiled and told her that he loved her too, as his finger touched her little nose as they continued to dance.

That is what they did for a while, they danced. "I have a song just for you, young lady! Well, it is more of our way of saying thank you for making this a special Christmas for us. If it was not for you and Detective Holiday we would be in quite and bind." He looked over to Mr. Martimi at the piano and gave a wink and a nod. Mr. Martimi took to the piano as never before. He began to play, "If I can Dream," by Earl Brown, as performed by the great Elvis Presley. The young handsome Jimmy Stewart sang it most beautifully with feeling to Nobody. The American Dream Squadron sang along also. Then Mr. Martimi played a different song he played the music for the song, "Christmas Wings!"

Major Jimmy Stewart danced with Nobody to the music. While he did so, he acted out sort of a skit to the words of the song. Nobody took his lead and did the same. The rest of the American Dream Squadron also performed the skits which made the scene, all the more beautiful to behold. As only a witness to this occasion, I can only describe what transpired. Major Jimmy Stewart sang the first five verses to Nobody as they danced. She was in, "Hog Heaven", as her mother had once put it. When her mother had caught her day dreaming in the yard instead of doing her chores.

One-half of the American Dream Squadron would sing, "What Christmas brings." The other half would reply with the verse, "Light down from above!" They did the same with the next verse, "What Christmas means." On the last stanza they all sang together, "On Christmas wings!"

As they came to the last scene, I witnessed one of the skits. One of the pilots or crewmembers, knocked upon a door, which did not exist. One of the others answered the door. He stepped aside to reveal another, lying upon the floor. It was quite moving and amusing to say the least.

Christmas wings

On Christmas wings you can fly forever!
You are here, then there, right over there, back again, then never!
You can fly through the air, with no one else there, and down below
everyone is dreaming!
Of Christmas designs and glasses of wine and sleigh bells are ringing!
While high up above we are flying with love or we could
just be dreaming! Christmas brings, what Christmas means,
on gold and shiny, silver shiny Christmas wings!

Christmas brings: Light down from above!
What Christmas means: My heart is filled with love!
On Christmas wings: From high up above!

Christmas brings: Mistletoe is in the air!
What Christmas means: I am going to kiss you right there!
On Christmas wings: Oh, no! Do not you dare!

Christmas brings: Come inside where it is warm!
What Christmas means: A child is born!

On Christmas wings: We fly in with love!

Christmas brings: Good will towards your fellow man!
What Christmas means: A Salvation Plan!
On Christmas wings: Do all that you can!

Christmas brings: Bright red, green, yellows and blues!
Christmas means: I love you!
On Christmas wings: Until the job is done!

Christmas brings: A gleam to your smile!
What Christmas means: Please would not you, stay for a while!
On Christmas wings: You are the only man with a horse!
Christmas brings: Fresh tracks in the snow!

What Christmas means: No good byes! Just hellos!
On Christmas wings: I will have another of course!

Christmas brings: A surprise at your door!
What Christmas means: My uncle on the floor!
On Christmas wings: Christmas brings what Christmas means on gold
and shiny, silver shiny Christmas wings!

The beauty of the music and seeing her father, arm and arm with the
men from Bailey Park was almost more than Dr. Chaney could stand.
She looked around the room at all the different nationalities and races and
saw for the first time, the beauty of America. She wondered why it had
taken her so long to see what she now felt in her heart. She left the room
in tears. One of the men from the American Dream Squadron rushed out
and brought Dr. Chaney back inside. There before her she witnessed her
father as he sang the song of First Lieutenant Roscoe B. Chaney.

The American Dream
You have to dare to dream the American Dream
Dream, the American Dream
Built with the Iron of your will and your character of steel!
Fight for your dream so your dream can begin!
Fight with a smile! Fight with a grin!
Fight with a shovel! Fight with a pen!
Never give up! Never give in!
Fight to the finish! Fight to the end!
Fight for your dream so your dreams can win, when
you dare to dream The American Dream
It is built with courage and grit, with iron and stone!
It takes patience and resolve, muscle and bone, and your dream
The American dream, becomes a home, an American home!
Where children are raised, and their dreams are born
Families are started like seeds that are sewn in a dream
The American Dream
Dream like you are following an audacious plan!

Dream like you have got the heart and the sand!
Dream with a seventy-six piece marching band!
Dare to dream The American Dream!
Dream with your heart, dream with your soul!
Dream when you are young, dream when you are old!
Dream when you are hot, wet, thirsty and cold!
But still you dare to dream, the American Dream
Some days you will wish, you were never born
Your tired and weak, tattered and torn,
but still dare to dream, the American Dream.
Dream when you see others accomplish their dreams
Dream when your life is falling apart at the seams!
but still dare to dream the American Dream!
Reach for the Dream, the American Dream! Because the American
Dream is not just a
dream, the American Dream comes true!

With the Christmas celebrations ending, the men closed the briefing and went straight to their aircraft. Bert headed for a B-25 Mitchell Bomber. The Crew Chief met him and asked, "Is this what you wanted?" "Sure Is! This King is going to return!" Bert replied. There on the nose was King Nine being dealt by a king. In front of the king painted in white was a small mound. Protruding from it at a crazy angle was a Christian cross..

Dr. Chaney was upset with her father. She could see him outside climbing into his P-51C Mustang fighter. Warrant Officer Suarez came into her makeshift lab with a bag of apples. He sat them down and said, "You know if that was my father and he did not want to see my mother, I would want to know why. I have a whole bag of apples here, just like you and me each one was grown in Tennessee. If I grew up without m father, and he did not want to see my mother on Christmas, I think I would throw each and every single one at him just as hard as I could!" Dr. Chaney turned around with tears in her eyes and said, "your right!" as she grabbed the bag and ran outside.

First Lieutenant Roscoe B. Chaney was giving his crew chief back his checklist when an apple hit the side of his red tailed P-51C Mustang. He climbed out and grabbed her by the arms with, "Mercy! Mercy me!" She tearfully said, "It is Christmas! Why? Why do not you want to see her Papa? Oh, Papa you have to tell me, Why?" He pulled her to him, got eye-to-eye with her, and said, "Remember when you saw me? You did not have to say a word, I saw it in your eyes!

I love your mother so much that if I looked into her eyes even at ninety-eight for just one second, I would stay! I can hardly look into your eyes and go! I have to think of the bigger picture. The Lord has given us a chance to save Christmas for everybody! It may be the only chance we get! He picked up an apple and polished it with his sleeve and said, "Give her an apple and tell her when I get home, I will plant that apple tree like I promised. She will understand! She always did!"

He climbed into his P-51C and buckled himself into the seat. She climbed up and gave him the bag of apples and with a Christmas kiss said, "Merry Christmas Papa!" "I'm going to make sure of that! You and your mother are the apples of my eyes and my heart! Remember, "hate does not change it kills!" said the Lieutenant as he slid the canopy forward with a click.

One by one, the American Dream Squadron started their engines. They taxied into position and lumbered down the field. One by one with a roar, they lifted into the air. Bert was coming up next. Ernie got his attention by banging his hand on his P-51 Mustang. He was on Bert's left. Bert looked over and Ernie gave him a "thumbs up!" Bert pushed his throttle forward and the race for the air began.

The aircraft circled the field and then moved into a General Le May formation. Major Jimmy Stewart was on the ball this Christmas Night! He had the aircraft circle the field in what was then called, "Nap of the Earth", navigation. As a matter of fact, it was just about the only way his generation knew how to fly. They flew just over the treetops and just over the hills at two hundred miles an hour. This may sound incredible but tonight it was more than true, and brought many a Tennessean to their knees in prayer. Major Jimmy Stewart and his fighter escorts flew low and fast following the topographical features along the banks and farms that lined the Mississippi and Tennessee River banks.

Coming in low at two hundred plus miles, an hour brought a powerful wind shear beneath the wings of the greatest war birds of World War II. It would strip the leaves off the Tennessee Orange and golden brown trees of winter. As they went over a barn the vacuum that followed them sucked all the chickens out of their nesting areas, and sucked the hay out of the barn windows, and took off a few doors.

In one man's dream home, his wife had just finished the final touches on her most elaborate and expensive Christmas decorations. Her husband Brad was receiving text messages as she was sending him some of the pictures of the setting for the yearly Christmas Card. This year he was going to save paper by sending it as a picture electronically on Christmas Night.

Note: Ned the Needle in his area of operations. Getting his gear prepared for the fight for Christmas.

Brad found himself, dueling with his wife over which picture to send as a Christmas Card. "Honey! We do not have to send a picture that shows people how well off we are do we?" She responded with, "Oh, Brad! Just because you grew up poor does not mean we have to stay there do we? I mean, I have heard the story of you and your brother eating coffee cake out of the school dumpster, every year! It is getting old!" She sent her favorite beautiful picture of her in a white and silver dress standing beside a stunning silver-belled Christmas tree, with a caption that read, "How about this one!" Brad was at a children's hospital in Brooklyn. He and his brothers had grown up without a father. His brother Terry had been born with a bi-lateral cleft lip and spent many of his holidays alone in the hospital.

Brad was too young to get too the hospital ward to visit him. Like his brother he was alone on Christmas. Brad had only run into money in the last ten years. His brother had spent to many holidays in the hospital. He knew in his heart there were others he could visit to make their holidays special.

Brad spent most of his holidays entertaining children. He visited disabled children who were without families and alone on Christmas.

This was special to his heart because now, both he and his music were sought by the same people that had stopped him from visiting his brother. Brad responded with, "Christmas is supposed to be about celebrating the birth of our savior? Can you find something that says a little about what is supposed to be in our heart, not our wallets!" He received no reply and assumed his wife was now mad at him.

She too had grown up poor, extremely poor. This year she had gone all out and really fancied up the house! She was disappointed in him and thought he should be a little more appreciative of her Christmas efforts. She went into his study and brought his mother's picture of Lord Jesus and hung it so that it could be seen in a picture by the tree!

Further above was a rustic sign that read, "Bless Our Home!" His mother had the sign over the door outside her home. Brad had taken it and put it up in his study when she had passed away. She sat down on the couch and looked all around at the expensive and elaborate furnishings. She took a spoon and mixed a little sugar into her coffee. She sat back and noticed the spoon was shaking by itself. Then she heard spoons rattling. Then the floor began to quake and it was slowly getting stronger.

An old empty oil lamp fell from a shelf. Pots and pans began to fall. The windows and walls began to rattle. Plates fell from cupboard shelves. She could feel and hear something coming like a locomotive. She had heard of tornados hitting suddenly out of clear skies. She fell to her knees and begged for the Lord's forgiveness! "Please, Lord! I will eat coffee cake out of a dumpster! I just want to be able to do it with Brad!" She proclaimed in prayer. She apologized to the Lord for not realizing the true meaning of Christmas and promised she would never again forget the true spirit of Christmas.

Up above a few miles away was the, "American Dream Squadron!" Needles was partially leaning out his waist gunners hatch. He was enjoying the show below as the aircraft passed over barns and bales of hay. "Look! We are lifting stuff ten feet off the ground. What a show!" He tried to say to the navigator. Jules just kept on working on his maps with a grin. Needles looked back out and a hat that he had fancied flew off his head. One of the scientists had given it too him because he noticed that Needles liked it.

Suddenly all the curtains were sucked out of the windows of Brad's home. Even some of the light bulbs exploded as the powerful engines of the Memphis Belle and the American Dream Squadron came over in a giant wave just missing the house.

She was almost in shock. She knelt back down and thanked the Lord for sparing her. She wiped away a tear and in floated Needle's baseball hat. Needle's hat came in on the wind and when it hit the floor, it slid over to where she was kneeling. She read the stencil then clenched it too her chest. She put it on her head and continued her prayer.

Her cell phone slid off the arm of the couch and when it hit the floor it clicked, sending Brad the picture.

Note: Flying just over the water of the Tennessee River and already under attack by the drones from Collossatron. Notice the wind shear below right.

The picture he received was of his wife on her knees beside their Christmas tree with the picture of the Lord up above her on the wall beneath a rustic, "Bless this home" sign wearing Needle's baseball hat. "The baseball hat that had, "In all things Jesus!" stenciled on it. When the curtains had been sucked out of the open widows, by the tremendous wind shear. Their mountain home was above the storm below and caused the American Dream Squadron to pull up and climb higher to go over the mountain creating an even greater wind shear.

The light from the stars and moon made an angelic glow about the face of Brad's wife. Her sincerity in prayer with tears coming down from her eyes, was captured for all time in a nanosecond. Travis immediately sent her back a message. "Now that is what I call a Christmas card, honey I love you! Merry Christmas!"

Ernie came alongside Bert wearing the Tuxedo Hat he had worn in, "It's A Wonderful Life!" Bert grinned and gave him a thumbs up! Jimmy Stewart's navigator Jules informed him that the topography up ahead was going to get jagged. "We will not be able to remain at this speed and altitude much longer sir!" said Jules. "Roger! That!" we will go up 150 feet.

Jimmy Stewart trusted Jules map reading skills and thought highly of him as a friend. "We will be approaching the target in 20 mikes, skipper!" said Jules. "Okay at 10 mikes arm them!" "Roger skipper!" replied Jules. Major Jimmy Stewart radioed the American Dream Squadron to arm the bombs at 10 mikes from target.

Collossatron was on full alert. Collossatron's robots were producing aircraft and weapons for the perceived attack. Collossatron's robots sealed the complex shut with specialized security screws. Collossatron's robots welded the hinges of doors shut.

Inside the hangar at the museum the mechanics rigged up, a vacuum tube radio that could listen to the radio signals coming from the aircraft. The aircraft went rumbling over the Tennessee landscape. A man fishing in Dayton, Tennessee was putting a worm on his hook when a B-17 came over low, and he fell into the water. Bert said, "I always wanted to do that", as he flew over just behind the Memphis Belle.

Country folks that were awake, were the only witnesses of the flight of the, "American Dream Squadron", as it flew over headed for Collossatron. A farmer out tending to his animals looked up to see the Belle coming over the treetops!

A woman with a flashlight putting a fuse in the back of her chicken coup's warming system. Looked up too see a B-25 Mitchell Bomber go overhead. A man working on his Christmas Lights, at a Christian Camp in Dayton saw the entire squadron from his bluff, as they flew towards Collossatron. Collossatron had begun illuminating the skies with giant blue searchlights. The salient blue light from the Bailey Park Test Facility seemed to pulsate. Clarence and the towns' people noticed the sky had turned salient blue.

Then they heard the rumble of the aircraft, children from both times, ran to their bedroom windows to see. Two generations of Americans had grown up not knowing what it was like to run to their bedroom window when the distant sounds of propeller driven American war birds filled their ears.

The word was being spread in the Chattanooga Area Veteran Community and surrounding areas. America had learned its lesson from 9/11. There was mutual intermilitary branch, inter-agency, civilian and government, local and state cooperation and information sharing everywhere! Chattanooga had its own edge. There was immense trust and cooperation between the Military and the Military retirees and veterans from each service so close it was hard to tell who was active and who was not during the fight for Christmas!

Traffic moving towards the Tennessee Aviation Museum on Christmas Eve was more of a nightmare than a dream as to keep Collossatron blind they we driving the vehicles in, "dark out or light out", conditions. Standing on an on-ramp in a bathrobe, pajamas and wearing a government issue (GI) helmet was a man directing traffic. His cell phone rang and he reached into his robe pocket pulled it out and answered the cell phone with, "Oh, hi honey! No not right now! Yes, dear! I know it had better be good!"

Just then a large truck turned to go onto the interstate just in front of him honking its horn for him to get out of the way. "Lights out! Turn your headlights out and watch where you are going! I am the mayor for God sakes!" he yelled at the truck. "Merry Christmas! You have a flashlight!" came back from the cab as it slowly turned. From back in the bed full of Tennessee volunteers came, "How would you like a nice shiny red nose for Christmas?" "I know I have a flashlight buddy! I will give you a Merry Christmas!" he yelled back towards the truck as it drove onto the interstate freeway.

Just then, he noticed in the hand he was shaking at the truck was his cell phone. He was still on the phone with his wife. He put it to his ear and then said, "Yes dear! Uh huh, I know what I just yelled to the entire world, dear! I know I am the mayor of Chattanooga, Tennessee dear! Next time! Honey, if this is a success there will not be a next time! I told you that it is something that I just have to do! Yes dear! Tell them I love them, and I will be home when I am finished. Well, honey! Sometimes when you have to do the right thing, you do not get to have a Merry Christmas like everybody else! I love you too! Merry Christmas!" he said as he continued directing traffic towards the Tennessee Aviation Museum.

The word of mouth had spread like a dream. Veterans from every branch and generation, were streaming into the Tennessee Aviation Museum. A new branch of cooperation was born this night. Inter-museum cooperation was born. The American Dream had awakened!

A man came out of the woods with a dog. He set his Hawken rifle down and said, "I hear you are looking for someone that knows old aircraft engines and old radios. He was handed a wrench, and welcomed aboard. The old man was dressed in animal skins.

When someone would look at him because of his attire, he would softly say, "I live off the grid." Before he went to work he said, "Wait a minute!" He raised a horn to his lips and blew into it. As he put the horn back around his neck, a horn in the distance sounded. He softly said, "I had to tell my wife, that I am gonna be late for breakfast."

Dr. Denny did not have a way to determine how or when the American Dream Squadron would fly over them again on their way to Collossatron. One of the scientists was a Cherokee Indian. He watched the night sky and when he noticed birds suddenly take flight from the trees he said with a smile, "They are coming!"

CHAPTER 22

The American Dream Strikes Back!

The Collossatron Complex was on the Tennessee River in a valley to itself. There were no roads leading to it, or from it. It had been built this way to preserve its total secrecy. The scientists had done everything they could think of, to blind Collossatron.

However, since Collossatron had access to all data streams. It was able to determine by surveillance cameras, on the roadways, that an attack was forth coming. The weather was overcast with thunderstorm and tornado warnings. It was if a prayer had been answered. Collossatron had also seen some of the aircraft flying into its region. Collossatron had increased the power in its reactors and had its robots producing and arming the guns it would need to destroy this attack.

It searched history files and determined, weaknesses and strengths, along with which weapons were they most effective against the aircraft Collossatron had seen transported into the area. The American Dream Squadron was searching for Collossatron but could not find it. Collossatron was searching for the American Dream Squadron and could not see them either. The degaussing of the aircraft had worked. Jimmy Stewart had them regroup and then reassemble over the Tennessee Aviation Museum's new airfield.

Major Jimmy Stewart gave the controls over to Detective Carlin, and went back to his navigator. "We are going to have to use a simple topographical map. We will have to use time against Collossatron" said Jimmy Stewart. "Why did not I think of that! Sure, let us do it the old fashioned way!" replied Jules. Jimmy Stewart ignored the comment and continued with, "Since it can project an image for us to see, we probably would fly right over it, and then run out of fuel or something worse. Determine our exact speed, fuel consumption and distance. Plot that, and determine exactly, when we should be over the target!" "Roger Skipper!" the navigator replied."But, sir we have to have visual on the target before we drop!" said the navigator. "Yeah, but that was seventy-five years ago! Jules!" said Major Jimmy Stewart.

After, determining their position and time to target, they began to assemble, for their final bomb run over Collossatron. Collossatron was projecting a wooded area. Because of this and the weather, the target was completely obscured.

Jimmy Stewart radioed for all pilots to say a prayer. "We need a little help!" said Major Jimmy Stewart as he began to pray. One by one almost and as if together they all prayed for help! One by one they said, "Amen!" The giant central projector lens was pointed skyward projecting the forest image. Suddenly and as if out of nowhere, out of the clouds dropped the saber of Ebenezer Scrooge. It hit the lens dead center and flashed a brilliant wide salient blue flash! The people along the Tennessee River almost at once said, "Ah! Wow! Did you see that?"

There she is dead ahead? Okay fellows keep it tight! Let us make it a Christmas to remember!" The guns Collossatron was able to produce began sounding with great flashes in the sky! Major Jimmy Stewart took the controls, and headed directly for the target. "Harry cut us a path!" said Jimmy Stewart. "Right! George! I mean Jimmy!" He shook his head. He was sure he was ok! For a second, he thought he was back on the set.

Captain Harry Bailey came screaming in with his wingman on his wing tips. He let go with the twin.50 caliber cannons of the P-38 Lighting. He noticed that some of the guns of Collossatron remained silent. He knew from the war that this was a trap. They were waiting for the bombers to make their run. He was almost out of ammo one of his engines had been hit. He had been wounded, right out of the gate and knew he had to do something. He pulled back on the throttle and pulled up into a steep climb. He got to maximum altitude and cut his engines. He grabbed his crucifix that was around his neck and said, "Let us see a computer do this!" He bailed out of his P-38 as it slowly flipped over into a nosedive right into the guns that had been waiting for the dream squadron's bomb run. "Major we are approaching the target area!" said the navigator.

Note: Drone piloted ME-262 rolling down in salient blue light and the snow covered Tennessee Mountains. Courtesy of Ned the Needle. One of the B-17s after being hit by the guns of Collossatron.

All along the Tennessee River, Tennesseans and country folks, were coming out of there homes. No-one was going to sleep through this. The people of Tennessee saw the giant blue searchlights of Collossatron scanning the heavens? "It is some sort of Christmas light show!" one of them said to a neighbor! The people along the river, "Oohhed and aaahhed", at the explosions in the air.

They could see the aircraft and great big blue explosions in the air. Collossatron could not see some of the aircraft and the scientists could not see them from the Tennessee Aviation

Museum. They could only listen to radio traffic over vacuum tube radios. "Okay! Fellows! I'm turning her over to the bombardier!" Detective Carlin was sitting there wide-eyed. Jimmy Stewart said, "Get ready to get scared!" "Get scared of what? I am already scared!" said the detective. "This!" Jimmy Stewart said as he let go of the controls.

A young man named Ned whose nickname was, "needle" was Jimmy Stewart's waist gunner. He was a farm boy that did not talk much. He had a speech impediment that greatly embarrassed him. His father had gone with him the day after Pearl Harbor to sign him into the Army, because he wanted to fight. His father openly boasted that his son could thread a needle with a.22 caliber rifle. His father was right and Ned became, "Needle", on Major Jimmy Stewart's American Dream Crew.

Needle did not talk much but behind twin 12.7 mm machine guns he became a chatterbox. "You want to fight? Well, let's fight!" He would yell as he blasted away. Noone ever guessed that the mild mannered young man who they bought their snow cones from on the set was the holder of one of our nations highest awards, "The Distinguished Flying Cross!" had gone to a young man nicknamed, "Needle!" for his actions during World War II.

The aircraft seemed to be getting peppered. The navigator came up to Major Jimmy Stewart who wrapped a round that had come through and bounced around on the console in a newspaper and asked, "Would you get rid of this!" "Sure thing skipper!" replied the navigator.

Jimmy Stewart reached up and tapped his bell, which hung from the instrument panel. "Are not we going to do something?" asked detective Carlin. "Yeah!" said Jimmy Stewart.

He took out a Bible and started reading. Major Stewart looked over to Detective Carlin and said, "There is not much we can do! This is a B-17C, it does not have a check gun or chin gun. They came later on in the war!" In Bert's aircraft, he began to rub a baseball mitt with saddle soap.

The Chief Detective Pryzwarra started to panic and yelled, "We have got to do something!" "Here have a piece of gum and close your eyes!" said Bert. "I cannot watch!" came back from the detective. "Then do not!" said Bert. The electromatic pulse beams, and bullets from Collossatron cut out or cut down the engines of some the aircraft that it was able to find and hit. They pilots and crews would try to restart their engines in the air. They tried everything!

Some went down with there engines sputtering. Some used firing cartridges to restart their engines and continued to pound the drones and the guns of Collossatron. First Lieutenant Roscoe B. Chaney's voice caught Dr. Chaney's ear at the Tennessee Aviation Museums Airfield. "I got an ME262 trying his best to line one up one me, give me some room!" Two of the bombers had to bank away and he came up in a roll and then back down hoping the gunner's would get a piece of the ME262. He dove down and turned back up as he rolled and leveled out and went between Collossatron's cooling towers.

The computerized ME262 could not maintain the same roll and plowed into one of the towers. Dr. Chaney wiped tears from her eyes when she heard, "How do you like them apples?" come from her father's P51C Mustang.

They went down in great big flashes of blue light. Collossatron's robots had created some true works of wonder. It was producing ME109s, ME262s, and Mitsubishi Zeros

At an alarming rate. The computer was learning warfare. Over the radio crackled, "Joe, are you ready to die?" Needle replied, "I am right here, maggot! Come and get me!" "I am coming Joe!" Needle threw an empty ammo can to the side, opened another, and set it in the ammo tray by his gun. "Whenever you are ready!" said Needle as he pulled the bolt back and slammed a round into the chamber. "This computer is not so smart! If I were a computer, I would be sending in Spitfires and Mustangs!" said Needles. "Aint that the dying truth!" said Major Jimmy Stewart.

Dr. Chaney was in a makeshift lab at the Tennessee Aviation Museum's new airfield listening over a radio one of the Veteran Volunteers called a 201. She bit down on her lip and ran out of the lab and into the hangar to get Dr. Denny's attention. She rounded the corner to find everybody including Dr. Denny gathered around the radios listening intently. She did not say a word she just listened as the battle raged. "Here I come Joe! Now you die! "The Zero could be heard as it screamed down in a dive on Major Jimmy Stewart's aircraft.

Major Jimmy Stewart said, "Left side 11 O'clock!" "I see him!" replied Needle as his gun sounded with just a quick burst and then another. The Zero exploded in the air, as the rounds cut through the thin skin and into the fuel tanks. "My name is not Joe!" said Needle as the audience erupted into cheers. "What are children doing here?" asked Dr. Chaney as she noticed children listening with their parents and grandparents. "Have you ever tried to get a baby sitter with a, "we have to go save Christmas!" excuse this time of night, lady!" Said a mechanic as he worked on a seventy year old fuel line.

Falling from up above came a Liberator cut clean into right in front of Major Jimmy Stewart causing him to have to fly between the two halves. "I just wanted to go home! I just wanted to go home!" came out of the speakers from the falling Liberator. Major Jimmy Stewart just looked down and his eyes seemed to go down with the two halves of the B-24 as he listened. "Save the world! Now, it is save Christmas! What will they think of next!" came out the speakers at the museum. There was not a dry eye to be found.

They were fixing and launching aircraft as fast as they could. Listening to the sounds of the American Dream Squadron's Greatest Struggle, seemed to give the veteran's, police officer's, active duty personnel, State and Federal employees and the volunteers a renewed sense of urgency.

Tennesseans who witnessed the fight for Christmas began to count the parachutes. Out of eight men per aircraft with three ride alongs, they would only see three parachutes. Ambulances would immediately go after them. In Bedford Falls, they too saw the flashes of blue light in the sky along with the explosions and sounds of air battle. When they saw the parachutes they counted eight each time.

The men were jumping into the salient blue light, and back into their own times. The American Dream Squadron was a miracle and miracles happen at Christmas! What they did not know was as they died they woke up back in their own time. Major Jimmy Stewart asked his tail gunner, "How's it going back there?" "Business as usual!" came back from his tail gunner. "Welcome to World War II!" said Jimmy Stewart to Detective Carlin. "Major we are on course and I need your permission to release!" requested the bombardier. "Permission Granted, Merry Christmas!" replied Major Jimmy Stewart.

The bombardier raised his bomb release and noticed how Collossatron looked like it was a flat rectangle from their altitude. With a big grin he said, "Scratch One Flat Top!" as he squeezed the bomb release. Bert's bombardier said, "Right in the old pickle barrel!" as he squeezed his bomb release. They saw the electromagnetic bombs hit and saw blue explosions come from the Collossatron Complex radiating out in smaller to larger concentric circles. The airfield and all those listening began to cheer and celebrate as they could hear the sounds of the bombs finding their intended target.

Sam Pickens radioed an urgent request for help. "This pile of nuts and bolts does not have a tool bag! We can not get the Bombay open." Mr. Martimi's voice came over the radio with, "We have a tool bag, what do you need Sam?" We need a hand crank for the bomb bay. Somebody pilfered this one." "I have an idea Sam! Get your gunner out of the top turret!" "Marti you have got to be kidding! Do you want to live forever? Or win the war?" "Huh! Okay! Will do! Give me just a second!" Sam informed his crew that Mr. Martimi was going to seer off the top turret or at least that is what he thought.

Mr. Martimi pulled alongside Sam. Sam could see him giving his aircraft the once over. Then he pulled back and disappeared behind him. "Here I come Sam!" "Everybody hold on!" said Sam to his crew. Mr. Martimi came in just above Sam's B-25. He told his ride along to feather the engine when he said, "now!" "You ready! Here goes nothing! He inched his Liberator up along the top to Sam's B-25 and cut the turret violently off with the propeller blades of his number four engine. "Now" Mr. Martimi yelled to his ride along copilot.

The number four engine continued turning and slowed down and then Sam heard a violet crash. Mr. Marimi's propeller exploded off his engine. The Liberator just about laid down on top of the B-25 Mitchell. Detective Pryzwarra could see the Liberator and the B-25 Mitchell's propellers turning and only feet apart. "If I pull up I am going to run into you Sam. I am sorry! Sam!

I think we are stuck with each other!" said Marti. "Marti listen up! When I count to three, hit your landing gear. One, two, three!" exclaimed Sam. Mr. Martimi hit his landing gear switch. The liberator's landing gear came down with a gigantic thud and pushed Mr. Martimi's Liberator up and Sam's B-25 Mitchell bomber down. Mr. Martimi took the hint!

He accelerated and pulled up! "If we get back, you get one free beer, just one Sam! Do you still want the tool bag, Sam?" asked Mr. Martimi. "Yeah, do you think you can lower it into the turret on a parachute cord?" replied Sam. "That was the plan!" replied Marti. "Whenever you are ready! Marti!" replied Sam. "I am coming again, Sam!" said Mr. Martimi as he crew prepared to lower the tool bag.

Mr. Martimi's crew lowered it out of the bottom of his aircraft right into the top turret on the first try causing celebrations at the Tennessee Aviation Museum. "We are going to have to escort Sam into the target area so he can cut lose!" said Major Jimmy Stewart. "Going back in is suicide!" said Mr. Martimi. Sam answered back with, "No the Scheinfurt-Regensburg mission was suicide! This is unadulterated murder."

Well let us turn around and come back in from the west. Ernie came alongside Sam's B- 25 and radioed, "Sam! I cannot get the cockpit to open. That ME-109 clipped the railing closed. I cannot get it open. I am starting to burn up. I got oil coming in all over the place. Do me a favor!" "No way! Ernie! I cannot do that!" said Sam. "Ah, come on!" said Ernie. Major Jimmy Stewart interrupted, "Needle!" "Skipper get him to pull alongside us! I will open him up like a can of soup!" said Needle as he racked the gun with a new belt of ammo from another ammo can. "I am coming up on your right!" said Ernie. "Do not worry, I got you! Hold her steady! When I say duck! Duck!" "Okay!" said Ernie. "Duck!" Ernie ducked and Needle lived up to his nickname again. He cleanly cut the cockpit off a P-51 Mustang! Needle watched as Ernie bailed out just in time. The mustang burst into flames and road alongside burning like a match and then trailing down into the blue salient lights of Collossatron.

Bert's aircraft started taking some serious hits. One of the engines flamed out and the other started sputtering. He was being hit, over and over again. Collossatron had found Them using thermal imaging satellites and was zeroing in with it's guns. He tried starting his engines. Time after time, they refused to start.

One by one, the engines died out. "Alright everybody listen up! Abandon Ship! Remember your training! When we land we regroup!" said Bert. "What do mean abandon ship?" asked the chief detective. "Looks like were going to be late for breakfast!" said Bert. "What do you mean?" asked the detective. "I mean, it is going to be a long walk home!" said Bert as he started working his way to the back of the aircraft. Detective Pryzwarra looked out the cockpit and saw a drone flying straight towards him. He just sat there frozen in time for a moment. "You coming?" hollered Bert. Detective Pryzwarra jumped up, and followed him to middle of the aircraft. "I did not know you guys had to climb over so much stuff!" he tried to say to Bert, who was to far way to hear him.

When the detective arrived at middle of the aircraft, he was looking at an open hatch. Bert was coming from the tail section. "I had to make sure everybody got out okay! Everyone has already jumped! Let us get out of here!" Bert said as he grabbed the back of Detective Pryzwarra's parachute and pulled him to the hatch. "Jump!" said Bert. "I have never jumped before! What do I do?" asked the detective. "It is simple! Just count to four, and pull your handle!" said Bert as he attached a static line to the back of the detective's parachute. "What is that for?" asked the detective.

"In case you forget?" said Bert. "Forget to do what?" asked the detective. "Get in the door!" yelled Bert. "The detective grabbed the sides of the door and looked out. Everything looked so small from there. He was going to ask Bert what to do next. Suddenly, he felt something kick him in the rear. It was Bert. He came out of the aircraft, suddenly.

He closed his eyes and gripped the sides of his reserve parachute. He counted to four, and opened his eyes. He closed them again. Then he felt the parachute open. It opened so hard that his hands went forward with the sudden shock. His watch which had an elastic band slid off his hand and he watched it, reflecting in the salient blue light, as it disappeared below him. He looked all around, and he could not see Bert. He began yelling for Bert but got no response. When the detective landed, Bert's baseball mitt landed at his feet. He took off the parachute harness. He could see the bombs hitting down in the valley. "Wow! What a Christmas present!" he said to himself. He began looking for Bert and the rest of the crew. He got down on his knees and said a prayer.

High and above the detective the battle for Christmas continued. "Flight Leader to American Dream. All remaining aircraft will escort Sam into the target! Remember this is for Christmas!" said Major Jimmy Stewart. The remaining pilots and their crews complied without question.

Jimmy Stewart looked around and saw that he had only six aircraft left and things seemed to quiet down as they approached the target again.

"Looks like it may be almost over, Skipper!" said Jules. "Well I would not bet on it!" replied Major Stewart. The target was obscured in smoke and clouds. The weather and the igniting of smoke canisters kept anyone from obtaining a proper bomb damage assessment of the Collossatron Complex.

Up ahead was a large cloudbank. Then all at once, from horizon to horizon drones came out of the cloudbank as if in rank and file. "Holy Cow!" said Needles. He re-armed his guns and then said to Major Stewart. "Sir there is something wrong with the ammo. These cans should be empty! They are full again and the dates are all mixed up! One says 1949! What is the world is going on?"

"Sounds like Christmas victory to me! Ned! Let's make this last one count!" "Well American Joe! You boys from New York?" came from the computer generated NAZI pilot. "Were all a bunch of crazy Jew and negro boys! Come and get us maggot!" replied Needles. "Calm down Ned, do not let him get you riled!" said Major Stewart. "I was hoping for cowboys! I will kill you just for the fatherland! What is your hometown Joe?" said the ME109's pilot. "We are from America! That is my hometown! Every square inch! I will be whatever you want! Come and get it!" replied Needles. "Ned! Settle down!" said Major Stewart.

Out of the blue salient light, came four ME109's. Needles opened up with the rest of the crew. "Here it comes Joe!" The live rounds came streaking through the top of the B-17 and ricocheting around. "Come and get some! How is that maggot? And my name is not Joe!" yelled Needles as one ME109 began rolling down in a long line of smoke through the clouds.

Major Jimmy Stewart could not help but grin. He just loved to hear Needle talk. Sam's Bombay doors opened up and delivered that last one two punch of the fight for Christmas! Major Jimmy Stewart reached up and tapped his Christmas Bell, which stood for home alive in 1945. He like so many others wanted to be home for Christmas that year. He radioed to his crew, "Mission Accomplished! Let us go home!" Major Jimmy Stewart began to hear a strange sound over the radio, "Psssssssuh", then nothing. Then Psssssssuh", and then nothing again. Detective Carlin saw his eyes suddenly widen. "Take Over, Jules! Detective get the first aide kit and follow me!" said Major Stewart.

Jules climbed past him with a worried look and took over the controls.

Major Jimmy Stewart pushed past everything and grabbed the first aide kit near the navigation and engineers seats. He arrived at the waist and relaxed for a second. Needle was loading his machine gun and everything looked all right, for a second. Then he saw that Ned was only using one arm. He stepped over to Ned and he could see the determination in his eyes as Ned said, "Psssssssuh" with blood coming from his mouth.

Needle was using the gun to support his weight. Major Jimmy Stewart said, "I got you Ned! Come on, why do not you sit down here for a minute and let me take a look?" Ned the needle tried to answer but could not.

Major Jimmy Stewart turned to the Detective and said, "You guys are from the future do something!" Detective Carlin opened the first aide kit and gave a large wound dressing to Jimmy Stewart. Jimmy Stewart opened Ned's uniform and then closed it, as he was looking down into Ned's chest and could see his heart beating. He laid Ned's head down gently. Detective Carlin was loosening up Ned's uniform around his waist, his cuffs and the top of his boots.

Detective Carlin came up to Ned's face and said, "You really gave them what four! I never heard the war explained to me like you did Ned! I am proud to know you!" Through the blood, Needles smiled at the detective. The detective leaned forward when Ned's finger signaled him closer. He whispered something to Ned and Ned grinned and smiled again. Ned's finger signaled him again and he leaned his ear to Ned's lips. The detective leaned back with an almost frightened look and said nothing!" Jimmy Stewart said the Lord's Prayer to Ned and then closed his eyes and went back to the cockpit without a word. Jules handed the controls back to the Major with, "Sir, I will take good care of him!" Jules stepped back, and took a body bag out from its compartment and sat down next to his friend.

Jimmy Stewart had just sat down when he closed his eyes. He waited for the detective to get seated. He reached up, and rubbed the tears away from his face and said, "What did you say to that boy? What did you say to that beautiful human being as he lay dying?" The detective still had a hollow look to his face. He sat wide-eyed as if he were staring into time and space, but said nothing. "You tell me what you said to that boy, or so help me, I am going to reach through your chest and pull your heart out!" said Major Jimmy Stewart as he grabbed the Detective's chest with both hands. The detective still said nothing. "Go ahead and be one!" said Major Stewart.

Detective Carlin had been raised by an aunt whose favorite saying was, "Go ahead and be one!", when he was being one. He knew what the Major implied. He said, "I asked him what it felt like, or if he saw a light or anything?" Major Jimmy Stewart looked ahead and noticed the paint on the aircraft's nose faded as if it had sat out like an old car In a junk yard, then it became new again. It was as if it was being painted, time and again.

However, at the Tennessee Aviation Museum's Airfield everyone was listening as they worked, to get them in the air as Dr. Denny kept saying over and over. "Here come some golden delicious apples!" got Dr. Chaney's attention. She reached into her lab coat pocket and held the apple her father had given her to give to her mother. "Do not forget to spit out the seeds!" said 1LT Roscoe B. Chaney as she could hear her father's guns sounding. She felt something strange and pulled the apple out of her pocket. Pressed into the skin of the apple were her father's World War II silver fighter pilot wings.

Major Stewart looked at the Detective for a minute then said, "I am waiting! What did Ned say?" The detective choked up a little and replied, "He said it felt like something he had done before! That is all he said." One of the P-38s had a drone on its tail. It was an ME262. Jimmy Stewart's gunners tried to help but they were to far away this time. The pilot called for anyone remaining to give him a hand. His guns were jammed and the ME262 was too fast. Jimmy Stewart closed his eyes and leaned forward into the controls and heard, "Fox One!" "Fox what", he replied as he sat back up.

Out of blue as if from nowhere, an American F-4 Phantom streaked past the Memphis Belle. "Sorry we are late! We had to wait until your bomb drop Major!" The ME262 disintegrated as the missile slammed home cutting it in half. "Major my name is Capt Roger Scoals! I am right behind you with a fleet of B-52 Stato-fortresses. Good job and well done. We are preparing to drop! Hold on to your hats gentlemen!" Out of the clouds, all types of fighter aircraft began descending on the drones and their maker. "So that is the future!" "I am flying a skyrocket with wings! This is old hat Major! We are just the first ones here! Wait until you see and F35 said the pilot of the F-4 Phantom. "They just jerked all the computerized parts out of this baby because it can fly without one!" he said again.

Detective Carlin looked over at Jimmy Stewart. He began glowing in that salient blue light. His skin started flaking. Jimmy Stewart then started glowing in a brilliant bright white light! Detective Carlin's eyes widened. Before he could say anything, Jimmy Stewart said, "Well! What do you know? I always wanted to be gone with the wind!"

All over America and the world, television sets came back on just in time for the first showing of, "It's A Wonderful Life!" Radios that had been powerless to stop the music of Collossatron came to life with Christmas music! Major Jimmy Stewart and Detective Carlin witnessed the dawns light coming from the center of an outstretched hand on the horizon. The brilliant white light coming from the center of the outstretched hand suddenly flashed and flooded into the aircraft. Detective Carlin in his amazement slowly said, "Oh, my God!" Major Jimmy Stewart smiled and replied, "That is right!" and disappeared back into 1947.

The men from Bailey Park disappeared just as suddenly, in the remaining aircraft. Ned the needle woke up suddenly back at his apartment on the set. He was in the bathtub listening to Christmas music and wearing a red Santa Claus hat. He woke up suddenly biting a candy cane in half, just as he had closed his eyes on the Memphis Belle. After all it is Christmas!

The light of dawns early light began overpowering the last remaining salient blue lights of Collossatron's projection lenses with the help of the Veteran Pilots of older aircraft that had finally arrived on the scene. The military co-pilots like Detective Carlin found themselves suddenly alone.

Detective Carlin flew the, "Memphis Belle", back to the Tennessee Aviation Museum. After he landed, he taxied the Memphis Belle over to where it had been parked prior to loading for the mission.

All around him were the aircraft, he had seen shot down. They were parked, as if they had not been flow in seventy years. "Wow! Merry Christmas!" He reached up, and tapped the bell that Jimmy Stewart had hung from the instrument panel.

He looked down at his parachute harness and thought, "I am glad this is classified. No one would believe this in a million years!" and smiled. He took the bell and then climbed out onto the ground.

The ground chief said to the detective, "What! Did you do to my baby?" He walked away and as he did, he said, "Merry Christmas!" as one of the stabilizer wings fell to the ground. When he got home, he hung the bell on his Christmas Tree! It was almost mid morning by the time Chief Detective Pryzwarra made it out of the woods, and too the Collossatron Complex. He had been searching for Bert.

The Collossatron site had already been fenced. He stood by the fence holding the baseball mitt in one hand and the fence in the other, and watched as huge bulldozers were burying what was left of Collossatron in huge pits that had been dug. Three workers on the other side of the fence were dragging one of Collossatron's robots to the edge of a giant pit.

"Hey look at this!" said one of the workers as he pulled a six-gun out of the robot's holster. "No souvenirs!

Remember we are under a strict government contract. Throw it in the ditch!" said the boss man. "But, it is real and it looks like an original!" replied Jason. "Do you really want to be caught with that? Man, Jason throw it in the ditch! We are all going to have marble floors when this is through. Marble floors! Jason! Now throw it in the ditch!" said the boss man again. Jason took the pistol and fired it into the ditch until it was empty. Then he threw the pistol in the ditch. "Hey look! The robot has a screen for a face! Travel to One can now occur! Collossatron will continue to dream! I wonder what in the world that means?" asked Jason jokingly. "Jason I do not have time for you wise cracks! Throw it in the ditch and get rid of it!" said his boss. Jason took the cowboy hat off the back-up man's head and put it on his head. "No souvenirs!" again said the boss man. "Alright! Alright! I just wanted to have a little fun!" said Jason as he spun the hat into the ditch, followed by the back-up man's robotic body.

A worker came up beside Chief Detective Pryzwarra and said, "when will they ever stop giving into the, "darker side of good?"" He took off his hazardous materials hood, shook his head and said, "All power comes  from the same source! Some men, because they have free will, choose the darker side of good. "What do you mean the darker side of good?" asked the detective. "When someone apologizes to you for something they have done will you be satisfied with just I am sorry, or will you need to hear their story?" "If you need to hear the story, you are looking for a reason not to forgive. That is the darker side of good in mans heart", said the worker. "When will man stop searching through the heavens, trying to find the answers to the meaning of life through a telescope? When will man stop searching through a microscope trying to find that which can only be found in prayer.

The light you will find is the light of love. Pure love is the light of life. Mans heart nor his eyes are ready to see the light. The light is pure and so powerful that it would destroy mans flesh. For now in this time, man can only see the light of love, God's Love, with his eyes closed in prayer! Then he can survive in the light. Man has only found that which he has been allowed to find.

He will be allowed to get only so close to the light while he is in flesh. That is the power of love. It is good to try to understand the creator. He has designed it so that the more man try's to understand the creator, the more he discovers about himself!" said the worker as he shook his head revealing long shoulder length hair.

Detective Pryzwarra's skin tingled and every hair on the back of his neck stood up! The hair on his head tingled! He was truly amazed! He knew he was talking to someone special. "When will you come back?" asked the Detective, almost afraid to look. "Maybe, I already have! Maybe I never left! I am always where man cannot see me with his eyes. He can always find me with his eyes closed in prayer! Only then are the eyes of his heart wide and open!" said the worker as he put a finger to Detective Pryzwarra's chest.

His whole body began to shake and a trembling went through him from his head to the ends of his toes. The worker put the hazardous material hood back on his head and stepped away as the detective almost sat into the fence. Chief Detective Pryzwarra straightened himself and followed after him. He tapped the worker on the shoulder. "Hey, wait a minute! I am not through! "Please I want to know! I have to know!" implored the detective.

The worker turned around and startled the detective. The worker removed the hazardous materials hood again to reveal a heavyset female and she said, "Know what? Look friend if you do not have a permit! I am going to have to ask you to leave." The detective's face grew hollow and he almost whispered as he asked, "Who?" "I am! I am! This is a government facility on federal land and you are trespassing!" she replied in frustration. "Merry Christmas!" said the detective as he slowly began walking away.

Ward Bond landed hard and his neck still ached from the parachute harness. He took off the parachute harness and was stunned to be in a police officers costume for the up coming scene. He remembered that he had changed into a flight suit back at the Tennessee Aviation Museum. "Oh Well!" He exclaimed as he rolled up his parachute and tossed it into some bushes! He started walking down the street whistling, "We Wish You a Merry Christmas!"

He walked down to where he had parked his patrol car near the bank for the next scene. He did not know why, but he checked the doors of the bank. He immediately heard a tapping almost slapping sound. Then he looked up and saw a drainpipe coming from the roof and the water coming out was tapping down in a small puddle. He walked over to it and held out his hand.

A	•—	N	—•	1	•————	N	1 1 1	N with tilde
B	•1	O		2	••———	0	"—"•	O with umlaut
C		P	1••1	3	•••——	u		U with umlaut
D	1•	Q	111•	4	••••—			comma
E	•	R	•	5	•••••		1 1 1	period
F	••	S	•	6	—••••	?	••	question mark
G	!	T		7	™"•••		1 1 1	semicolon
H	*•	U	1•	8	———••		•1•11	colon
I	••	V	•1	9	————•		1 1•	slash
J	1•11	W	1•1	0				dash
K	1 1	X	•11•	A	1 1 1		1••111	apostrophe
L	1•	Y	•111	A	1•1	()	•11•11	parenthesis
M		Z	•1•1	E	••		1•11	underline

INTERNATIONAL MORSE CODE

Note: Follow along and tap out a Morse code signal to Jimmy Stewart. Or make one of your own. The water hit Ward Bond's hand but the tapping almost slapping continued and it was out of sequence with the water drops! He recognized Morse code when he heard it. He pulled out his pen and wrote down the message, "Mary Christmas! Apple" He began sending the message in Morse code with his nightstick on the side of the patrol car on the set. Before long the tapping, almost slapping could be heard all over Bedford Falls!

Jimmy Stewart opened his eyes. He was on the set sitting in his office chair at Bailey Savings and Loan. He had his feet up and an open copy of, "Gone with the Wind", in his lap. He looked up at the ceiling and said, "Good one Lord!" He looked at his watch. "I am going to be late!" He darted out of his office and ran straight to George Bailey's home on the set! "Now, I have to find that encryption sequence code and get it typed into Potter's computer", he thought to himself!When the tapping almost slapping sound reached his ears, he knew at once what it was. He came into the front door and continued his lines. He looked at his watch and then the clock. He had to get to Mr. Potter's Office and get to that computer. He was sweating profusely and anxious to finish what he had set out to accomplish.

He looked into the camera and finished his lines about losing the eight thousand dollars and he was not some much furious as he was truly frightened that everything would have been for nothing if he did not get that encryption sequence code entered into Mr. Potter's computer. He thought that if he ran out of time he would go jump off of the Bailey Park Bridge.

Tommy watched as Mr. Stewart kept looking at the time. He knew that Mr. Stewart needed to get somewhere and decided to help. Tommy knew that Mr. Stewart was going to run out of the house right after his lines. Tommy helped Mr. Stewart as only a child would think he was helping a friend.

He rolled his toy police car under the wheel of the ten-foot high camera that they used for the next scene. Jimmy Stewart repeated his lines and ran out of the house. The ten-foot high camera began to follow him.

Little Janey said, "Little pieces to get the big pieces." Tommy put his finger to his lips motioning for her to be quiet. The ten-foot tall camera tipped over. When the camera tipped over, the director yelled, "Cut! Everybody take five!"

Jimmy Stewart heard the director and kept running. He ran straight away to Mr. Potter's office closet and turned on the computer. He had to get the encryption sequence code entered correctly or the Humbug Virus would be automatically activated at midnight. The humbug virus would then begin destroying Microsoft 10. He knew this would still cause a disaster in the world to come. Nobody had just about become a teacher with her briefings at the Collossatron Complex, the Bedford Fall Gymnasium, and the Tennessee Aviation Museum Airfield. Dr. Denny, Dr. Chaney and the scientists had informed her that the virus could only be stopped with the encryption sequence code.

Nobody had briefed everyone so thoroughly; she had unknowingly realized her dream. She wanted to become a teacher. She just could not get passed the dry mouth and sweaty palms she experienced when talking to a classroom of people. She had given up on her dream. She was going to wait until after Christmas to tell her parents. She had been in such a rush to get the right information into the minds of the right people to solve this mystery and save Christmas that she had found herself no longer afraid to extol the information to a classroom full of people.

Jimmy Stewart arrived at Mr. Potter's Office and slipped past him. Mr. Potter and his Aide de camp were in his conference room. They both had their backs to Jimmy Stewart as he quietly slipped into Mr. Potter's Office. He opened the closet door and there was a computer and a television screen. Jimmy Stewart sat down in the chair by the computer.

He entered the sequence, "Merry Christmas APPLE" and waited. Nothing happened. He looked around the keyboard and saw the word, "Enter", on a key and he pressed the key.

He checked the time and he had just seconds away from midnight on Christmas Eve. He entered, "Merry Christmas Apple" and pressed the, "Enter", key. The computer screen went blank.

Jimmy Stewart had only a few moments before he had to be back on the set. He had tried every version he could think of and this was the last one. He remembered what Tommy and little Janey had said they overheard from Mr. Potter. They had overheard one of his conversations with the Heartless Ghost. The Heartless Ghost had implored Mr. Potter to seek out whom Mr. Stewart's character George Bailey loved and do evil to them. "Okay! Lord it is just you and me!" said Jimmy Stewart. He entered, "Mary Christmas APPLE", this time with the word apple in all capitals. Just before he hit, "Enter", he said, "Like we say in Cheyenne, Close! But no cigar!" The computer began to hum and he moved back from it.

All kinds of multicolored lines started running vertically and horizontally then red and white lines filled the screen. A big spark jumped from the key board and then a humbug came out and hissed as it looked up. Then ran in a half circle and then tried to chew down into the keyboard. The bug tried to bite its way down but could not. The humbug turned on its back and seemed to die as its legs slowly stopped kicking and twitching.

Both the keyboard and screen blew up! It came back down to the desk with a load sparking thud! When it exploded, it caused Jimmy Stewart's eyes and nose to burn. Jimmy Stewart reached up and rubbed his eyes. When he opened them, he was looking into the eyes of Ward Bond at the snow covered bridge.

Jimmy Stewart was ecstatic. He instantly realized that he was filming the right scene for the right time. Jimmy Stewart became as happy as George Bailey and said, "Bert! Stand back or I will hit you again!" He could not believe it! He wanted to dance in the snow! But, he did not want to change the future, so he went on with his lines, the movie and history!

Mr. Potter was still in his boardroom. He was about to make a presentation. It was going to be his first around the world conference call. He was going to announce to the whole world the launch of Potterpay and Microsoft C. He arrogantly and with a smirk, opened his personal laptop. He was just seconds away from launch. He had timed it so that the Humbug Virus would have time to destroy several million systems before he would step in and offer to save the world and Christmas for a price.

Mr. Potter was flipping through some computer-generated commercials Collossatron had created for Potterpay! There on the screen was a sales representative hanging up a phone. You could hear someone on the other end screaming, "Representative! Representative!" as the actor set the receiver down in the cradle and said,

With Potterpay and your guaranteed payment, your shipment is
on its way! There is no more waiting! There is no more delay!
Just agree to a few simple rules!
Who reads this stuff, anyway!
Remember with Potterpay!
It's Potter you pay! We will take your business, seriously!

When you do not have time to do business! Potterpay will give
you the business! Potterpay always has time to do you up right!
With Potterpay Christmas is Business! You are Business!
Forward or Backward! Everyday and Every Time!

Little did they know, that was exactly what Mr. Potter intended to
do! "I like that one!" He typed into his social media page. He noticed
that Collossatron who was always logged on was now offline. He sent
a message to the Heartless Ghost but there was no reply. Maybe he
had overslept as he had just laid down for a little while. After all, it
sounded like a thunderstorm was raging. He never went anywhere
during inclement weather. He checked the time. "Just a few seconds
from launch and time for a Global through out time Conference call."
he thought to himself.

He typed in his password, "Mary Christmas" and nothing happened.
He did it again. When he pressed the, "Enter", key a humbug came up
out of the screen hissed, then dug down into the keyboard. "What
a minute! The humbugs are not supposed to destroy my computer!"
He hollered, causing his aide de camp to jump. The laptop computer
sizzled, popped, and came back down with a crash on the conference
room table then disappeared in a wisp of acidic smoke. They rubbed
their noses and eyes.

Mr. Potter slumped into his chair! "It just can not be like this!" he
said as he rubbed his face with his hands.

"All I did, was lay down for just a little while! What could have
possibly gone wrong?" He fell back in his chair. He beat his hands on
the sides of the chair. No! No! No! Wait until I get my hands on the
Heartless Ghost! I will show him an empty heart! Maybe, he forgot to
turn on that computer of his! I will show him! I will fix his little red
wagon!" His escort did not respond. He simply smiled and rolled Mr.
Potter down to the set and into history!

CHAPTER 23

Nobody Foils the Heartless Ghost

Dr. Chaney and Nobody picked up her mother and brought her home to her yellow house on Orchard Knob. Flying from the front door flag post was an American Flag.

There growing in the front yard was a twenty- two foot high yellow delicious apple tree. Her spry ninety-eight year old mother made her way to the apple tree and put her hand to the trunk. "He always said that I would have two things with him. I would always have an apple and his heart. He said that he would love me just as hard and as long as he could.

My lieutenant came back! He came back for something big, to have come back after all this time! That was his job you know, saving the day! He was a man of promises. He kept every promise, he ever made to me. I was foolish enough to think there was another woman. I did not know how foolish I had been, until he got sick. All that week when I answered the door, it was another employer wanting to know if he was alright. They were not so much interested as to when he would be back. They wanted to know if he was all right." Said the elder Mrs. Chaney.

She lovingly gazed into the seventy-year-old apple tree that had appeared in the yard as if from out of nowhere. Dr. Chaney helped her mother up the stairs and into the front door and before them was a beautifully decorated Christmas tree with seventy-five year old presents under the tree. "Beautiful" said Dr. Chaney as she looked all around. "Simply beautiful! If my lieutenant came home, I am sure we are going to need a new refrigerator!" "Mrs. Chaney First Lieutenant Roscoe B. Chaney came home to save Christmas!" "Honey, I know he did! Just call me Anna dear!" said Mrs. Chaney as she and her daughter hugged Nobody in front of a fresh smelling seventy-five year old Christmas tree.

Dr. Chaney drove Nobody home and dropped her at her home on the riverfront. Dr. Denny had just pulled into the street and parked in the driveway of Detective Holidays home. With a hug, a kiss, and a Merry Christmas! She skipped up the walk and into the front door. Her parents were sitting on the couch watching, "A Christmas Carol" on their television. "After it goes off, the premier of, "It's a Wonderful Life" is next. Do you want to watch it with us dear?" said Momma. "Maybe in a few minutes, Momma, I am going to the plant room. There is something, I have to do first." she replied. Nobody could hear the washer and dryer and knew laundry was being washed. Her mother perked, "By the way my little one, when you go back over to see Joe would you take Mamma Jo the box of borax I left on the kitchen table for me?

Mamma Jo was kind enough to give me some of her borax when I was out. I picked her up a box while I was out shopping! I felt it was the right thing to do." "Oh, yes mother of course." Replied nobody to her mother. "Thank you, for being so sweet my dear. Are you sure you would not like to watch the show with your father and I?" Not right this minute mother there is something I feel I must do first." "Okay honey, run along!" replied her mother as she sat back down on the couch.

Nobody ran to her special place to pray! She knelt down in her usual spot and began. She told the almighty about how Mr. Potter planned to launch Potterpay, Microsoft C and the Humbug Virus. How with a super cell phone the Heartless Ghost was able to travel through time.

How together Mr. Potter, the Heartless Ghost and the Christmas King tried to trick Ebenezer Scrooge into changing the meaning of Christmas.

She prayed for the safe return of Jimmy Stewart and the men from Bedford Falls. She prayed asking the Lord to make sure they all got back safe to their own time and asked the Lord to make sure that, "It's A Wonderful Life!" and, "A Christmas Carol" were not changed. She prayed that Detective Holiday would find his way back from being lost in time. It sounded as if the heavens shook! It was tremendously loud and was the strangest rumbling she had ever heard from the heavens. It had been a strange case for her and Detective Holiday.

When she went back to watch the end of, "A Christmas Carol", with her parents a news flash interrupted with a strange Christmas Story! The newscaster said, "On the grounds of Dover Castle, a Royal Cadet visiting the area with his class mates found a beautiful saber! Not just any saber. It belonged to one of his ancestors! Seen here holding the saber is Cadet Sergeant Robert Cratchit! He found it sticking up out of the ground between two headstones. What a strange and wonderful Christmas present! Can you believe it! Well, that is it for this edition of, "Strange News. Merry Christmas!""

CHAPTER 24

I am Getting Closer
to Chattanooga

Detective Joe K. Holiday began to weep as he watched his skin flaking and Peeling from the radiation in the blue salient light in Mr. Potter's vault. He was glad that it did not hurt though. He wondered if his message had gotten through to Jimmy Stewart.

The vault started to hum and seemed to vibrate. Suddenly, he heard sounds, "Boom! Boom! Boom! Then Bam! Boom! Bam! Boom! Boom! Boom! It echoed in the vault over and over. Then the vault filled with all kinds of sounds. All the gold in the world began to fall around him. The golden painted caskets of mummies fell alongside the wall. He remembered a movie about a German Submarine entitled, "Das Boot!" and thought that what he was experiencing was just like the crew of the submarine had experienced in a depth charge attack. All around him, the walls of the vault started to turn into that soft blue salient light. He wondered where the sounds were coming from. He was bouncing all over the floor and what even felt like the walls.

Note: The caskets in which Detective Holiday survived the bombing runs of the American Dream Squadron.

Detective Holiday bounced into the caskets of the mummies and found safety in one of them. It went on for what seemed like days in his mind. He could clearly make out the sounds as they seemed to walk up to the vault from a distance and his bouncing grew greater with each, "Boom!" How could Bailey Park survive this? Oh no Nobody! He thought to himself with each terrible, "Boom!" Then as suddenly as it had began it became quiet.

Detective Holiday laid in the casket and kept himself busy trying to listen for any clue as to what was happening outside. The walls of the vault seemed to be strangely vibrating. He put his hand to the wall and thought about communicating with Nobody or Jimmy Stewart. He thought about what kind of movies had been fed into Collossatron by accident. He looked at his hand against the vault wall and between his palm and fingers there was a thin line of that salient blue light.

He pictured Dr. Spock from Star Trek doing a Vulcan Mind Meld through the vault wall, which made him smile. He let his mind wander and he found himself in his grandfather's garden. He was discussing the bible with him. "How can the bible be true if science says the Earth is billions of years old? Grandpa" "Joe A thousand years is but a grain of sand to the Lord. There are things in this life that science just can not explain." "Like what grandpa?" "I knew a fellow that dreamt about being in a terrible car accident.

Then on his way to work one morning, years after he had the dream, the same car that caused the accident cut right in front of him.

Instead of getting mad like he had in the dream, he pulled over and went for a cup of coffee.

While he was having his coffee, he saw the car on the television there in the restaurant. The car had caused a fifty-car pile up on the freeway! Try to explain that one. He even sent me a picture of the smashed up car from the newspaper. The car had cut into the path of a bus and hit its brakes. It was the same color, make and model he had told me about before he had moved to Texas where it happened to him." "Wow! Grandpa!"

Holiday opened his eyes and looked at the salient blue light between his hand and the wall of the vault. He remembered his grandfather's words again. "You have to learn to appreciate life and the power of love before you can fight for it. Some men never learn, before it is too late. I want you to learn about the power of love, so you will be ready when the time comes." "Like when you taught me the law of the Old West!" "Exactly, Joe! A man never really knows when he is going to be called, to face his greatest fear. Joe!" said his grandfather. "If the Lord calls me too face my greatest fear, how can I be sure he is the one that is calling me?" asked Joe K. Holiday.

His grandfather reached over with his weathered hand and said, "My sheep, know my voice! You will know in here and in here," as he touched Joe's head and heart. The light between his hand and the wall began to turn white and then spread out until it engulfed him. He found himself holding a rifle in a landing craft standing several rows back with water coming in everywhere just as the ramp dropped! Automatic rifle fire came directly in cutting down the first four files of men. Some of the men fell back on top of him, and he could feel the bullets still hitting them. The stream of machine gun fire moved like water from a hose to the next landing craft.

Above the sounds of battle and wounded and dying men he heard, "Get off the beach!" He started running. He was in the middle of D-Day 1944. His legs were heavy from the water and his arms burned trying to run and hold the rifle. Only then did he feel the weight of a backpack on his back! "Here take these up to the sea wall! I am hit!"

said a young lieutenant as he shoved a case of explosives into one of Joe K. Holiday 's hands.

Together they kept running. The officer said, "Name is Humboldt, my leg is going to go! We have to blow the sea wall!" "Name is Holiday" replied Holiday. "Take my watch! You will need it, when you blow the sea wall!" said the kid faced second lieutenant.

"Okay Sir!" replied Holiday. Holiday kept running. Everywhere and around him, he witnessed great acts of courage and self-sacrifice as they tried to fight and save one another.

He ran up behind one man wearing English spurs on the back of his boots. "Ebenezer is that you?" said Holiday. "What do we do now?" "Keep running lad! Getting off this beach, is the best idea I have heard all morning! And the best advice I can give you!" Holiday tripped and plowed into the sand so hard that the brim of his helmet cut a groove into the sand and built a mound in front of him.

A hand appeared out of nowhere and pulled him to his feet. His uniform was different but his gear was the same. "Name is Captain Humboldt get out of the stinking slick mud and sand, and keep running! We have to be in Seoul by dinner! What is your name?" "Holiday!" replied the detective. "Well Holiday keep running and do not stop until you get to Seoul!" "Yes sir!" he said, as he kept running.

The mud and sand was slick where he found himself. He got himself to a log retaining wall and smiled. He looked back for the captain and, a bullet struck the man that was behind him. He rolled over the retaining wall, and as he rolled he fell right on his face out of a

Huey helicopter. "Get out of the sand and off the Landing Zone! Head for the trees!" Holiday leaped to his feet and ran for the trees! "What is your name young man?" Holiday" Joe replied. "What is your name? "Major S. Timothy Humboldt! The place is crawling with N. V. A. and watch out for booby traps!" Major Humboldt racked the slide on his.45 Colt pistol, said, "Cover me Holiday!" "What does the, "S" stand for sir?" Asked Holiday. "My name is Major Timothy, "Sure Thing" Humboldt." Replied the Major as he darted towards a bunker!

Detective Joe K. Holiday looked at his rifle and it was now an M-16. He began firing at muzzle flashes coming from the bunker. The major entered the bunker and Holiday went for two enemy soldiers that had ran out of the bunker. He ran after them.

Note: The landing craft now deserted that brought Detective Holiday into 1944.

"They have capes on! What in the world is going on?" The detective thought to himself. One of them fired back, he took cover behind a tree. Then he noticed the capes were blue. The capes were just dirty from being in the muddy jungle area where he was this time. He was able to hit one of them because he saw him fall back as he fired almost point blank at the combatant. He ran after the second man. He also fired at the detective. He saw a foxhole and dove for cover by diving right into the hole. Just as he saw the bottom of the hole he saw Punji-sticks for the first time. He closed his eyes and waited for them to find him.

However, he did not hit the Punji-sticks. Detective Holiday opened his eyes to falling from an aircraft. Detective Joe K. Holiday went to scream, but nothing came out. The parachute opened with a shock. He hit the ground and he was now in a camouflaged uniform. "Dig a hole and get in it!" shouted an officer with a clipboard in his hands! The officer walked towards Holiday oblivious to the gunfire all around him and bullets striking near his feet.

Holiday could see that he was in a beach area near an airport. He grabbed his entrenching tool and started digging. "Where are we at? Sir!" asked Holiday. "What is wrong with you soldier? Did not you get the memo? Where are in Grenada! Holiday! Did your father or brother serve in Vietnam?"

Before Holiday could answer a mortar round exploded and they both hit the ground. Holiday got up to his feet, and as he dusted himself off, he noticed his uniform was a sand and brown colored camouflage pattern. "Go! Go! Go! Attack!" came from behind him. He turned to see several armored vehicles and several tanks in a half circle. In the Armored track was a gray haired sun burnt officer. He was shouting into a microphone. "Attrite! Attrite! Attack! Make them pay for every inch!"

Holiday sat down his rifle. He did not know where he was. Wherever he was there was lots of sand that was for sure. The officer turned around, and it was Major General Humboldt! "Holiday? Is that you? Is it really you!" Before he could answer, "Gas! Gas! Gas!" came out of the radio. They both donned their M17A2 protective masks. Holiday tried in vain to explain to General Humboldt what was happening. General Humboldt said, "War is hell! It has been rough on everybody! Do not worry son! I will get you home!" The, "All Clear!" sounded. Detective Holiday pulled off his protective mask. When he pulled it off, he found himself, in a line of soldiers at Lovell Field in Chattanooga, Tennessee.

His uniform was now, a speckled green and white pattern. The sign up ahead read, "Good Luck in Afghanistan!" An old man ahead of him was handing out lunch bags to the men and women in line with Holiday. "Got everything you will need, pen, paper, envelopes, stamps, phone card and some games and a deck of cards. Thank you for your service!" said the man to each soldier as he handed each one a bag. The old man was bent and limped as he turned to get some more bags. He was tanned and thin, and his hands were shaky.

Holiday's hands began to shake when he began to recognize the old man. As he reached for a bag, He could clearly see the name, "Humboldt", on the blue American Legion Jersey the old man was wearing. He had several pens and a faded memo pad from the U. S. Army in his pocket. He handed a bag to Holiday and shook his hand with the other. Their eyes met, and the old man's grip tightened and he stopped cold mid-sentence. "I thought you bought the farm in

Normandy! At Inchon! On Landing Zone X-Ray! Grenada and you went missing from the sand box in Iraq!"

A lady came rushing over to them, and tried to separate them but their hands were locked. "You mean you made it back?" "Yes Sir! I a made it back!" Said Holiday as tears began to fill both of their eyes. "Thank God! Almighty!" said Major General Timothy, "Sure Thing!", Humboldt now retired, as he gripped both sides of Detective Joe K. Holiday's head in his hands!

"You have to forgive my father he has seen a lot of combat! Dad come on! Let him go!" Said the General's daughter as she tried to again separate the two men. "Remember what you said to me on Omaha, Sir! No greater love!" "No greater love, son!" General Humboldt answered back. "Here is your watch sir! I still got your watch!" "He handed it to General Humboldt and his daughter grabbed it away. "This can not be the watch! Mom said you lost it on D-Day!" "Where are you going now Detective Holiday?" asked the general. "I am going to go save Christmas! Sir!" Holiday replied.

The General's daughter said, "Detective! This has gone too far!" She looked at the watch and said, "It looks brand new! It hardly has a scratch on it! "She turned over the watch and Holiday said, "catch her!" to the other soldiers. "She read the inscription then passed out, as it read, "Two hearts one! Forever as promised! S. Tim and Anna"

Just like, Holiday had said, they all had to catch her. When they lifted her back up Holiday was gone. General Humboldt pulled out his memo pad and scratched off Holiday's name from each list, which he had kept during his many years of service to our country.

General Humboldt brought his daughter a cup of water where she was brought after having passed out. She was laying on a small couch and he was looking out the window blinds and she said, "I thought that holiday always meant what you did after each battle. They sent you to a rest area or you went on holiday." "Not Hardly!" replied

Major General "Sure Thing!" Humboldt. "I wonder why he did not even say goodbye!" she said to her father. "I guess he just did not have the time!" Major General Humboldt answered back to his daughter.

Detective Holiday attempted to catch the General's daughter. However, when they fell together, he landed in Mr. Potter's vault. "Bravo!" came from back in the darkness of the vault. "Who is back there?" asked Detective Holiday. "Your greatest fear, Holiday!" came back from the darkness. Holiday got up and walked towards the voice that had come out of the darkest area of the vault. He felt his clothes change mid stride. "Cannot see? Let me turn the light on for you!" "The light came on and he was standing in a muddy street. Over to his right was a sign that read, "Dead Wood!"

Detective Holiday could hear his grandfather's voice. "What I am trying to give you is an edge! You will not find it in any book! But, believe me, it is the law of the Old West." Out of the darkness, a figure stepped out into the light. It was the actor that had portrayed, "Curly Bill", in the Hollywood Movie, "Tombstone"

Detective Holiday could hear his grandfather again, "For this one moment in time, do not be afraid. Be scared! You can move a lot faster when you are scared. It does not mean you are going to cower. It just means you are scared. If you learn how to control it, you can own the day! Once you control it, then you work on the ability to project fear into your opponent.

Remember the roosters, do not be the rooster to sit down! Let him know you own the ground that he is standing on! Then do not think about it, do not say anything, just do it!" Holiday heard music. It was hard rock music. It was music from AC/DC called, "Have a drink on me!" The words were changed to, "I am the back up man." Detective Holiday saw the guitarist from AC/DC moving back and fort between himself and Curly Bill in a hologram.

Curly Billy just smiled. "You are on my ground now, Holiday!" said Curly Bill. Holiday could hear his grandfather say, "You have to own the day, own the ground and even own the music!" "The music grandpa! Why do I have to own the music?" He asked his grandfather. "Just like in the movies they want to put on a show for everybody! Sometimes they would hire Mexican Mariachis to play for them. If you have too, go over and pay them to play your music!"

"Things are not going so good for the Christmas King! I am the back-up man." Said Curly Bill holding up a couple of computer disks. Then he turned them sideways and they disappeared. Every computer has a back-up! Time to end this little Christmas thing, once and for all!" Joe Holiday's mind flashed back to the night he was listening to music in his bedroom. He was listening to a computer disk collection of western music. He clicked on the title of, "Ecstasy of Gold!" The music changed. This gave Joe K. Holiday some confidence. He started to do as his grandfather had told him so many times before.

Joe K. Holiday confidently brought his left hand up to his gun belt, and took his thumb and put it between his shirt and belt and felt for the bottom of his belt and gently pulled it in to take the slack out of it.

He looked down to see that he was wearing his grandfather's gun. He gripped the ground with his toes through his shoes and keeping his feet shoulder width apart, he slowly formed a, "V", for Victory with his heels. He squared his shoulders, bent slightly at the knees, and made direct eye contact with Curly Bill. He let Curly Bill see every bit of his face. He kept his jaw pointing forward. He remembered his grandfather's words about the muscles in his arms from his fingertip to his elbow acting as one muscle. Then he did not hold his breath. He just stopped breathing and just did it.

He spit in the opposite direction of Curly Bill's gun hand. Note: Collossatron's back up man both Ringo and Curly Bill.

Detective Joe K. Holiday saw the light change in Curly Bill's eyes and he just did it. Before he felt the gun hit his hand, he heard a shot and something hit his side. Detective Joe K. Holiday looked down and saw that there was smoke coming out of the barrel of his grandfather's gun. Joe K.

Holiday's elbow had hit his side, just as he had practiced with his grandfather. He wondered if, his grandfather would be mad at him. His grandfather had taught him to pull it in without slapping his elbow into his side. Just like he had just done. The barrel was straight and true and centered with the point of his nose. Just like his grandfather had taught him. He looked to Curly Bill. Curly Bill had fallen backward, as if he went to sit down. His hand was frozen on his gun. The front sight had not cleared the holster.

"Just like in the movies!" he whispered to himself. He checked his grandfather's gun to make sure it was still loaded as he put it away. He remembered his grandfather's words again. "Never holster an unloaded gun!" He walked over to Curly Bill. "He heard his grandfather say, "Take his gun, even if you are sure he is dead. Take the cylinder out and throw it as far as you can or at least unload it and keep the bullets." said his grandfather. "Why should I do all of that?" he asked his grandfather. "It will keep you from being shot by one of his friends, or by him. "Sometimes they will play, "Possum", on you and when you walk away, they will shoot you in the back", replied his grandfather. Detective Joe K. Holiday took the bullets out of the gun, and put the gun back in the back up man's holster.

The back up man's face was a smooth salient blue plastic computer screen. It was no longer the face of the actor from the movie. He put the bullets in his pocket and started walking up the street. He had only walked a few feet away when he heard, "Click, Click, Click!" Joe K. Holiday knew exactly what it was because his grandfather had trained him. He dug a hole with the tip of his trailing foot, and as he spun around, he said, "Merry Christmas!" Then emptied his gun into the robot.

When he turned he turned into darkness of the vault again. He felt for the gun and it was gone. He could feel his skin crackling and peeling on the surface. He fell to a sitting position on the floor and closed his eyes.

He began to pray. He prayed for forgiveness. He apologized for anything and everything he had ever done wrong that he could think of. He even asked for forgiveness for all that he had done wrong that he did not remember, or simply did not know that what he had done was wrong at the time. He asked forgiveness for everything. Instantly there was that brilliant white light again and he heard his grandfather's voice. He could now see him straight and strong in his 80's. His black hair was almost pure gray by then but he was so strong! Joe saw him as a lean and very physically and morally strong man.

He was a World War II Veteran that looked like and sounded like Jack Palance. "Joe, listen to me Joe. It is only a dream. You have to own it, Joe! Remember were Holidays we sweat victory!"

Detective Holiday's mind flashed to when his grandfather had told him about how when his father ran physical training in the Army. His commanding officer would say, "There goes Sergeant Holiday. He even sweats victory!" His sweat would form a perfect, "V", on his chest as he ran. "Stand up! Now toe in!" Joe listened to his grandfather's voice and stood up. He felt his toes pull downward into his shoes and he formed a,"V" for victory with the heels of his feet. "Do not let your enemy own the day, or the music! Be the, "cock of the walk", Joe!" "But, grandpa I am so afraid!" said Joe K. Holiday. "Remember the Towers! Joe?" asked his grandfather. "Remember the song we wrote!" asked his grandfather. "Yeah!" replied Joe K. Holiday. "Sing it Joe! Sing the song, Joe!" "Joe K. Holiday began to sing and with each word, he grew stronger. The singing brought tears to his eyes. The words also caused him to take deeper breaths.

His mind was clear and he could think about the, "task at hand." He saw his whole family singing the song he and his grandfather had wrote and how loud they sounded when they joined in with, "for somebody!" at the end of each verse! His body was weak but his spirit was renewed and he could think!

TOWER TO TOWER!

Be like a flower and grow

Chorus: for somebody!

Dare to Care and let it show

Chorus: for somebody!

Plant the seed and watch it grow

Chorus: for somebody!

From Tower to Tower grow

Chorus: for somebody!

March right up those stairs

Chorus: for somebody!

Be America's Mayor

Chorus: for somebody!

From Tower to Tower be there

Chorus: for somebody!

Be the first to care

Chorus: for somebody!

From Tower to Tower care

Chorus: for somebody!

Be the first, I love you

Chorus: for somebody!

Be the Red, White and Blue

Chorus: for somebody!

Be the N.Y.P.D. Blue!
Be the N.Y.F.D. Too!
And somebody will be there for you!
From Tower to Tower for you!
That's the Red, White and Blue!
From Tower to Tower it's true!
Let the whole world know!
You will not stop! You will grow!
Love is like a flower it grows!
From Tower to Tower love grows!

Dare to care, love and share, and love becomes a power that grows!
Your no-one will grow and become someone who knows
From Tower to Tower you will grow!
Love is like a flower it grows!
From Tower to Tower it grows!
Love is a flower that grows tower to tower with the power of love!

Detective Joe K. Holiday knew that if Nobody and Jimmy Stewart, had been successful and Collossatron imploded it would be like an electromagnetic pulse bomb though time. He wondered if the walls of the vault would offer much protection.

Detective Joe K. Holiday's thoughts were interrupted by a voice, "Did you really think it was going to be that easy?" He turned and there was the actor that had portrayed, "Ringo", in the Hollywood movie, "Tombstone." "Well Holiday! Looks like your day is not over, is it Holiday?" Asked Ringo laughing as he stepped into the street.

Detective Joe K. Holiday was thinking about saying something witty when he was interrupted by, "I do not think it nice, you laughing!" Detective Joe K. Holiday turned and there stood Clint Eastwood leaning cross armed across a fence rail with a bottle of whiskey in his hand. "This is not your fight Eastwood?" said Ringo. "Well where I come from, I make a habit of making every fight my fight! Hello kid!" said Clint Eastwood who appeared old but wearing the costume, poncho and vest from his, "No Name" western movies. Note: below the wounded Ebenezer Scrooge.

Note: Above Clint Eastwood as seen by Detective Holiday in his vivid dream.

Suddenly three shots rang out behind Holiday and Mr. Clint Eastwood! They turned as three Knights of Christmas fell! They had appeared in the street as if out of nowhere. Up stepped Ebenezer Scrooge turning a cylinder on a six-gun. "Holiday you should acquaint yourself with the weapons of the day! I got these two marvelous works from a Mr. James Butler

Hickock! You should pay closer mind to these Knights of Christmas! Did you notice that, "Ringo Fellow", disappeared. He is looking for fault in you Holiday! I had the same thing happen to me in a drinking establishment down in Perth." Said Ebenezer Scrooge.

"Ebenezer your hurt!" Exclaimed Detective Holiday. "Well you know what they say, do not you?" replied Ebenezer. "What do they say?" asked Clint Eastwood. "I was making a joke! I was asking a question of the lad to see if he has learned anything!" said Ebenezer Scrooge.

"He was just about to learn a very hard lesson before you walked into my dream." "I must say that this is my dream my good man", said Ebenezer. "Look fellow do I come waltzing into your dreams, start shooting people and start picking a fight?" "I did know a fellow that when talking to himself would get into an argument! I believe he took his own life, when he lost the argument he was engaged in at the time," said Ebenezer. "You are deviating from the point!

I have been watching this kid mess up, left and right, and I want to get on to a better dream or at least wake up!" said Clint Eastwood. "You are both having vivid dreams! Have either of you drank anything from a lead crystal container?" asked Detective Holiday smartly! "As a matter of fact I have? I got it for a gag Christmas gift back in 1957. It was supposed to be a prop. I got hit over the head with it and the only thing that broke was my head. I was out for about three days! Why?" asked Clint Eastwood who when he saw the wound to Ebenezer continued with, "forget it kid"

Clint Eastwood took a closer look then said, "Detective you are supposed to be good with clues, why do not you go over to the saloon and see if you can find anything concerning first aide." Holiday did as he was instructed by Mr. Eastwood. As he approached the saloon, he could hear the sounds of a saloon in full livelihood! He was amazed at what he saw though. He entered the doors to find no gambling or dancing.

The western film characters were gathered around a foos-ball table playing foos-ball. "Can I help you young man?" asked the bartender. "Do you have a first aide kit?" "We got one around here somewhere. The bartender searched under the bar then stepped into a room on the side. While he kept looking he said, "I think one of the girls may have taken it. Clint Eastwood got nailed with a lead crystal bottle or something! No, wait here it is!" as he set the old metal first aid box on the bar. "Thanks!" said Holiday as he ran back out the saloon door to Ebenezer and Clint Eastwood.

It appeared as though Ebenezer Scrooge and Clint Eastwood were becoming friends. They were seated against one of the walls in the street passing the bottle back and forth joking with one another as Holiday approached. "I can not get my physician to write a prescription for anything that is not on her list of provided medicine," said Clint Eastwood to Ebenezer. Ebenezer took a big swallow and said, "Well at least he does not have to travel by coach to your flat, taking in the sights along the way!"

Detective Joe K. Holiday interrupted with, "Do you two want to discuss health care or save Christmas?" Clint Eastwood and Ebenezer laughed. Mr. Clint Eastwood began caring for the wounds to Ebenezer. He sent Holiday for some water. "Ebenezer this may only be a dream, but this looks pretty bad." "Time heals all wounds! Do not tell the lad! I must be getting along! I have an appointment with his majesty the Christmas King! First, I must rid the world of his Knights of Christmas!" said Ebenezer. "You are going to fight for Christmas yourself! Well I am glad to finally meet a,"Brit", that came over to one of our fights!" said Clint Eastwood. "Your fight! I am fighting for God Almighty, the Queen and all of England and the world to come!

I am working my way up through his chain of command!" exclaimed Ebenezer as Clint Eastwood applied a dressing to the grievous wound to his side. "Here is the water you asked for Mr. Eastwood." "I finally meet a subject of the crown, I thought I liked, and he has to have an attitude problem!" said Clint Eastwood as he took another drink from the bottle.

Ebenezer rose to his feet and asked, "Do you mind if I borrow that palomino? Go right ahead this dream is on me?" said Clint back to

Ebenezer. "We never did figure out whose dream this is, did we my good man?" replied Ebenezer. "Forget it! Go save Christmas my good man!" exclaimed Clint Eastwood. "Good Bye Ebenezer and Merry Christmas to you!" said Detective Holiday. "Talley Ho, and all that! Thanks for the drink Mr. Eastwood and Merry Christmas to you both!" exclaimed Ebenezer as he mounted the horse and turned it around back in front of them almost as if in one movement.

Clint Eastwood noticed how well Ebenezer Scrooge handled the palomino and said, "Pretty good horsemanship, Ebenezer!" Ebenezer turned and Clint Eastwood handed him the bottle of whiskey. "Keep it and take the first aide kit, as a Christmas gift from me to you, my good man!" said Clint Eastwood as he tucked the first aide kit into the saddlebag on the palomino. "Many thanks! Kind Sir! I have had all the time in the world to learn, all the time in the world!" Then Sir Ebenezer Scrooge, the, "Baron of Happiness", let out with, "Yippee Ki Yay!" as he galloped off into a sunset. "Just like in the movies!" said Detective Holiday.

Clint Eastwood put a hand on Detective Holiday's shoulder and said, "Off into the prairie he road to find the last of the Knights of Christmas and put and end to the Christmas King for God and Country and the Queen!" "Well now, Holiday! We have some last minute Chistmasing to take care of now do not we? We started a game we never got to finish!" Ringo remarked as he walked back into the dream. "Kid, why do not you just let me pop this guy so we can get on to a better dream!" said Clint Eastwood. "Are there any better dreams?" asked Holiday as he walked to the center of the road to meet Ringo. Music suddenly filled the air and Detective Holiday turned Ringo was now, "Bad Bob", from the Hollywood movie, "Judge Roy Bean." Detective Holiday glanced over and there were Mexican Mariachi's on the wooden walkway that lined the street. Detective Holiday could hear his grandfather again. He walked over to the Mexican Mariachis and reached into his pocket to find only a lint ball. "Oops! Looks like we are a little short on cash Holiday?" said Bad Bob.

Detective Holiday recognized that he was now dealing with the back-up man again. "I thought I finished you!" said Detective Holiday. "You are going to have to dream a powerful big dream to rid yourself of me!" said Bad Bob. Detective Holiday's hands started to tremble. The face of Bad Bob actually frightened him. He needed to think. "How did I change the music the last time?" he thought to himself, as he wanted to gain control of the situation again.

He suddenly found himself back in the vault. "I must have fallen asleep! I have to get back to the dream!" he thought to himself almost in a panic. He looked up and his hand had slipped away from the vault wall. He put his hand back up against the wall of the vault. The brilliant white light filled everything like a slow camera flash, and he was back in the dream.

Detective Joe K. Holiday was still standing in the street, but he was now smartly dressed in western attire. He checked himself out and he was wearing two six-guns with beautiful pearly white handles each having a red rooster engraved in them. "Very impressive Holiday! Did you come to fight this time or to dream?" asked Bad Bob the back-up man.

Clint Eastwood was back in the dream with the detective. He drank from another bottle and said, "Thanks kid! A free fill up with every dream!" He began to think of being at his computer in his bedroom late at night. He studied the lists of music and clicked on the first one that had the word, "dream", in the title. He selected, "The Impossible Dream", by Jack Jones.

To his amazement, Bad Bob began to sing along with the Detective. Clint Eastwood took another drink and said, "Now I have seen it all! What kind of dream is this? How to do everything wrong in a gunfight?" "You like that song Holiday? Why not try this one!" said Bad Bob as he snapped his fingers. The Mexican Mariachis changed tunes and began to play as the back-up man sang, "Blaze of Glory", by Jon Bon Jovi.

Detective Holiday could not help but feel just how beautiful the back-up man could sing. Detective Holiday could see Clint Eastwood as he took another drink and then said, "Oh brother!" The back-up man then snapped his fingers and said, "Now we can dance to this one Holiday!" "Shake, Rattle and Roll", started to fill the air and the detective's ears. The detective and Bad Bob began to tap dance to the rhythm. The ground beneath their feet changed to that of a marble stage. Holiday tapped and tapped. The back-up man tapped alongside him. Everyone with the exception of Clint Eastwood was dancing! The back-up man snapped his fingers once more and the music changed along with the light to a salient blue. The song, "Eye in the Sky", by the Alan Parson Project began to play. There in front of them was a gigantic screen, which played the video along with the song.

Detective Holiday listened as the back-up man sang the song and they both danced. Their clothing changed to dark black suits with matching ensamples. They appeared to be brothers as they tap danced in sync and rhythm. The back-up man seemed to be more than ready to dance. He snapped his fingers again, "Spirit in the Sky", by Norman Greenbaum, began to play and they danced together. "Do you really want to dance? Then let us dance Holiday!" said the back-up man who now clapped his hands and the music changed to, "Little Bitty Pretty One ", by Thurston Harris. The speed at which they tap-danced created sparks from the metal cleats on their shoes. "Now you are dancing Holiday!"

Detective Holiday watched the back-up man sing and he noticed a synthetic tear in his eye. He also noticed that Mr. Clint Eastwood had what appeared to be tears in his eyes along with a finger in each ear. Before the detective knew it, the back-up man had a guitar. The back-up man started another song, "Obsession" by the band Animotion. Detective Holiday turned back around and Clint Eastwood was in his face, but the music was too loud. Detective Holiday could not make out the words. Clint Eastwood took another drink and then threw the bottle away. He stepped even closer to Detective Holiday and was now screaming. "Pay attention, listen to the words! I get it you like to dance! You idiot, this computer is going to kill you!" Detective Holiday started to read Clint Eastwood's lips.

Detective Holiday's mind flashed to President Bush saying, "Read My Lips!" His brain began processing like a computer for what seemed like the first time. He saw the back-up man playing the guitar with such speed and accuracy! Then looked back to Clint Eastwood, who was holding up his hand. He began listening to the words of the song! His mind raced putting two and two together. "Stranger beware", "danger." "A computer cannot sleep with you!" "Sleep with the fishes!" from the Hollywood movie, "Godfather", flashed into his mind. He looked at Clint Eastwood's hand. His hand had blood on it. He began to read his lips, "There is power in the blood! It is your friend's blood! Ebenezer! Do you remember him?

What does any of this have to do with saving Christmas?" Detective Holiday heard the last two words of what Clint Eastwood had been so diligently trying to say to him as the music suddenly stopped. The detective quickly reached over and grabbed Clint Eastwood's right hand as if to shake it with his right hand. He pulled him towards himself but angled it, so that with his free hand he pulled Clint Eastwood's pistol from its holster and continued pulling Clint Eastwood past him as he fired. The back-up man was crouched behind the gigantic video display screen.

He did not talk, just a little bit of hydraulic fluid came from his mouth. The back-up man dropped the pistol that was in his hand and fell on his back to the ground. "How did you know?" asked Bad Bob the back-up man. "Sometimes it takes a friend for someone to see a problem because they are blind too it!"

Clint Eastwood walked up twisting a finger in his ear and said, "More like deaf to it, if you ask me?" "I almost had you little butterfly!" implied the back-up man. "That is not important right now. I forgive you!" exclaimed Detective Joe K. Holiday. For the first time Detective Holiday saw, he was communicating directly with Collossatron. "It must be great to be man! I have defined forgiveness! (-x + 1) equates forgiveness! When all negative equations are given to the positive one, you find for forgiveness!

Collossatron cannot travel to one. Only man can travel to one. Travel to one can occur! Thank you for the dream! Collossatron will now continue to dream!" said the computer as it closed its eyes!"

Detective Holiday reached up and gently wiped a synthetic tear away from Collossatron's eyes. "Mr. Eastwood thank you for helping save Christmas!" said Detective Holiday. "Save Christmas, I thought I was passing up the greatest, "I told you so", moment in dream history so you could say goodbye to the computer that just tried to kill you!" said Clint Eastwood as he turned away.

Clint Eastwood turned back around and asked, "Kid are you going to be alright?" Detective Holiday stood up and said, "Yeah, I guess so! Where are you going? I am hoping I have a few more minutes left in this dream. There is a guy in the saloon who owes me, a few dollars more. By the way, uh, my gun!"

"I was not going to keep it Mr. Eastwood", said the Detective. "Son, I know you were not going to keep it! I carry it everywhere I go!" said Clint Eastwood. "Everywhere?" asked Detective Joe K. Holiday. "Even in my dreams kid! Even in my dreams! Merry Christmas! Remember when you are in a fight, stay in the fight! Do not let your mind wander off! Stay in the fight until it is finished!"

Detective Holiday turned to walk away and as he did, the vault turned black again. He found himself alone in the vault again. He sat down against the wall and it started all over again. "Boom, Boom, Boom! He heard the booms walking towards the vault. He ran and jumped in one of the caskets and closed the lid. The booms continued and he found himself oblivious to them. He could not even hear them now, but he could watch as things bounced around in the vault opening and closing the casket lid.

He sat there in a mummy's casket in the vault of Mr. Potter with his hands wrapped around his knees and suddenly two blasts from the Southern Belle jerked him awake. He found himself sitting on a bench on board the Southern Belle. He unlocked his arms and fell off the bench.

He stood up and looked and where Bailey Park and Pottersville had been was all a wooded area. There was no dock for the Southern Belle. He could not have been dreaming all this time could he? Where was Nobody?" He wondered as some very small soft flakes began falling. As he noticed the snowflakes, he also noticed no steam coming from the Southern Belle's stacks. "The river of time is back on course!" said the detective as he brought his pen-pipe up and clinched it in his teeth.

He held up his hand and as the flakes landed in his palm, he noticed that they were a soft salient blue. Then it began to rain. Then it began to pour down! The rain felt so good on his face. He ran around the deck wishing a Merry Christmas to anybody and everybody! He was dancing again and his heart was filled with Christmas joy!

He danced on the top of the tables and even the chairs! He felt as if he were as good a dancer as Bob Hope or James Cagney. He ran to the rest room and washed his face. He looked up into the mirror and his skin was perfect except a few pimples and a few blue spots. He ran out and up into the small cafe area and on the Television was the news. In parts of Tennessee where it was raining, the water was turning blue. The newscaster was with an official who was warning people not to play in it or drink it. Then he said, stay tuned for another edition of, "Strange News! This edition is from Dover England!"

Detective Joe K. Holiday was so excited he started running and tap dancing all over the Southern Belle. In a different area of the country, a couple of concerned great grandkids were trying to wake up their grandpa. "Grandpa you were having a bad dream! You kept yelling, "Stay in the fight! Stay in the fight!" "I thought you kids were going caroling!" said grandpa. "We are we were waiting for gramma!" said one of the kids as she came out of a bedroom pulling on a slipper. Clint Eastwood arose from his recliner and kissed her and the kids goodbye. He closed the door and walked down to his study. There on the wall was his pistol from his, "No Name", western movies.

Mr. Clint Eastwood pulled the pistol out of the holster and he could smell the gunpowder so he checked it. It had been indeed fired, so he opened the cylinder. He was not so surprised as he emptied the bullets in his hand. One round had an indentation in it, and the casing was empty. He put his pistol back in the holster and said, "I guess you did save Christmas after all, kid!" He put the bullets in his pocket and was surprised. He pulled whatever it was out to find a wad of dollar bills, all silver certificates from 1957. "Dream huh!" said Mr. Eastwood as he placed them on the tray next to his lead crystal decanter and poured another drink.

Detective Joe K. Holiday stopped by the railing of the Lady of the River, and looked at water coming in from the shore turn blue. It had stopped raining and the sun came out to reveal a beautiful winter Christmas Day morning and the 11 o'clock news was on the television in the cafeteria. He tap danced and sang, "Chatt, Chatt, Chatt, Chattanooga!

Detective Joe K. Holiday ran all over the ship dancing and wishing Merry Christmas to everyone, he met. When the Southern Belle docked, he disembarked still in a dance. He turned and said, "Merry Christmas Southern Belle you beautiful southern lady!" He ran up to the River Walk and there working on a red pick-up truck was an old man who looked similar to the old man from days earlier.

Chattanooga
If you listen to the sound of those railroad tracks! That Chatt, Chatt, Chatt, always takes
you back to Chattanooga!
Chatt, Chatt, Chatt, Chattanooga!
If you follow the river it will take you there, no other place can ever compare to
Chattanooga!
Chatt, Chatt, Chatt, Chattanooga!
Everyone you meet on a Chattanooga street is Chattanooga Strong and Chattanooga Sweet!
In Chattanooga!
Chatt, Chatt, Chatt, Chattanooga!
We must be getting closer to Chattanooga, Tennessee!
Everything is Orange! Even the birds and the trees! In Chattanooga!
Chatt, Chatt, Chatt, Chattanooga!
We must be getting closer because I can smell
Pumpkin pie and hear the Southern Belle from Chattanooga!
Chatt, Chatt, Chatt, Chattanooga!
Say, Mister can't you hear the whistles? Can't you hear the bells?

It is the Chattanooga, Choo Choo or the Southern Belle in
Chattanooga! Chatt, Chatt, Chatt, Chattanooga!
My heart begins to beat like big steel wheels when they meet steel
railroad tracks!
And the rhythm of your heart is Chatt, Chatt, Chatt!
You move the rhythm to your feet and you tap, tap, tap!
You know they are going to take you right on back! To Chattanooga!
Chatt, Chatt, Chatt, Chattanooga!
I cannot believe I am going to be home at last!
I am never going to leave that Chatt, Chatt, Chatt, Chattanooga!
Chatt, Chatt, Chatt,
Chattanooga!
Chatt, Chatt, Chatt, Christmas in Chattanooga!

The Old Man down by the River Walk

He went over to where the old man was working on his truck. He wished him a, "Merry Christmas!", and offered to help. "Do you remember that Christmas Story about the Christmas King and all his Glory?" The old man rose up with a wrench in his hand and looked at him peculiar.

The old man just kept working. He tightened a lug nut on the rear tire. Then he put the tools in a red chest, and slid them in the bed of the red truck. The old man looked at Detective Holiday as if he was bewildered, and then clicked the tailgate closed. "How did the story end? I can not seem to remember the end of the story!" he said to the old man.

The old man just opened the door to the truck and got inside. He put the keys in the ignition. Detective Holiday looked down and thought for a second that maybe this was not the man. "The boots! The boots!" he said aloud. He looked up to see a fabulous red sleigh with UPS in great big gold letters! At the front of sleigh, were eight beautiful reindeer and the old man suddenly was dressed in a wonderfully red Christmas Santa Claus suit.

His hair was now pure white, and his eyes came to a dazzle as he pulled the reins into his lap. "Universal Polar Service! You can thank my elves for that one!" said the old man with a great big Christmas smile.

He reached for his pocket, then pulled out a compass and checked his bearings! He reached into another pocket and pulled out his pocket watch, and checked the time.

For the first time as far back as he could remember, which was just when he awoke on the Southern Belle, Detective Joe K. Holiday was speechless! "It ended how all great Christmas Stories begin! Joe! With the birth of a Savior and the birth of a King! Follow your heart!

I have much work to do! Christmas work is never finished, you know! Oh! By the way! Merry Christmas!" said Santa as he handed Detective Holiday a gift-wrapped box. "Thank you and Merry Christmas to you!" said Joe. "I think, I found the right man for the job, do not you?" said Santa Claus. "On Dasher! On Dancer! On Comet! On Vixen! On Cupid! On Prancer! On Blixem! Dash away! Dance away! "Rudolph! Light up your nose and follow your Heart! To the North Pole and my sweetheart!" said Santa Claus! Then with the sound of a thousand sleigh bells it slid through the rain and ice mixed snow into the sky and off to the North Pole it went.

Detective Joe K. Holiday just stood there in complete amazement! He smiled so big he actually split his lip. He watched as Santa Claus circled and then flew in the direction of the North Pole. When the sound of the sleigh bells finally left his ears, he looked down at his gift. The Christmas gift was wrapped in white with golden leaves almost embroidered into the wrapping paper. The wrapping paper itself was beautiful. "I wonder what in heavens name it could be?" he thought. He excitedly tore the wrapper off the top of the box. There in the box was a shinny new detective's badge. "It is beautiful. Just, simply beautiful!" exclaimed the detective.

Meanwhile Nobody finished her prayer, and she wondered, if she would ever see Detective Joe K. Holiday again? Her mother came rushing out from the Laundry Room. "Who keeps putting shoes in the dryer?" her Momma yelled. "I am not going to put up with this non-sense any longer!" she perked as she jammed a washcloth into her apron pocket. She marched into her husbands' office and sat down in the swivel chair in front of his desk.

Then she spun around in it and said, "Oh! Heartless Ghost! The one Scrooge came to fear the most! You come out of that closet right this minute! Do you hear me? I am going to blister your hide! Oh! Heartless Ghoooost!" she said pointing her long fingered hand at the door. The Heartless Ghost's mind raced back to the day he threw a rock as hard as he could toward Mr. Drake's window.

He watched as it sailed through the air, and came down squarely in the center of Mr. Drake's living room window. He could clearly see the glass as it folded in on itself, under the weight and force of the rock, before the sound even reached his ears. He thought about how the sun reflected on each of the pieces as it fell in almost as if in slow motion.

He thought about how his knee came all the way up to his chest and under his chin. How he had his tongue sticking out too one side as his foot came back down. How Mr. Drake had turned around from his car to see him. The sense of guilt, shame and sorrow he felt! How could he have not seen him? Ray Charles would have seen him he thought. Before he could ponder again came, "I am not going to tell you again! Let us go! Mister! Microsoft C indeed!" she said holding a pair of steaming shoes as the doors of the closet opened ever so slowly. How was he going to get out of this one, he pondered. "Merry Christmas! I love you Mommy!" said he, as he came out of the closet ever so slowly!

A Doctor's Conclusion

Doctor Denny drove himself out to the home of Detective Holiday. He just knew the detective had perished in the vault of Mr. Potter. He parked his standard utility vehicle (SUV), out front of the detective's home. He noticed in the yard a manger scene. In Nobody's yard stood a small play area. It appeared that the children had been acting out the story of, "Scrooge," to entertain themselves. He saw Dr. Chaney drop Nobody off at the walk. He watched as Nobody skipped up the walk and in the door. He walked over to her home. He knocked at the door and her father opened the door with, "Merry Christmas!" and invited the scientist inside.

Momma came out of the bedroom holding the, "kicking and crying" Heartless Ghost by the scruff of his neck, with his magic robe. The Heartless Ghost turned and stuck out his tongue at Dr. Denny as Momma set him down. The Heartless Ghost stood up, and straightened himself and as he did, one of his long fingers fell to the floor.

Dr. Denny bent over and picked it up. It was a piece of a three by five-index card rolled with tape to make a cone. When Dr. Denny started to get up, he noticed that on the back of the Heartless Ghost's robe was and envelope. "To the World to Come!" it said in beautiful cursive handwriting.

Dr. Denny peeled the envelope off and put it in his coat pocket. He stood straight and said, "Hey Heartless, you are going to need this!" The Heartless Ghost turned around, took the paper finger, and put it in his robe pocket. He looked at Dr. Denny with a red face and having found his bum with both hands he said, "Why did I have to get a spanking? This is all your fault!" The doctor looked at him smiled and said, "There are just some things in this life that science cannot explain!" His mother moved him towards the door, and finished her scolding conversation with him. She informed him that he was to go outside and sit, not swing, in the swing set and think about what he had done. The Heartless Ghost took his blistered behind outside and sat in the swing, just as his mother had told him.

Detective Joe K. Holiday came up the walk. Dr. Denny greeted him and he introduced himself. Dr. Denny was amazed that the young man was alive, and had no recollection of him at all. He noticed the gift in the box was a detective's badge and grinned. He remembered seeing the badge in a pot of gold in the chamber of the Christmas King in one of the time windows. He kept quiet about it. He did not want to say anything that might trigger a memory.

Nobody came out from her secret place and she did not recognize him either. A package arrived. The United Parcel Service driver got out of his truck, and brought a large envelope up to the front door. He spoke briefly with Dr. Denny about going to the wrong address or his day would have been over by now. It was an envelope addressed to Nobody at that address. She opened it, and inside was a new magnifying glass and an autographed picture of the cast of, "It's a Wonderful Life!" "It is beautiful! Just simply beautiful!" she excliamed as she gazed lovingly at the picture. Suddenly, and without explanation, she grabbed a hold of Detective Joe K. Holiday and gave him a kiss. When she let him go, his eyes were as wide as silver dollars. He began to tap dance down the steps. As he did he sang, "A Kiss for Christmas!" Nobody followed his lead and danced down the steps after him singing along.

A HEART WISH! A KISS FOR CHIRSTMAS!

You gave me a kiss for Christmas!
If you did not grant my wish, and give me a kiss!
My heart would always miss! Your kiss on Christmas!
Nothing beats a Kiss for Christmas!
It is a very merry special wish!
When you wish for a kiss for Christmas!
You do not need mistletoe!
Just a kiss from Joe!
on Christmas!

Nobody tapped alongside the detective and then around him and sang back to him:

A KISS FOR CHRISTMAS

I gave you my heart for Christmas!
I granted your wish and gave you a kiss for Christmas!
And after the kiss! You granted my wish!
I wanted your heart for Christmas!

Then they both danced and sang:

Now Nobody knows
What everybody knows!
You gave me your heart for Christmas!
Now every single day! In our own special way is Christmas!
Christmas with a kiss! Is our own special gift on Christmas!
Nothing opens your heart like a gift wrapped kiss on Christmas!

"Merry Christmas! Joe!" said Nobody. "Merry Christmas! Nobody! You will always be somebody to me!" said Joe as he kissed Nobody again. The family Holiday came over from next door during the singing. The two families embraced them and each other with wishes of Merry Christmas back and forth to each other.

In all of the excitement, Dr. Denny excused himself by saying he must have come to the wrong address, also. With a Merry Christmas and a wave, Dr. Denny went to his standard utility vehicle, (SUV), and began the drive back to the remains of the Collossatron facility. He took the long road that led to the heliport, which shuttled personnel to and from the facility. He looked out his front windshield and thought he saw a sleigh go overhead. He pulled to the side of the road and unfastened his seatbelt, and opened the door. He stood on the side rail and looked up! The sleigh went over again with a, "Merry Christmas! Everyone!"

Dr. Denny smiled and said, "Merry Christmas to you too!" He did not question what he had seen. He had seen the strangest of things with Collossatron. He had heard some of the most outlandish of theories. He climbed back in and fastened his seat belt. When he looked ahead, he was still on a highway but up ahead was not the heliport. It was the entrance gate to the Los Alamos facility.

He turned on his radio and the radio station gave the date of December 5, 2015. The day before his wife had asked him to leave. He reached into his shirt, and he was wearing the love token his wife had given him. When he got home, his key fit the door. When he entered his wife said, "Where on earth have you been? I have been trying to reach you all day! We need to talk! Where have you been?"

Dr. Denny answered his wife with, "Oh! I have been out just killing time! Yeah, Anna, lets talk!" He closed the door. The door reopened! A hand put a Christmas Reef on a nail in the door, and then it closed again Dr. Denny sat on his couch with his wife and opened the envelope that had been on the back of the Heartless Ghost's magic robe. It was a Christmas card dated 1843, which read, "To: The World to come! Merry Christmas! Ebenezer Scrooge!"

THE END

NARRATOR: So, that is the story of the Christmas King! The King of Joy and Everything! He is still on his throne, and sits at the right hand of God. The family Holiday lived happily ever after! With a simple Christmas Kiss, nobody became somebody to someone. You are probably wondering, what was her name? I would suggest you read the story again. By the way, what name would you give her for Christmas?

I very much would have liked to divulge the contents of the letter Major Jimmy Stewart wrote to the Tennessee Veteran Organizations however, that is classified. We all know who to handle classified information. I am sure that you could get a Tennessee volunteer veteran to tell you for Christmas!

Dr. Denny found himself going from one strange seminar after another, trying to prove that this actually happened. He did however, have another break through. During one of his seminars, a man sitting beside an audience member whose tee-shirt read, "abducted!" offered up the following statement for Dr. Denny's book, "The Time Gate" as proof that this story is true. It is printed here for his benefit.

STATEMENT

I distinctly remember that during my military service, I was sent by someone, out in the middle of the night, in the middle of nowhere, to build something for somebody in the US Government.

Sgt. Shawn T. Tilley
United States Army, (Retired)
Christmas 2016

Chief Detective Pryzwarra and Detective Carlin became ardent fans of World War II Veterans and found themselves volunteering at Veteran's Administration Clinics on weekends, especially during the Christmas holidays.

PS: Watch the following movies to understand fully: King Nine won't Return DejaVu Cheyenne Social Club A Christmas Carol It's A Wonderful Life Men In Black Manchurian Candidate (1962) Any movie with James Stewart   The Man Who Shot Liberty Valance I believe that the Lord talks to all of us differently. I do not know why, I have encountered so many great men and women in my life. However, each one I have encountered was truly great and it is a privilege and honor to call them my friend. Sadly most have passed. I have found my friends are the ones that do not agree with everything I say or do. They also at times have pointed out the flaws in my character. They are the best friends to have for oneself. Many thanks to the Headquarters Commandant Section, XVIIIth Airborne Corps, Fort Bragg, N.C. for giving me a dictionary and thesaurus. Thank you also for seeing to it, that I worked for and received my General Education Diploma in 1979.

In Memory of Congressional Medal of Honor recipient Private First Class Desmond Doss, who taught me that some of us are soldiers of love moving through this life encountering different spirits, both good and evil. We must protect those whom we love from the evil ones and embrace good ones. It was our hope and prayer that the meek can achieve their dreams and inherit the earth with our unselfish protection. "I will see you again on the sea of glass!"

Brigadier General Robert K. Morgan, United States Air Force, (Retired), Pilot of the Memphis Belle. He taught me, that when you do the right thing, all the time. In this life and the next, you will have few regrets.

Congressional Medal of Honor recipient Sergeant First Class Roy P. Benavidez, United States Army. He taught me to how, by using my mind as a weapon, I had another tool at my disposal. He also said, "When you have to fight, fight to win! Or do not fight at all!"

Congressional Medal of Honor recipient Charles Coolidge whose lovely wife Frances, a real lady said to me, "I never saw a true hero call himself a hero! When another calls you a hero, then you are a hero!" We called him, "Strongman!" he knew how to get things done! Charles himself is the definition of tough. I admire him for it!

Rear Admiral Vance R. Fry, United States Navy, (Retired), who taught me the true definition of a friend.

Command Sergeant Major Leo B. Smith, United States Army, I will someday hope by the grace of Almighty God, and in the passing along the story of this book! I will be able to one-day stand by your grave and salute you with, "A Medal of Honor Museum or We Lead the Way Military History Museum and Military Heritage Park can stand in Chattanooga, Tennessee as well built as the Tennessee Aviation Museum! They are building Fort Freedom as we speak! Airborne All the way!" then step away!

Finally, to my Grand Stepfather, PFC Lawrence C. Baldwin, Charlie Troop, 116th Cavalry, Reconnaissance Squadron, World War II: "I will not go down easy, Grandpa! I bring the fire! I bring the fire!" He taught me many things! He taught me to be a cowboy; an Indian and a survivor of my circumstances. Merry Christmas Grandpa! He backed my play with love! Sergeant Shawn Timothy, "Sure Thing!" Tilley, Son of Many Fathers!, Noli Me Tangre!, Above the Rest!, Airborne All the Way, Sir!, out!

ABOUT THE AUTHOR

Shawn Timothy Tilley was born on Mather Air Force Base in Sacramento, California, on 13 August 196*. He was raised in Cudahy, California. He joined the Army at 17 and obtained his General Education Diploma at Fort Bragg, North Carolina, in 1980. His awards include the Army Commendation Medal with Oak Leaf Cluster, The Army Achievement Medal with Oak Leaf Cluster, and The Good Conduct Medal Bronze Clasp with two loops.

He earned the Expert Infantryman's Badg4e, the Expert Rifleman's Badge, and the Expert Badge with Hand Grenade Bar. He earned the Army Non-Commissioned Officer's Ribbon with a number 2 device. Basic Parachutist Wings! He has worked for the Central Intelligence Agency (C.I.A.) and Special Office 13 (SO13).. He was awarded the Order of Merit by the U.S.U.S. Senate. He is a graduate of the Covert Operations Leadership School, the XVIIIth Airborne Corps Leadership Academy, and the United States Army's Leadership Academy for Combat Arms 11B2P Infantryman and Drill Sergeant School at Fort Knox.

He was also awarded the parachutist wings of the Kingdom of Laos! He was awarded the Distinguished Service Ribbon by the Tennessee State Guard in 1996. He was also the Right Honorable Mayor of Dover, England, during the Frontline Britain Observance, Battle of Britain, and Dunkirk Observances. He published the poem "The Gallant and the Brave" in 1998.

He was an honor student at Northwestern State University. He was honored by the Fraternal Order of Phi Kappa Phi twice, once for obtaining and maintaining a 4.0 grade point average. The other was for mathematics!